RED PLANET RISING

RED PLANET RISING

ANDREW M. SEDDON

CROSSWAY BOOKS • WHEATON, ILLINOIS
A DIVISION OF GOOD NEWS PUBLISHERS

Red Planet Rising

Copyright © 1995 by Andrew Seddon

Published by Crossway Books
       a division of Good News Publishers
       1300 Crescent Street
       Wheaton, Illinois 60187.

Cover illustration: Rick Courtney

Art Direction / Design: Mark Schramm

First printing, 1995

Printed in the United States of America

Library of Congress Cataloging-in-Publication Data
Seddon, Andrew M., 1959-
    Red planet rising / Andrew M. Seddon
       p.   cm.
ISBN 0-89107-825-8
    I. Title.
PS3569.E3145C79 1995
813'.54—dc20   95-31030

03	02	01	00	99	98	97	96	95
15	14	13	12	11	10	9 8	7 6	5 4	3 2	1

To my parents, Ernest and Cynthia Seddon,
for their support, encouragement, proofreading,
and brainstorming sessions.
And to Judy and David
for not interrupting me too awfully much.

AUTHOR'S NOTE:

Since the Martian year, at 687 days, is almost twice that of an Earth year, all dates are given as the corresponding Earthdate.

PROLOGUE

The faint, scent-laden breeze that wafted through the drooping limbs of the dark cypresses left the still waters of the reflecting pool unrippled. The day was warm but not unbearably so, the sky not yet baked to the brittle blue of summer. Ghalji Maranan stood silently at the water's edge, loathe to disturb the tranquility of the scene.

Purists abominated the trees, planted the previous century, claiming they spoiled the serenity of the reflections. To Maranan, they added a personality—an aura—of their own.

The reflection of his face, framed by a pair of cypress trunks, stared back at him, mirror clear. He studied his image intently, as if for the first time. Perhaps it was the first; was he truly the same person as before?

Assuming his memory did not play him false, he was vaguely bemused to find that all was as he remembered. The scars and trauma of his recent rehabilitation were internal, leaving no evidence on the skin for eyes to appreciate. Short brown hair was brushed back from a high forehead. Faint crinkles radiating from the corners of his eyes would not harden into the crows' feet of the aged for many years. Unduly thick lips created a sensuous—almost feminine—appearance. He had ceased to be concerned about his ears, unusually protuberant, long ago.

He accepted himself.

His eyes, olive green, partly hidden beneath heavy, langorous lids, searched deeper.

Rehabilitation, they called it.

It was not he who needed rehabilitating but all those who did not understand him, who failed to comprehend the importance of his mission.

For he had a mission, of that he was sure. Not all the therapists, analysts, and treatments a sophisticated society could offer had been able to shake his assurance in who he was and what he had been called to do.

They thought he was cured.

Maranan smiled. Perfectly formed teeth flashed white in the sunlight, cleaving the pale brown of his complexion.

His pale blue *choga* shrugged off his hairless shoulders, Maranan wore only a *dhoti*, enjoying the warmth of the sunshine on his naked skin. It was a symbol of his oneness with all to go clad in nothing but a loincloth. Cloak and loincloth; simple clothes.

He folded the *choga* into a neat square, laid it on the grass, and collapsed his legs into a lotus position. Pressing his palms together before his chest, he willed his breathing to slow. Deep breaths, in and out . . . in and out . . . in and out . . . .

He shut out the warmth of the sun, the cool touch of the breeze, the fragrance of cypress and flower, the cheerful call of birdsong.

His gaze centered on the waters of the lake. From this position the gleaming towers of the Taj Mahal crowned his vision, pure marble capped by a sparkling dome. He allowed his spirit freedom. Feeling his body fall behind, he passed into the water, between the towers, through a portal inlaid with ornaments of agate and jasper. Beyond the portal he traveled ever deeper, ever within.

The two sarcophagi, softly illuminated by beams of light filtering through screens of carved marble, rose into view.

Shah Jehan and his wife, Mumtaz Mahal.

A love story.

Today, there was a third with them, another presence in the octagonal room.

Ghalji Maranan bowed low in the presence of his Guide, conscious of a tingle, a visceral thrill in his spirit. It was always thus when he met his Guide. Once he had been unsure, a doubtful young man perplexed by the spiritual. Doubting, as when his Guide had told him he could no longer be married, that the wife he—not his parents—had chosen, would be a hindrance.

At first, he had refused to accept his Guide's counsel, choosing to follow the dictates of his heart. But then his wife had joined a new religion, forsaking their peoples' long-cherished beliefs. Worse, she had tried to recruit him to her newfound ways—to belief in one God.

To the love of one called Jesus Christ.

He had put her away. Sent her to be executed.

There had been other women since, many. But she—Mumtaz, named after Jehan's wife—had been the first. Regret tinged the embers of memory. If only the Christians hadn't turned her head and her heart!

"I will never forgive you for what you took from me," he said in the voice of his mind.

He could still visualize his wife's face as the frowning, grim-faced police led her away. Accusation, hatred, disbelief—he could have dealt with them. But her face was loving, her eyes sorrowful—though not for herself.

For him.

"I will pray for you, Ghalji," she had said. "And I will always love you."

He hated the Christians even more.

The remembrance flitted through his mind in a moment and was gone. The voice of his Guide broke in upon him, recalling him to the present.

"Greetings, Ghalji. It has been long." The voice, low and resonant, reverberated up his spine like the voice of one of the ancient gods. Shiva, perhaps, or Vayu.

"Indeed. My mind was full of drugs, and I was unable to find the way."

"That is past now. Are you still possessed of purpose, Ghalji Maranan?"

"I am."

He tried to read the expression on his Guide's face, but as always was prevented by the radiance emanating from the glowing form.

"Our Mother has need of you. But the way will be long and hard. Are you willing to sacrifice all?"

Maranan felt a knot tighten inside of him, a sudden spasm of fear. Something told him there was still time; he could still go back. It was not irreversible . . . yet. Mumtaz' voice called to him from the infinite, urging him, warning him. . . . .

He hardened his resolve.

"I am," he whispered, feeling as he did so that he crossed an invisible threshold from which there would be no return.

"Good," replied his Guide, inclining assent. "Very good."

Earthdate: August 30, 2166
Mars, Hellas Planitia, The Enclave

Lin Grainger entered the final code sequence and leaned back, her chair adjusting its configuration to suit her new position. In nanoseconds the computer had completed its calculation; the screen illuminated with a multicolored display. She added the latest overlay to those she had already completed and studied the result, her eyes tracing the intricate network of patterns.

"Looks good."

INITIATE? (YES) NO

"Initiate." She set the program running. The Tokahatsu-3 Biosynthesizer would do the rest.

There you go again, Lin. Playing God.

The doubts seemed to be coming more frequently these days, just when a definite end was in sight!

She forced down the nagging of her conscience.

Perhaps she was playing God. If so, why not? Was that so bad?

Playing God: Adjusting and recombining human genes in ways nature had never attempted, creating new combinations in the search for an improved genotype—a new, superior breed of humanity.

Were they still human?

In brain function and intellect, yes. They hadn't been tampered with.

A soul?

She didn't know for herself, let alone a construct.

Lin pushed her chair back from the console.

What was a scientist doing, thinking about souls? Leave that for the philosophers and mystics.

Lin rose and strolled to one of the nutrient growth tanks. The cloudy, viscous liquid defied description. It was all colors, reflecting light in rainbow iridescence. Interior currents riffled the surface. The status board showed a rank of green lights—heart rate, temperature, respirations, brainwave activity; all normal.

The indistinct form of a construct lay submerged near the bottom of the tank. A mass of sensors, wires, and tubes connected the tank to the computer array. Some penetrated the clear plastic to attach directly to the organism—monitoring, adjusting, feeding.

She patted the top of the tank. Lin made it habit to talk to the constructs. Whether or not they heard her—? She thought perhaps they did.

"Hi, Spock. How'ya doing today? You're getting big. Won't be too much longer and we'll have you out of there. Bet you'll be glad, huh?"

Lin's collection of old two-dimensional shows, (known as "TV" to connoisseurs) was prohibited in the Enclave; abominated by Maranan as inconducive to correct spiritual discipline. Not that anyone else had facilities to play them even if they wanted to.

But Lin had her computers, and she'd smuggled in a few chips of her favorite shows, watching them on her monitors in the privacy of the inner lab. It seemed appropriate to name her constructs after favorite characters.

Murmuring a word of encouragement to each one, she checked the other tanks. All were functioning within normal parameters.

You are good, Lin reassured herself. *Very good. The best biotechnician on Mars.*

She chuckled wryly.

She was the only biotechnician on Mars; leastways the only one working with humans. The crew over at GenAg didn't count. All they did was plants. Turnip-tenders.

This laboratory and the one adjoining were her domain. She ruled here. Not even Erik Klassen knew of this room. The thought gave her a feeling of power—in this place she was safe. It helped her forget that in all other respects she was a prisoner, the one person forbidden to leave the Enclave.

Surely Maranan was blind where Klassen was concerned!

Lin dimmed the lights for the evening. The nutrient growth tanks sat silently in the gloom, like a row of coffins. But inside them was not death but life.

The late-model biosynthesizer—not yet commercially available—would run on its own, assembling molecules of adenine, thymine, guanine, and cytosine along phosphate bridges into a helical strand of DNA. The DNA would make genes. The genes, chromosomes. And the chromosomes—with any luck, if her programming was accurate, a being that could tolerate the bitter surface conditions of Mars without protection. A true Martian, not an Earth-human scratching out a living on the dry and dusty surface of a dead, unforgiving planet.

Pantropy.

The word had a magical sound to it.

Earth scientists had abandoned human genetic engineering a century ago. She—Lin Grainger—had resurrected a lost art, determined to carve for herself a place in the history of this new world.

The first pantropist!

With Maranan's help.

He had recruited her, sensed her potential, knew her need. He had created this place, providing the equipment, technology, and raw materials. Grainger owed the master a debt of gratitude. Without him, she might be another turnip-tender, spending her days churning out fruits and veggies for a thankless population.

In the main lab, computer banks chattered incessantly to each other. Complex webs of mathematical symbols scrolled endlessly down half a dozen screens.

Lin felt a tremor of insecurity.

This room was much harder to justify to herself. Surely the master knew best, but still . . .

Lin paused before one of the half-dozen occupied couches. Strapped to its soft, contoured surface was a woman. Lin regarded the handsome, oriental features, so much younger looking than her own. She raised a hand to her own cheek, brushing back a strand of limp, flaxen hair, conscious, when faced with this woman's serene beauty, of her own imperfections.

This woman commanded attention; she had power, money, social status. A legion of admirers followed her every move and action.

Lin had no one she could call her own.

The glassy, almond eyes fixed in a vacant stare, lost in the depths of infinity. A metal composite helmet, affixed to a computer array by the pale, ruby glow of a communications laser obscured the scalp. From the computer's complex circuits, a continual flow of information fed into the brain, becoming a part of the living tissue, of the developing consciousness.

The master said it was necessary. A regrettable evil necessary to accomplish a higher purpose.

What of those who were destined to be replaced?

You don't know, do you? You're a coward, Lin. Afraid of the answer. Afraid to ask.

She checked her chrono. It was late. Time for bed.

Making sure the lab door was properly secure, she padded softly down the hall.

Lin hoped Klassen wouldn't call. The thought made her shudder.

She fingered her cheek, where the fading bruise from last time was still tender.

Please God, she half-prayed. *Not tonight.*

ONE

The waves, crystal clear and pure as glass, caressed the shore, lapping over brilliant white sands. So clear the water, only when depth had imparted a shade of indescribably beautiful azure did the rocky bottom at last merge into obscurity.

A breeze laden with scent blew from the heather-clad hillside. The tang of saltwater mingled with the fragrance of mown hay, the pungent, acrid odor of sheep, and a hint of peat. Fluffy forms dotted the green pasture slopes of the *machair*, spreading like a velvet blanket up the gentle mound of Dun I.

The porcelain sky, dotted by a few clouds of fleecy cotton wafting high overhead, stretched in an arc of bird-egg blue from horizon to horizon. It was impossible to determine whether the sea mirrored the sky or if the sky was but a pale reflection of its watery cousin.

On this pleasantly cool day, warm sunshine glinted off the crests of the waves, flickering and dancing.

Carolyn McCourt, muffled in a lavender sweater of good Scottish wool, inhaled, savoring the scents and the scene, struggling to implant them firmly in her memory. The breeze ruffled her flaming red hair, twining strands about her shoulders. She sighed with contentment.

"Isn't it wonderful?" she exclaimed, her eyes bright. "I'm so glad we could come. Thank you."

She reached up and placed a kiss on her husband's cheek.

Duchesne, who had been watching the ferry retreat slowly across the sound toward Fionnphort, draped his arm around her shoulders and drew her close.

"It's not what I imagined," he replied. His back to the ferry, he regarded the huddle of immaculately maintained stone buildings fronting the shore. Dark slate roofs contrasted with whitewash. "It's like a world out of time," he continued. "I want to pinch myself to see if it's real."

"I bet it hasn't changed in a hundred years."

"More like four hundred."

"One hundred, four hundred, who cares? Come on, J.I., let's explore."

She tugged on his arm. He followed obediently. He flicked open his reader and inserted the guidebook he had acquired at a souvenir-laden store in Oban.

"According to this, the nunnery is directly up the hill. The Cathedral, obviously, is off to the right," he pointed.

"Look at the flowers!"

Carolyn dropped his arm to run ahead. She bent down to sniff the scarlet and white blossoms that enclosed the nunnery ruins in a floral frame. Duchesne rested his hand on the rough, moss-covered rock and gazed to where a roofless arch pointed mutely heavenward. A narrow slit of window imprisoned a small fragment of sky.

He could feel a weight slipping off his shoulders, a weight which he had been denying for the better part of two years. Contemplating the simplicity of the island, he felt an enthusiasm for life returning, a vigor and contentment of spirit that he had lacked and lacked all the more for not knowing he had lacked it.

Their vacation had actually begun in the south of England, with the obligatory inspection of Stonehenge. Duchesne had not been overly inclined to visit the monument, unofficial symbol of the United World Church, but Carolyn had said it would help them to appreciate Iona more.

" . . . *a dismal cirque*

of Druid Stones upon a forlorn moor," she'd quoted helpfully from the shadow of a monolith.

Duchesne had paused in his circumnavigation long enough to raise his eyebrows.

"John Keats. Poetic if inaccurate."

From Stonehenge they'd visited several of the great cathedrals—Wells, Canterbury, Salisbury—before heading north.

Carolyn rose to her feet, a bouquet of flowers in her hand.

She saw the expression on her husband's face and smiled.

He caught the look. Carolyn had been worrying about him; he hadn't needed a degree in psychology to know that.

"You feel it too, don't you?" she asked.

Duchesne returned her smile. "Yes. I guess you were right to insist we take a vacation. I'm glad to be here. There's a quality. Almost . . ." he paused, searching for the right word.

"Spiritual?"

"Yes, that's it. As though evil has never touched this place."

He took a purple flower from her hand and arranged it in her hair. "There you are. It suits you."

Carolyn returned the favor, slipping a blossom into the pocket of his jacket. "And you. Let's head up to the Cathedral. I want to make sure we see it today."

"There's no rush. We have plenty of time."

"I know. But the day is so perfect. They say the only thing you can count on about Scottish weather is its unpredictability."

Perched on the gunwales of their wooden boats, several fishermen tended their nets. The small vessels, red, white, and black paint peeling in strips, were drawn up above the tide-line amid a welter of fishing gear.

Duchesne waved. One of the men raised a hand in reply.

"Do you suppose they really fish?" Carolyn asked.

"Like their ancestors before them for hundreds of years. It's a special privilege to be allowed to live on an island like this."

"Local color for tourists? I hope it's more than that. What are those boxes?"

A stack of wooden-framed contraptions leaned drunkenly, strands of drying seaweed tangled through their mesh sides.

"I have no idea. Why don't you ask one of the fishermen?"

The fisherman looked to be in his eighties, weathered face lined and wrinkled from years of exposure to wind and spray, but was probably much younger. He wore a cable sweater of pea-green and sturdy sea-boots. His gnarled hands plied the recalcitrant twine with a suppleness one would not have supposed they possessed.

"Excuse me." Carolyn paused on the shingle. "I'm sorry to interrupt, but what are those twine boxes?"

The man chuckled, baring a rank of stained and eroded teeth. "They're lobster pots, lass."

"Lobsters?"

"Aye, lobsters." He repeated. "Lobsters. Do ye no ken lobsters?"

"I've never had lobster."

The man looked at her strangely. "Never had lobsters? Where de ye hie from?"

"We're from Mars," Carolyn explained. "We're on vacation."

The fisherman spat on the ground. "Ye're a long ways from home. An' ye're neither little nor green nor a man." He chuckled again.

Carolyn smiled politely. The joke was an old one. "My ancestors were Scottish. Generations ago, of course."

"That's different." He picked up a knife and cut the strand. "Is yon lad ye're husband then?"

"He is."

Carolyn rejoined J. I. "He says they're lobster pots."

Duchesne nodded. "They must still be allowed to catch them. We'll have to add lobster to our list of specialties to try. Perhaps Ardraig Cottage will have some."

"You're not getting me to eat haggis, though."

"It was good."

"Ugh!"

Leaving the small village in their wake they strolled toward the cathedral, its gray bulk rising sharply out of the manicured grass.

"Fifteen hundred years," Carolyn whispered.

"Huh? What was that?"

"Fifteen hundred years," Carolyn repeated, holding his hand to warm her own. "This has been a place of Christian worship for fifteen hundred years."

"A long time. Especially in this day and age."

"It has never stopped. Even in the days when Christianity was suppressed, it never ceased to be a place of worship."

"The United World Church owned it for a while, don't forget."

"But at least the Christians were allowed to get it back, even if only as a museum preserve. One place in all the world."

"You know what this is going to do, don't you?" Duchesne asked, as they approached a low mound off to the side.

"What's that, J. I.?"

"Make us think again."

"I've been telling you that for two years, honey."

Duchesne shrugged. "I'll get around to it."

"That's what you always say."

"So I'm not a religious gadfly."

"I haven't been either; not since I found that old Bible."

"Figures that the one religion you'd be interested in is unauthorized."

Carolyn squeezed his hand. "Let's not fight, okay? What does the sign say?" She pointed to a small, incised wooden board.

"*Reilig Oran*," Duchesne replied. "If you'll pardon my Gaelic, which I'm sure is wretched. It says here," he consulted the book, "that it is the burial place of the kings. Macbeth and sundry other assorted kings of Scotland, Ireland, and Norway."

"And this," he indicated the cobblestoned track they were following, "is *Sraid nam Marbh*. The street of the dead. Macabre, don't you think?"

Carolyn suppressed a shiver. "I hope we're not walking on top of them."

"Don't worry, the bones disappeared long ago."

His eyes followed the coastline, tracing the outline of the low islands, grass-covered rocks barely rising above the restless sea. "It's hard to imagine, isn't it? Those white sands being the scene of a massacre."

Carolyn failed to quell another shiver. "When was that?"

"In C.E. 806. The monks were butchered by marauding Vikings."

"It looks so peaceful now," mused Carolyn. "Perhaps that's part of the magic of Iona."

"I don't follow." Duchesne frowned.

"Not that it's untouched by evil," Carolyn explained, "but that good has overcome evil."

"You may be right."

"It's ironic, isn't it?" she continued.

"How's that?"

"Well, Christianity started off persecuted by the Romans, then it became the dominant world religion, then oppressed again by the neo-pagans. A repeating cycle."

"I'll take your word for it. I heard rumors before we left home of some trouble involving the Christian community. Nothing serious, mind you. Just complaints that they don't care for Mars, whatever that means."

"Probably nothing."

Two great Celtic crosses guarded the cathedral doors. The cross of redemption penetrating the circle of the world, said the guidebook in a surprising moment of candor, quoting an unidentified but presumably sympathetic source. Another quote claimed the circle represented the sun.

Situated left of the entrance, St. Columba's shrine was a spare, featureless room. Duchesne leaned through the half-opened door. A lone candle burned in an alcove. Columba, a prince of the royal blood who relinquished his heritage to don a missionary's robe. No starry-eyed weakling, but tough, uncompromising, yet gentle in spirit.

Shafts of light angled into the dim cathedral through narrow, clear glass windows, warming to russet the massive cut-block walls of gray, black and maroon stone that spread up to dark wooden rafters. Plain and unpretentious, the Cathedral exerted its power through simplicity rather than overwhelming pomp.

The interior stones were as worn as those outside, witnessed to the days when the neglected cathedral had existed as a roofless ruin, exposed to the ravages of the harsh Hebridean weather.

Carolyn and Duchesne wandered quietly through the structure, conscious of their footfalls. Although they tried to move as silently as possible, the deep stillness made every noise a sacrilege, an affront to the holy.

Overwhelmed by awe, Duchesne felt acutely that he was in the presence of something greater than himself. The thought dismayed him. Carolyn parked herself on a chair near the front of the nave, contemplating the altar.

Duchesne sat behind her. "Happy?" he whispered.

He could feel Carolyn smile although her face was away from him.

"Very." She fixed her eyes on the unadorned silver cross surmounting the altar. "Very."

>

The afternoon passed quickly. Only as dusk crept over from the Ross of Mull did they leave the Cathedral to navigate their way to Ardraig Cottage, one of the ivy-encrusted houses lining The Street. The landlady greeted them warmly. She was a small woman even by Earth standards, barely over five feet tall and dwarfed by her lanky guests. Duchesne had almost expected to see her kilt-clad, but the elderly woman wore a faded hand-made dress with a floral pattern.

"Com' in dears, com' in. My, but we're glad tae see ye. My name is Glenda. Ye'll be the Duchesnes?"

She stood aside to let them enter.

"That's right. This is Carolyn, and I'm J. I." Duchesne bent his neck to avoid hitting his head on the low ceiling.

"J. I.? What sort of a name is that, then?"

"It's better than what the initials stand for," Duchesne said, forestalling any comment Carolyn might have made.

"Is this ye're first visit to Iona?" Dropping the subject of names, Mrs. Williams closed the door on the dusk. "My, but it's chilly tonight."

Duchesne smiled. What would Mrs. Williams make of a day on Mars? Venturing outside without the protection afforded by an environmental suit took some getting used to.

"That it is," Carolyn agreed. "It's a beautiful island."

"Aye. I've lived here all m'life, I have. Been alone for nigh on thirty years since my Kenneth died. Would you like to freshen up before dinner?"

"Yes, please. It's been a long day," said Carolyn.

"Mind ye're heads on the stairs," Glenda cautioned, leading the way up the narrow, creaking steps. Carolyn and Duchesne followed Glenda's plump figure, exchanging amused glances.

Glenda Williams continued to prattle cheerfully. "Not many people stay overnight on the island, ye know, though many are day visitors. Most com' from Oban or Tobermoray jest tae look aroond, an' gae back at evening. Ye must be important folks tae be able tae stay."

Carolyn cast a look back over her shoulder; Duchesne was quite content to let her answer.

"Well, not *that* important. But we do have a few friends here on Earth. We're from off-world."

Carolyn did not mention their vocations, which Duchesne thought wise. Security officers were not likely to be frequent— or welcome—visitors to Iona.

"Aye? I couldna place ye're accents."

"We're from Mars."

"Born there?"

"Born and bred."

"I don't believe I've met anyone from Mars before. There's not many who mak' sooch a long trip."

"It's not that long," replied Carolyn, glancing at J. I. He rolled his eyes. "But it can be expensive."

"Aye? Well I hope ye lak it. Here's ye're room. Watch the step."

"Thank you."

"Dinner will be ready in half an hour. Com' on doon when ye're ready." Glenda Williams wended her way back down stairs.

Carolyn collapsed on the bed. "It feels good to lie down. My feet are killing me."

"I thought you would have remembered." Duchesne pulled off his shoes and rubbed his feet. "The gravity is murder on the arches. And the legs." He yawned. "It helps to know you're coming and have time to prepare."

"True, but I thought we were in good shape."

"We are. But it's a large adjustment nonetheless. Our bone structure isn't made for this." He stretched, feeling the soreness of his back muscles.

"Tell me about it. I feel like a giant; everyone is so short."

Dinner was not lobster. Instead, served on an antique wooden table covered by an embroidered cloth, the meal consisted of Scotch broth, shepherd's pie, and a sponge cake for dessert. Glenda Williams's conversation enlivened the meal. She seemed to know everyone and everything on Iona.

Technology intruded little on the island. The food was real, not synthesized. The appearance of antiquity was scrupulously maintained, from the antique ferry to the period furniture. Only a vidphone terminal sequestered in a curtained-off alcove spoiled the illusion.

After refusing yet another helping of cake, Duchesne and Carolyn took their tea through to the sitting room where a peat fire crackled. Duchesne sipped his tea, listening to the hissing and popping of the fire and the sounds of Mrs. Williams bustling in the kitchen.

When they were done, fed, comfortable, and relaxed, they retired to their tiny bedroom.

One of the consequences of rustic simplicity was an unmodernized heating system. Duchesne could reach out his arm and touch the whitewashed stone wall.

Low ceilings, chill rooms, and a lumpy mattress. Duchesne pulled the douvet up to his neck, glad of its downy warmth.

"I'm glad I don't have to live in the past forever," he murmured. "Even the Academy had better beds than this."

"Go to sleep."

"See what happens to a man when he gets married?" he teased. "Your wife drags you across the solar system to a high-gravity planet."

Carolyn rolled over and pillowed her head on his arm. "I have to listen to you giving the orders the rest of the time, don't I?"

>

"Finally, a honeymoon," Carolyn said. "After two years." They spent the next several days relaxing, strolling the sheep tracks over the low hills, ending up at the Beach of the Seat or the Port of the Coracle. Reclining on rocks by the shore, feet buried in the warm sand, hours passed unnoticed in contemplation of the ocean.

"Was it worth the wait?"

Carolyn kissed him.

They drank, laughingly, from the Well of Eternal Youth. One unforgettable, magical evening they watched the sunset from the hummocky summit of Cnoc Mor, arms entwined, enraptured as the sun was extinguished with a blaze of glory by the conquering, burning sea.

At evening, feet propped before the peat fire after one of Glenda Williams's hearty meals, they compared experiences and warmed the aches and pains.

One breezy day, clinging to the thwarts of a small boat bouncing over the chop, they visited Staffa. Fingal's Cave, hewn out of the tough, hexagonal basaltic pillars by the relentless action of the waves, impressed Duchesne as much as Iona's man-made cathedral. Inside the cave the ocean boomed and roared, larger waves flinging spray high into the air.

Duchesne regretted when the day came to depart.

"Must we?" Carolyn's eyes pleaded.

Duchesne forced himself not to yield. "I'm afraid so. It's a long trip back, you know, and we're not rushing as it is."

"What's the matter? Afraid that Boris will get into trouble if he's left alone too long?"

Duchesne laughed. "If I know him, he'll have the staff eating caviar and speaking Russian by the time we get back."

"Maybe you should have left Cohen in charge."

"Oh, sure. What do you think she'd have done?"

"I retract the suggestion."

Glenda Williams seemed genuinely sorry to see them leave. "Com' back agin, won't ye?" she asked.

"We'll try," Carolyn promised.

Leaning on the metal rail of the ferry as the island shrunk behind them, Carolyn watched with somber eyes.

"When in some future time," she murmured, "I shall sit in some madly crowded assembly with music and dancing round me, and the wish arises to retire into the loneliest loneliness, I shall think of Iona."

"Was that a quotation?" Duchesne asked.

"Aye, laddie. Mendelssohn."

"The composer Mendelssohn?"

"Aye."

Earthdate: October 26, 2166

One of the very few trains left in operation, the Flying Scotsman, chugged southward. For people used to aircars, monorails, or whisking across the world in hypersonic planes, the slow traversal of the landscape provided a pleasant diversion.

Great Britain, in Duchesne's opinion, had done the best job of preserving its heritage of history. To be sure, the great cities of London, Glasgow, Liverpool-Manchester were gleaming metropoli of soaring skyscrapers and vast underground complexes. The sea-city of New Canterbury was a marvel of design, engineering, and construction.

But the British had been determined not to lose their past to new technology. Vast areas of the country appeared as they had for centuries: Old villages, ancient landmarks, the land itself lovingly preserved or carefully restored. Virtually alone amongst the nations of Earth, the British Isles represented a page from history. No matter that under the surface, subterranean cities grew and spread. On the surface, the past reigned.

Contrast that with Japan or the European continent. There, cities like monstrous octopi had swallowed vast tracts of land. Japan was simply one huge city, all remnants of its past bludgeoned beneath the inexorable advance of the swelling population.

NorthAm was the place to go for unspoiled wilderness; Great Britain for history.

The countryside slipped by. All too soon Duchesne followed Carolyn off the train into Paddington Station. "Major Duchesne?"

A stocky man in Security black and gray elbowed his way out of the crowd and strode toward them.

Duchesne identified himself.

The man saluted. "Corporal Rogers, sir." He acknowledged Carolyn. "Captain McCourt. I'm from the London branch of the European Commonwealth. I have a message for you."

Duchesne looked about the crowded platform. "Come over here." He beckoned toward an unoccupied bench.

"What's this all about, Corporal?"

"Don't know, sir. I was given your description and instructed to wait for you, and then deliver this message." He passed over an information chip.

"Do you have a reader, sir?"

"Yes," Duchesne replied. He pulled the instrument from his pocket and slipped in the chip, followed by his ID code. The small screen illuminated. He read the message then whistled, conscious of Carolyn's unspoken question.

"It's from Forbes."

"What does the colonel want?"

"We're to report directly to him in the New York headquarters. Leave is cancelled."

"I have an aircar, sir," said Rogers, "and there's a plane on standby. I'll make sure your bags follow."

"Lead on, Corporal," said Duchesne.

Rogers directed them out of the terminal.

"What's up?" whispered Carolyn.

"Trouble back home," Duchesne replied, equally quietly. "A group called the Revitalists."

Mars, Hellas Planitia, The Enclave

Gerhart Hannik cast a glance over his shoulder as he jogged furtively along the deserted corridor. Lights dimmed for nighttime, the normally brightly lit corridor was deep in shadow. Glow-strips at floor and shoulder level provided the only illumination. Hannik hoped his progress was noiseless, that nothing would wake the adherents sleeping soundly behind the closed and numbered doors that he passed. His breath rasped in his ears.

His hands slippery with sweat, he hadn't felt this nervous in a long time. Perhaps he was getting too old for this kind of activity. He knew the taste of fear, but he wasn't afraid at the moment—only nervous.

It was imperative he escape the Enclave undetected.

He hadn't encountered anyone else roaming the corridors. He paused, listening, but no sound met his ears, and he continued on. It would be awkward having to explain his presence at this time of night, when all were required to be at rest. He couldn't think of a convenient excuse; he was, after all, only a neophyte Revitalist. Previous nocturnal expeditions had gone undetected; he hoped his luck would continue.

He rounded a corner and flattened himself against the wall. The shadow of a guard patrolling the junction in front of the entrance to the motorpool swung across the floor.

Hannik cursed to himself. He hadn't expected the entrance to be guarded during the night shift. He'd never seen a guard here before. Could the hierarchy somehow have suspicions of him? He leaned back against the cool of the wall, willing his breathing to slow, his mind to think. Fool! Of course the door would be guarded! They wouldn't want adherents coming and going at will. Access to the motorpool was restricted to those deemed absolutely trustworthy, who had authorized functions to perform. He had just missed the guard when making his reconnaissance, that was all. Perhaps the man had other places to watch as well.

Hannik sneaked a look around the corner, trying to estimate the length of time it took the guard to go from one end of the cross-corridor to the other. When he judged the time was right, he dashed forward, stopping just short of the corridor. He was just in time. Seconds later the guard passed Hannik from his right, not sparing a glance to his left.

Hannik sprang. The guard never saw the blur from the darkness. He grunted softly as he slumped against Hannik. Hannik lowered the man's unconscious body to the floor and breathed a sigh of relief.

A moment's work on the lock, and the door to the motorpool slid open. Hannik grabbed the guard beneath the armpits and dragged the man in behind him. The man would be unconscious for some time. Hannik didn't want to take any chances; it would be fatal if the alarm was raised.

He switched on the lights and scanned the motorpool. The featureless rectangle had probably been a storage facility during the Enclave's construction. Storerooms lined the perimeter. Vehicles were parked in the center.

He wanted a flitter, but there were none to be seen. The Enclave possessed several, but they must all have been taken out. That was unfortunate.

But his decision was made. He had to escape tonight. The presence of the guard had seen to that.

Hannik dismissed the construction equipment offhand. The crawlers were attractive, but too slow. His best chance would be one of the lightweight speeders. He examined the several that were present, and found one with charged batteries and full water tanks. In the supply depot he located an environmental suit, respirator, and survival tent.

Hannik hoisted the guard into the storage compartment of a crawler and locked it. With any sort of luck, the man wouldn't be discovered for hours. He donned the e-suit, hooked up the respirator, made sure it was functioning correctly, and stowed the tent on the speeder.

The vehicle started immediately—the low hum of the electric motor reverberated in the cavernous space of the motor pool. Hannik drove it into the air lock and closed the doors behind him. The air lock cycled, and the outer doors opened to the surface of Mars.

Hannick gunned the motor and sped away. A cloud of dust rose in his wake, illuminated by the pale orb of the sun struggling to climb above the horizon.

>

Lin Grainger eased cautiously into the inner lab through a concealed entrance, clinging to the security of the wall. An eerie blue glow from the nutrient tanks suffused the gloom, imparting a spectral appearance to the banks of equipment.

She blinked and stifled a yawn.

Concealed behind a tank, she waited, senses alert, wishing her night vision was more acute.

Perhaps I was just dreaming, she thought.

She heard only the normal murmuring of the tanks, the hum of the computers, an occasional bleep from one of the monitors.

Satisfied she was alone, Lin inspected the array of monitors. The readings registered within normal limits.

She shook her head, annoyed with herself for giving way to nerves. She'd awoken from a sound sleep with the sense that something was amiss.

Stupid. There was nothing here.

A cough broke the stillness.

Lin whirled toward the outer lab. Forgetting her unease she rushed into the room to be met again by silence.

Another cough.

Lin realized belatedly it was the Asian woman on the central couch. She gave a nervous laugh.

Calm down, Lin. You'll give yourself a stroke at this rate.

The woman seemed to be well, the input feeding in smoothly. Lin patted her hand.

"You're okay."

Lin closed the lab and walked slowly to her room. She wondered if Hal was on guard duty tonight. Perhaps she should go and see? He had acted interested over lunch in the commonroom.

No. Better not. She didn't want to risk getting him into

trouble. If Klassen found out . . . there was no telling what he might do.

She slid beneath the sheets and fell back into a troubled slumber.

October 27, 2166
The Enclave

For most of his adult life, Ghalji Maranan had been a man of patience. An uncompromisingly phlegmatic nature had been seized upon by his parents, who saw patience as a desirable trait for their eldest son. More importantly, however, patience was a means to an end. Had he not possessed patience, he would not now, after nearly thirty years of labor, be seeing the fruits of his life dream lying almost within reach.

Many had considered Maranan, because of his placid demeanor, to be lacking ambition.

He smiled.

That was a mistake.

His green eyes half-closed by heavy lids, he studied the man seated opposite him. Curly black hair framed a face dominated by a too-wide nose and dark, deeply recessed eyes. A poorly repaired scar puckered the left cheek.

If only Erik would learn patience! He could see it written in his subordinate's eyes, the impatience, the anxiety, the desperate need to be always busy, to be forever at work. Klassen was the perfect man of action, a complement to Maranan's intellectualism, but if only he could learn . . .

Lately, he thought Klassen was losing that battle. Something seemed to have snapped, leaving the younger man at the mercy of anger, unable to control the passions that raged within.

Klassen's whole posture spoke of tenseness. The nails of his right thumb and index finger worried each other, a nervous mannerism that indicated some deeper conflict. Etched crow's-feet radiated from the corners of his eyes, contrasting with Maranan's smooth and unlined face.

Perhaps it was due to age. Klassen was about forty. For fifteen of those years he had been by Maranan's side. Maranan had known as soon as he had met Klassen that here was a man who would go places. He had carefully recruited the young man, nurtured him, led him through the hierarchy, until at last Klassen became his right hand man. Someday, Klassen would even be the leader of the Revitalists.

If only he could restrain his impatience.

"Well?" Klassen asked.

"We have been over this before, Erik. The time is not ready."

"When will the time be ready? For years you have been saying the time is not ready. What more do you want? We have more than enough people in positions of influence. Another one or two will make no difference. Let us strike now."

"Not yet, Erik. To act prematurely could mean the ruin of all we have striven for. Let us be patient."

"Patient!" Klassen spat. "I am sick of that word. We may lose all if we delay too long. We are fortunate to have escaped notice so far. I find it hard to credit that Security hasn't stumbled onto some leak since Garcia was removed."

Maranan pursed his lips. "That was unfortunate," he replied. "We had a man in Garcia whom we could control. Unfortunate that he was incompetent enough to be replaced. The new man, Duchesne, I do not think we can control. And you are right, it is curious that Security has not been interested in us."

"That's because Duchesne has been busy straightening out his mess at home. We can be thankful that Garcia left him enough to occupy his attention. Once he's finished, he'll be free to turn his attentions to us."

"Perhaps. But still I think you worry too much. So far, we've done nothing to excite attention. We mind our business and play cautiously until the time is right to come out into the open."

"What if he does become suspicious?"

Maranan's eyes were bland. "Then you take care of him."

"Always later! Act now!"

Maranan sighed. "The disappearance, compromise, or assassination of a Security officer would be certain to bring disaster. We cannot afford any mistakes. If Duchesne becomes aware of our activities, a convenient accident may have to be arranged. But only if necessary.

"We will deal with Security in good time, Erik. But first we remove the Christians. I know that you do not believe it, but they pose a far greater threat to our success than a handful of Security troops."

Klassen laughed coarsely. "Them? That crew of love-your-neighbor mystics? One hint of trouble and they'll melt away."

"Yes, Erik, them. If you were wise you would realize that there is more power in the spiritual realm than you think."

Klassen snorted. "Religion is for fools and weaklings. Or a means to an end. Can you give me any idea when we can move?"

"The time for action will be soon, Erik. That I promise you. Perhaps within a fortnight."

"Good. I wish to see this occur in my lifetime."

"As do I, Erik."

The annunciator on the door chimed. Maranan released the lock. "Come."

A chunky man in faded green coveralls preceded a young woman who remained standing in the background. The man's eyes flickered between the two leaders. It was to Maranan he nodded deference.

"What is it, Forrest?" Maranan inquired.

"There's a landspeeder missing from the motorpool," the man replied. "The guard was found unconscious."

Klassen lept to his feet. His face flushed. "Stolen?!"

"A neophyte adherent named Hannik is missing."

"I told you!" Klassen whirled on Maranan, stabbing a finger. "I *told* you that man was not to be trusted. You should have listened to me. I knew there was something not right about him."

Maranan spoke calmly. "That is past. Recriminations will avail nothing. He must be found. We cannot allow word to escape at this juncture."

"What are you waiting for?" Klassen yelled toward the waiting Forrest. "Find him!" Forrest headed for the door.

"Wait. When did he leave?"

Forrest paused on the threshold. "During sleep period."

Klassen cursed. "Too long! He'll have several hours head-start. Speeders will be too slow. Take out the hoverjet."

"The plane may be spotted," Maranan cautioned.

"That can't be helped. Hannik mustn't be allowed to escape and break word of the Plan." Klassen turned back to Forrest.

"Find him. I want Hannik dead! And see that the guard is punished."

Forrest nodded and disappeared.

With a final glare toward Maranan, Klassen stalked out.

Maranan sighed again. It was becoming increasingly difficult to control Klassen. He hoped it wouldn't become necessary to remove him. He would truly regret it if anything had to happen to Klassen. But he would wait and see. There was ample time for corrective measures.

One must never act in haste.

Maranan regarded the young woman who had entered with Forrest. "Come in, Lin. I hope you are not bringing me more bad news."

Lin's straw-colored bangs bobbed. "No, Master. I merely want to tell you that the newest replacement is ready."

"Sue Li-Shin? Good. I will arrange for her to be inserted."

Maranan saw the concerned look on Grainger's face. "What is it, Lin?" he asked gently. "Is something the matter?"

"Master—" Lin's eyes were downcast. "I don't think I can do this anymore."

"Why? What is wrong?"

"I—how can it be right to create these copies? And the originals—" She faltered, not meeting Maranan's gaze. "What happens to them?"

"Why the sudden concern, Lin? Do you reject your constructs also?"

Her eyes flashed. "No. They are my creation, a new form of life."

"Then why the others?"

"Because . . . because they're human."

"Look at me, Lin," Maranan commanded. "Look at me."

Lin responded to the force of his words, raising her eyes to lock with his green ones.

"They are no different than any other created life form. They have no more intrinsic value than, let us say, a fetus which we create and destroy at will. Their value lies in what we give them."

"But . . . a soul? Do they have souls?"

"Souls, Lin? We have no soul. We have a body that is part of the world, and a mind that is part of the universal all. The immortal soul is a fiction created by certain groups to maintain a hold over their followers by threats of eternal damnation in some supposed future existence."

"I feel—I feel like I'm playing God, usurping someone else's prerogatives—"

Maranan laughed, a deep, unearthly sound. "*You are* god, Lin! *I* am god. We are all god, all part of the divine. You are only doing what divinity is called to do."

"But—"

"What is the definition of a clone, Lin?"

"The asexual progeny of a single cell," she said. "A group of cells descended from a single cell."

"That is all these are. They are not human. They are tools. Tools which we use in our quest to restore Mars to its proper state. Without them, your pantropes have no meaning."

Maranan laid a hand on her shoulder. Lin pulled back.

"You have been working hard, Lin. Go and rest."

"Will there be more?" Lin asked, her voice drooping.

"A few. Not many. Soon we will have control, and then we—the Revitalists—will take only what we need from our Mother. We will be self-sufficient. We will not plunder Mars to help Earth."

"I wish I'd never laid eyes on them! It wasn't my—"

"I know," Maranan interrupted. "It was Dr. Farrer's work. But he is dead, and you must continue his work. I need you, Lin. I rely on you to bring the Plan to fruition."

"What about Klassen?" Lin flared. "I thought he was your next-in-line."

Maranan regarded Grainger thoughtfully. Clearly her feelings ran deeper than he had imagined. He would have to ask his Guide about this.

"Erik is a tool, also, Lin. He is useful. But he is not a thinker, not a planner. You, Lin, are much more essential than he."

"Then why don't you tell him to leave me alone?" Lin accused, the wetness of angry tears in her eyes.

She turned on her heel and left Maranan standing alone in the room.

TWO

The nose of the hypersonic plane dipped as it commenced its descent to New York. True to Corporal Rogers's word, the plane had been waiting at a Security airfield just outside London. More used to interplanetary vessels designed for function rather than aesthetics, the plane's sleek lines pleased Duchesne. Its swept-forward wings imparted the impression of restlessness, the jet chafing at being earthbound, eager to depart the runpad for its true home in the sky.

Forty minutes of cloudscape later, New York streaked into sight.

Small windows gave a restricted view, but in the limited space available over Carolyn's shoulders, Duchesne could still see enough to be impressed. The megalopolis encompassed what had once been separate cities in their own right—Philadelphia, Baltimore, Washington, Newark, Wilmington.

Two years had passed quickly—it seemed just yesterday that he had been completing a dangerous mission in this city. But would he trade Lowell for it? No.

Look at it this way: Washington-New York had lots of people, but his jurisdiction—Mars, Asteroids, moons of Jupiter, Titan—vastly eclipsed it in terms of sheer volume.

Beside him, Carolyn's breathing quickened at the remembered view. Her snub nose pressed against the window.

"Big, isn't it?" Duchesne understated.

"I still have a hard time conceiving it. It certainly puts Lowell to shame."

"One hundred million people. A hundred times as many as Lowell." He laughed. "We've only got two in the whole Outer System."

The plane descended vertically for a gentle landing.

A pair of Security troopers, caduceus and star insignias emblazoned on their uniforms, waited on the landing pad. Both saluted; the senior stepped forward as Duchesne and Carolyn descended.

"Major Duchesne?" her voice carried over the fading whine of the plane's engines. "Trooper Chu. Colonel Forbes sent us to escort you. Car's over this way, sir."

"Let's not keep him waiting. Lead on."

The weather in Scotland had been unseasonably perfect, sunny and relatively mild. Thanks to a freak heat wave, New York hit them like a furnace. Even this late in the year, the sun broiled down. The humidity was drenching, as if competing with the temperature to see which could debilitate Mars-humans the most.

The city's towering skyscrapers failed to block the sun to any appreciable extent, reflecting and amplifying the heat.

In moments, Duchesne's shirt clung to his back.

Carolyn wiped her forehead on her sleeve. "I wish I'd put my sweater in the luggage."

"Uh-huh."

"Terrible climate control," she remarked to trooper Chu. "You should complain to the environmental department."

"Is it always like this?" Duchesne asked.

"No, sir!" Chu replied grinning. "In summer, it gets hot."

Duchesne grimaced.

Chu turned up the air conditioning.

The speaker in the aircar rattled to life.

"YOU ARE ENTERING RESTRICTED AIRSPACE. TRAVEL BEYOND THIS POINT IS RESTRICTED WITHOUT PROPER SECURITY CLEAR-ANCE. WARNING. YOU ARE ENTERING RESTRICTED AIRSPACE . . ."

Chu entered her code; the warning gargled to a halt in mid-sentence.

The bulk of the city had disappeared; they were now at the north end, just beyond New York. For a few moments, the car traversed the verdant green of foliage. Rising stepwise above the trees, Security HQ stood alone in a clearing, isolated from the city by several kilometers of parkland, perimeter guards, and airspace restrictions.

The temperature was noticeably cooler as they stepped out of the car onto the landing pad. A trace of breeze disturbed the air.

Passing through security and ID checks at the entrance, Chu escorted them to the lifter. It rose quickly up the building.

"Still at the top?" Duchesne asked.

"Yes, sir," Chu replied. "One hundred and eighty-eight."

Chu announced Duchesne at Forbes's office, and then turned to Carolyn. "There's an officers' lounge one floor down, if you'd like me to show you, Captain."

"I'll find you when I'm done," said Duchesne.

"Okay." Carolyn followed Chu.

Forbes's aide, a competent-appearing corporal, scrutinized Duchesne as if expecting a Martian to appear different in some way. "You can go on in, sir," he said. "Colonel Forbes is expecting you."

Duchesne felt a twinge of apprehension. It had been two years since he had last met Forbes in the flesh. Official dispatches via delayed comm laser from Lowell were more efficient but less personal.

Forbes had commanded Security for nearly twenty years, surviving changes of government, political climates and societal perturbations with the skills of a chameleon. How he had managed to remain in power when many presidents and World Council members and ministers had come and gone was his own secret.

Despite contrary winds of change Forbes had turned Security into his own private enterprise, personally training many higher ranking staff officers. Security bore the stamp of Gerald Forbes's personality.

Duchesne well knew that while Forbes could tolerate an honest mistake, incompetence or laziness would drive him to extremes of rage.

The fiasco involving ex-major Garcia had seen the Forbes wrath rise to unprecedented levels.

The door opened; Duchesne strode in. "Commander, Outer Planets, reporting, sir," he began formally.

Forbes stood up and extended a bear-paw of a hand toward him. "Duchesne, welcome to New York," he growled. "Good to see you again."

"You are looking well, sir." Duchesne returned Forbes's excruciating grip, hoping no bones would crack. "Please pardon the lack of uniform. I wasn't expecting—"

"Think no more about it." Forbes waved off the explanation. "Take a seat."

Forbes returned behind his desk. A massively built man, the colonel's uniform strained to constrain his mixture of muscle and girth. Thick, black eyebrows proliferated above narrow, shrewd eyes. A perpetual scowl creased Forbes's forehead. Most striking of all was the colonel's moustache; Duchesne had never seen its like.

Forbes's malignant eyes glittered. "What kind of a vacation are you taking, poking around Christian sites?"

Duchesne was nonplussed before remembering that Forbes cultivated an intimidating presence as assiduously as he did his moustache. "It's partly research," he replied, deciding that at least some honesty was necessary. "There's anti-Christian sentiment in Lowell, and I thought it would be helpful to gain a better understanding of what the other side is about."

"And the other part?" Forbes menaced.

"My wife is of Scottish extraction. She wanted to dig into her roots."

Forbes huffed. "See that's all it is. Mark my words, Duchesne, too much interest can be unhealthy. It'll get you into trouble. Christians are known to do funny things."

Duchesne had once conducted a funeral service for a trooper killed on assignment. Major Garcia had been furious. A Christian service? Defying the UWC?

Curious how Christianity kept intruding into his life.

" . . . marrying a fellow officer, Duchesne. Highly irregular," Forbes was saying.

Duchesne grinned and wiped it from his face in the same movement. "These things happen, sir."

"Do they, now. Quite a job you're doing, Duchesne."

Forbes took him off-balance again. Duchesne wasn't quite sure how the words were meant. He decided it was a compliment.

"Uh . . . thank you, sir."

Forbes scowled. "You're doing nothing but creating waves. Do you know how many reports of resignations and transfers

I've received? Not to mention complaints from several officers with influential connections. Eh?" he glared. "Do you know?"

"I did what I felt was necessary," Duchesne replied wood-enly, "to clean up the mess I was handed. Do you have a complaint with the efficiency of my command, sir?"

Forbes smiled. "Good. I like a man who makes waves. And one who doesn't apologize when he's right. From the reports, it seems you've weeded out a lot of bad eggs." Forbes emitted a gusty sigh. "I had no idea conditions had sunk so low. Garcia was an imbecile but a clever imbecile with connections. It would have been devilishly difficult to have removed him without clear-cut cause. His family connections succeeded in ensuring that negative reports never made it to my attention. At least he finally provided a reason that was incontrovertible."

Duchesne said nothing.

"But that's old history. There's something a lot more serious afoot." Forbes inserted a computer wafer into his workstation and swiveled the high resolution screen around to face Duchesne. "Do you recognize this man?"

Duchesne regarded the features that stared back at him. A middle-aged male, dusky complected, short brown hair cropped unevenly over unusually large ears. He wore a fixed, expressionless smile, conveying no emotion, and a shapeless, robe-like garment. The out-of-focus background looked vaguely like somewhere on the Indian subcontinent.

He had seen the man somewhere—a news broadcast, perhaps?

"Seems familiar." The name came to him. "Maranan?"

"Precisely." Forbes nodded. "Ghalji Maranan. Founder and leader of the Revitalists."

Duchesne was puzzled. "I've heard of them, of course. An insignificant cult. Why the recall?"

"I'll review the history for you. The Revitalists were founded by Maranan about thirty years ago, as a registered member of the United World Church. As far as I know, they still are, although one could hardly call them mainstream. The movement began here on Earth, but for reasons that have never been fully explained, Maranan packed up and moved to Mars with those of his members who chose to follow. For a while, nothing was heard of them.

"About ten years later, they became aggressive, actively proselytizing. This lasted for a period of several years, until the group again became quiescent. They have remained that way since, contenting themselves with staging the occasional protest and promoting the writings of their leader. His views have become progressively more radical.

"Their numbers have remained small. There are believed to be not above two hundred full members, although there are undoubtedly more adherents. Numbers of those remaining on Earth are not available.

"They have remained law abiding and peaceful."

"Until now?" Duchesne anticipated.

"Until now." Forbes flashed another picture on the screen. Duchesne shook his head. "As far as I know, I've never seen this man."

"No reason you should. His name is—or was—Hannik. Gerhart Hannik. He was an investigative reporter for Newsnet."

Forbes twirled one side of his moustache between a thumb and index finger. "He was also an ex-Security agent."

Duchesne looked up sharply. Reporters were an accepted nuisance. One who had retired—or been discharged—from Security. . . . "And you think—"

"His last report indicated he was pursuing a lead concerning the Revitalists."

Forbes pulled out the wafer and handed it to Duchesne. "He believed that they had become significantly less peaceful, and, in fact, were engaged in some kind of conspiracy."

"A conspiracy? On *Mars*?"

"We don't know. Newsnet reports that no word has been received from Hannik for over two months, long past the deadline when he was to report back. We must presume that he was caught and silenced."

"Has there been any Security involvement?"

"Not officially. But before Hannik left, he was contacted unofficially and advised to report anything of a potential threat to the public."

"Did he?"

"He said he believed the Revitalists had formed an enclave toward Hellas Planitia, and he was going to investigate. That was all."

Duchesne nodded. "The Enclave exists, I know that for a fact. It's a long ways from Lowell, out in the middle of nowhere. There's never been any need for official investigation. We'd have to check their permits, but I'd assume they're all legal."

Duchesne thought for a moment. "I don't follow. A missing reporter, a fringe cultic group, unsubstantiated rumors of a conspiracy. Mikhaelovitch is perfectly capable of following up Hannik's whereabouts."

Forbes looked grim. "Ordinarily, you would be correct. You probably haven't heard the news broadcasts."

Duchesne shook his head. "My wife has made me avoid them."

"There has been a governmental crisis on Mars. The Thorston administration is threatening to topple under heavy accusations. Legislators have renounced party affiliations."

"And?"

"There are reports that the Revitalists claim they are taking control."

Duchesne's jaw dropped. "What's their reason?"

"That's what we'd like to know."

Duchesne rubbed his lip. "That's out of the ordinary, isn't it, sir? Governmental or religious matters; surely the Minister of Religion—"

"Hang the Minister of Religion!" Forbes shouted, slamming a fist onto his desk. "I don't care what that bunch of kooks believes! They can waltz around in their robes and sing and chant until their throats wither!"

He fixed Duchesne with a steely glare. "Administrator Thorston is an old friend. He called me for help. You're it."

Mars, Hellas Planitia

The landspeeder bucked and bounced over the uneven terrain, twisting and convulsing like a wild thing. His neck snapped back and forth. Hannik gritted his teeth as yet another crazy yaw threatened to hurl him off. Clenching his hands, he kept a tight grip on the controls, his fingers going numb from the pressure. He was thankful for the restraining straps which were all that kept him in the control seat.

The perpetual motion made it difficult to steer a straight course between the rubble.

Once, to impress a half-forgotten girlfriend, he had ridden a bucking bronco at a rodeo in Calgary, justifying it to himself as background color for a story. The bronco had nothing on the speeder. He couldn't remember if the story had sold.

He raised his eyes from the ground ahead—no hard matter—in order to cast an anxious look back over his shoulder. A trail of dust stretched behind him, ascending into the thin air. An arrow, with him as its apex, an easy sign for any pursuers to follow. And there would be pursuers, he was certain of that.

Why couldn't there be a wind today to disperse the dust?

His only hope was to reach the mountains before nightfall. In the rugged, boulder-strewn terrain his ability to elude pursuit would improve, even though travel would be difficult. Hannik did not delude himself—his chances of survival were slim.

The tanks on the speeder provided a week's worth of water. Food was a different matter. He had been able to abstract only a few rations, stuffed into his pockets. That didn't bother him; he could survive without food. What he couldn't do was survive without shelter—he needed somewhere secure to erect his tent. It would do no good to pitch it in the open, in plain sight of whoever was following.

The speeder crashed to earth after a wild bounce flung it momentarily airborne. Hannik swerved to avoid a gully which opened wide. The wheels crumbled along the edge before pulling away. He almost wished he had opted for an enclosed crawler, designed for rough travel, instead of the speeder. A pity crawlers were so slow. The speeder—not much more than a frame, engine, and wheels—was much faster, but it meant he would have to spend the whole time in his environmental suit. Speed over comfort.

The proximity alarm on the landspeeder's console began blinking a fateful red. Hannik muttered an exclamation of annoyance.

Too soon!

Far too soon!

The mountains were close; he could make out the darker shade of the foothills ahead, rising out of the rust-red of the rocky plain.

He cast around, trying to see what the alarm was indicating. A speeder couldn't have caught him so quickly, unless his departure had been discovered within minutes. A flitter, more likely.

A faint whine sounded overhead. Hannik searched the sky and in a moment picked up an ominous profile.

A hoverjet!

He wasn't aware that the Enclave possessed a hoverjet; he'd been expecting only ground pursuit. Had he known there was a plane, he would have tried for it. He could pilot—not well, but competently enough for an escape flight.

The whine increased. The shadow of the plane, cast by the setting sun, sped across the sand, heading unerringly toward him.

He peered upward, eyes narrowed against the glare, seeing the black form of the plane coming in low and fast. The red flash of laser fire illuminated the sky a split second before it hit the ground a few meters to his left. A spurt of rock and dust spewed into the air. Hannik jinked the speeder, trying to disrupt their aim. He was momentarily successful; another bolt burst wide. With a roar, the hoverjet passed directly overhead, almost close enough for him to catch a glimpse of the pilot in the cockpit. The dust of its passage enveloped the speeder, adding to the cloud raised by the spinning wheels.

The hills were closer. Just a few more minutes. . . .

The front wheels hit a rut. Hannik fought for control. The speeder slewed around, and for a moment he was heading back the way he had come, wasting precious seconds. He brought it about on two wheels and resumed his course. But now the plane was between him and the hills, coming about in a large curve.

He gunned the motor as hard as he could, heedless of the punishment the suspension was absorbing.

A trickle of sweat ran down his forehead. Hannik wished he could wipe it away. He realized he was hyperventilating and tried to slow his breathing.

The plane aimed directly at him, the laser ports winking like flashing eyes. Hannik gritted his teeth. The blast, when it came, blinded him with searing light. The shot impacted the front of the speeder. His restraints parted. The speeder upended. Hannik somersaulted backward into space. He had a brief glimpse of the world spinning crazily before the ground rushed up to meet him with bone-crunching force.

Consciousness returned in a flare of pain and blurred vision. Hannik forced his eyes to focus. He saw that he was lying behind a low hummock, only a few meters from the crumpled wreck of the speeder, which spurted puffs of flame and smoke as combustible parts tried to burn in the oxygen-poor air. A glance sufficed to tell him that it was ruined beyond repair. His vision fuzzed again.

The hoverjet settled down on a level patch beyond the wreck.

Hannik moved gingerly and winced. Pain lanced through his right arm. He probed it with the other, grimacing as another spasm took him near the shoulder. He couldn't move it. Probably broken. Otherwise, he seemed to have escaped with bruises and flash burns. His e-suit was scuffed but intact, and he gave thanks for that small mercy. A star shivered his faceplate, but the tough plastic had survived the impact. Dark blotches showed where light-dampeners had burned out from the laser blast, but not before saving his sight.

Raising himself to his knees he supported himself with his good arm. He had landed close to the edge of a ravine, almost out of sight-line of the speeder. The swirling dust helped to conceal him, plastered as he was with the stuff.

The port on the hoverjet dropped open. Two figures descended. It wasn't hard to discern the rifles they carried. Ambling across the desert they inspected the wreck of the speeder. Hannik crawled as rapidly as he could to the brink of the ravine. Feet first, he eased over the lip and skidded and slid to the level bottom.

He leaned against the side, catching his breath and waiting for the stabs of pain from his broken arm to subside.

Loosening the strap supporting his life-support pack, he slid his injured arm underneath. He used his good hand to tighten the strap and bind the fracture to his chest, creating a makeshift sling. It wasn't good, but better than nothing.

Hannik set off at a slow trot down the course of the ancient waterway, trying to put as much distance as he could between himself and his pursuers.

A faint, muffled shout echoed behind him. The two men had abandoned their investigation of the speeder and stood on the edge of the ravine. One unlimbered his rifle. A bolt of red fire streaked after Hannik, splattering the ravine wall beside him and showering him with needle-sharp fragments.

Every jarring step sent renewed waves of pain coursing through him. Hannik ignored the discomfort and tried to present as elusive a target as possible. Another shot seared at his heels, and then the canyon took a sharp turn. He was out of sight. Grimly, he ran on, numbly placing one foot ahead of the other.

He flicked on the receiver in his helmet, picking up voices.

"Come on! He can't move fast. Did you see the way he was clutching his arm?"

"Let him go."

"Are you crazy, Szalny? Klassen told us to make sure he was dead."

"You said it; he's as good as dead already. Where's he going to go, Forrest? He's got no food, no supplies, no transportation, and it's the better part of two thousand kilometers to Lowell. His tent was on the speeder. He won't survive the night unprotected." The man laughed. "There's no way he'll make it to Lowell—he was a fool to think he could try. Leave him to freeze to death. Let's you and me get back before dark."

"Good thinking."

The transmission fuzzed.

Hannik heard the whine of the plane powering up. His first thought was that they were going to hunt him from the air. He was unsure whether to continue, or to hide himself between boulders and hope he wouldn't be spotted. He was spared the decision. The roar of the plane faded into the distance. They really were leaving him. He considered returning to the speeder, but the men wouldn't have left anything worthwhile behind. He was on his own.

He plodded along in the general direction of Lowell, knowing he had no chance for survival. That had been taken away from him.

Could he have planned his escape differently?

His only hope was to get close enough that someone would find his body—and what he carried.

➤

TO: MIKHAELOVITCH, BORIS, LT., SECOUTPLANHQ, LOWELL CITY, MARS.

FROM: DUCHESNE, J.I., MAJOR., COMOUTPLAN,
IN TRANSIT, SST *Aries*, EARTH REG. 1-LK-665.

EARTHDATE: OCTOBER 27, 2166.
TRANSMISSION 2300 GMT

SECURITY ENCRYPTEYES ONLY***
PRIORITY 1 DIRECTIVE

TEXT: [SUMMARY] DIRECTIVE: INSTITUTE DISCRETE
INQUIRIES LOCATION SUBJECT GERHART HANNIK
(DESCRIPTION FOLLOWS), POSSIBLE AREA HELLAS PLANITIA.

DIRECTIVE: INSTITUTE DISCRETE INQUIRIES GHALJI
MARANAN (DESCRIPTION FOLLOWS), REVITALIST MOVE-
MENT, ATTENTION TO CURRENT GOVERNMENTAL CRISIS.

DIRECTIVE: UNDER NO CIRCUMSTANCES IS
EXISTENCE/NATURE OF INQUIRIES TO BE MADE KNOWN.
ABSOLUTE SECRECY ESSENTIAL.

COMPLETE TEXT FOLLOWS

The message would go out with the next batch of transmissions to Mars. Duchesne retired to join Carolyn in their
quarters, his body thoroughly confused by the repeated time
changes. New York to Gander Spaceport to Security Naval
Spacedock to transport *Aries*. A bad meal; a transport lieutenant
surly at being delayed until he learned the identity of his two
passengers.

"Are you ready to tell me yet?" Carolyn asked. She reclined
on a couch in the small compartment.

Duchesne dropped onto the bed. Earth was receding into
the blackness of space, the transport under steady, low acceler-
ation. He had skimmed through the contents of the wafer earlier while the wave-washed coastlines of Maine and Nova Scotia
passed below.

"Is it that obvious?"

"It's perfectly obvious that you're chafing at being aboard
ship while something is going on that you can't do anything
about."

Duchesne allowed a flicker of a smile to cross his lips.
"Can't hide it, can I? Tell me, what do you know about the
Revitalists?"

Carolyn wrinkled her brow. "Fringe group, beliefs comprised of the usual mixture of reincarnation—I think—ecological concerns, communication with 'ascended masters', self-advancement and the like. The type of group that crops up following a charismatic leader and fades away when he or she dies."

Duchesne looked askance.

"Hey, I did a lot of reading on different religious groups, remember?"

"How could I forget? For a while there you were a member of the religion-of-the-month club. But you're absolutely correct. Up until now they were no more than a curiosity and a not particularly interesting one at that."

"What's new?"

"Did you hear about the governmental crisis back home?"

"Yeah. The comm officer picked up a Marsnews feed for me."

"Well, Forbes appears to think the Revitalists are behind the crisis."

"You're kidding!"

"Perfectly serious." He handed her the wafer. "You can read through this if you like. I'll be needing your input. There's not much concrete on here, but it makes me feel very uneasy."

"Why does a minority religous group suddenly want to take over the government? They've never been persecuted or suppressed, have they?"

"Not that I know of. And goodness knows the United World Church gives enough leeway to believe almost anything you want to. The Revitalists seem to have maintained a low profile, minding their own business."

"What does Forbes want you to do about it?"

"Goodness only knows."

Duchesne sat in thought for a few minutes, finally bringing his fist down on the arm of the couch. "The Revitalists must have an agenda. But what is it?"

THREE

Erik Klassen received the report from Forrest and Szalny with satisfaction.

"You are certain the traitor is dead?" he persisted, flexing a stylus in his large fist, his feet reclined on the corner of his desk.

"Sure," said Szalny. "There wasn't much left of him after the speeder went up." He moved his hands in the air to indicate an explosion.

Forrest chuckled. "Not much at all."

"We buried the pieces in a ravine. There's no chance they'll be spotted."

Klassen swung his feet down to the floor and leaned forward. His eyes flashed from one man to the other.

"All right. That's one problem solved. Now the next item is this. There's another substitution to make."

"Who is it this time, boss?" Forrest asked.

"Sue Li-Shin."

Forrest whistled. He cast a nervous look toward Szalny. "It won't be easy—"

"I didn't say it would be!" Klassen shouted. The stylus snapped in two with a sharp crack.

Forrest took a step back.

"You two are being paid enough," said Klassen, regaining an icy calm. "Or would you rather I found someone else to do it?"

The unspoken implication was clear.

"We can do it," Szalny nodded. He motioned to Forrest to stay quiet.

"I'll make your job easier," said Klassen, "though I don't know why I should. She's making an inspection of the detail at

Olympus in a couple of days; security will be looser than at Lowell HQ. You'll find a couple of uniforms in supply that should fit you."

He bared his teeth in a chill smile. "Think you two dolts can impersonate police officers?"

"Sure," said Forrest. "It'll be fun."

"I don't care if it's fun or not!" Klassen raged. "Just see that it's done."

"Right, boss."

Szalny tugged on Forrest's sleeve. "We'll get right on it."

When they were gone, Klassen regarded the broken stylus.

"Or so help me . . ." he said, methodically snapping the implement into smaller and smaller pieces.

>

The salmon pink of the evening sky darkened brick red, deepening to star-speckled black. No gradual sunset as on Earth, where dusk merged imperceptibly into twilight. Night came quickly.

Hannik stumbled through lengthening shadows. Each step had to be calculated; no taking for granted that the shadows concealed level ground. A misstep meant a fall; a fall meant a possible tear in his suit from a knife-sharp rock-edge; a tear in the suit meant a quick death as his blood boiled in the low air pressure, even as he froze in the sub-zero temperature.

Would that be so bad?

Hannik was tempted. Death was inevitable. Would it matter so much if it was fast or slow?

He wished there was a sunset to enjoy.

The temperature dropped steadily. The tiny motor of the e-suit whined in protest, straining to put out every last erg of heat. How much longer would the batteries last? Even though fully charged when he left, they weren't intended to endure indefinitely. If he hadn't been detected and the speeder destroyed, he could have recharged them from either the speeder's larger batteries or its solar collecting system.

His cold muscles threatened to cramp. The sweat that had broken out earlier when he was fleeing from his pursuers had dried on his skin, contributing to the chill that gnawed at his vitals. He checked the heater, but as he expected, it was set on maximum. His stomach ached with hunger, but that he could ignore. The fatigue and cold he could not. He took a sip of water to moisten his mouth.

He knew he couldn't continue much longer.

His mind felt as sluggish as his legs, a sure sign of impending hypothermia. Soon his body temperature would drop further, and he'd lose consciousness and drift into a sleep from which he would never wake.

Perhaps if he had strapped the tent on top of the oxygen tanks on his back like a backpack, instead of tossing it onto the carrier deck of the speeder . . .

Perhaps if he had left earlier in the evening, placing more distance between himself and the Enclave, widening the area that would have to be searched . . .

Perhaps if he had reconnoitered more thoroughly and discovered the hoverjet instead of taking a speeder . . .

Perhaps . . . perhaps. . . .

One mistake was too many. That made three.

If only he'd found another way to communicate with the outside, but the single communications room at the Enclave was manned continually. Try as he might, he hadn't been able to access the equipment.

Recriminations were useless. He shook his head to try to clear his mind. He had known the danger when he had embarked on this enterprise. He had taken risks all his life, begun assignments from which other, more cautious reporters shied away. Always he had come out on top. Another scoop for Gerhart Hannik.

Until now.

He squinted to make out the irregularities of ground immediately before him. The walls of the gully in which he ran cut out most of what little sunlight remained, reducing the sky to a narrow gray strip strung overhead. Deimos and Phobos were far too small to illuminate the night; absorbing, not reflecting light. But for the stars, Martian night was pitch black.

The gully ended abruptly in a wall of rubble. Hannik halted his momentum just in time to avoid running into the rockslide. He saw no other egress. He clambered awkwardly up the crumbly rock onto level ground. Breathing heavily, he looked westward. The last fleeting rays of the impaled sun dipped below the stark peaks on the horizon. Hannick wrapped his arms around himself and shivered.

The end was near.

In a little while, the temperature would fall to fifty degrees below zero Fahrenheit. Unprotected, he could not survive. Hannik kept moving, prolonging the inevitable, willing one more step from his cold, tired muscles.

Why keep on? How much would another few kilometers at best make? Even though he could cover ground faster than on Earth, the distance would be miniscule compared to what was left.

The closer he was to Lowell, the more likely someone would find him.

Perhaps a prospector . . .

Would anybody even bother to look?

Perhaps.

Perhaps, when he didn't return from assignment, Newsnet would inform the authorities. Newsnet wouldn't be overly concerned about a missing freelancer, not enough to bother investigating themselves. But maybe they would notify Security.

There was no one else to care. Hannik had no wife, no family, no one he could call a friend. Not even a dog. He had prized his isolation, his privacy, his self-sufficiency.

No one would miss him.

Perhaps Security would look.

Unless they had other, more pressing matters to occupy them.

Like the Revitalists.

If they found him in time . . .

Please God, Hannik thought, *let them find me in time.*

His chest burning in the cold, no longer able to see the ground in front of him, Gerhart Hannik stumbled on into the icy dark of the Martian night.

➤

Lin Grainger slapped a centimeter-sized patch onto the left side of the Oriental woman's neck, making sure she centered it over the vigorous pulsations of the carotid artery. She smoothed the edges down, blending them into the flawless skin. The flesh-colored patch would be nearly invisible, especially when the woman's dark hair hung over her shoulders.

Just to be sure, Lin shrugged up the collar of the brown uniform enclosing Li-Shin's shapely form.

Li-Shin's face had a glassy expression, her eyes blank. The woman made no move as Lin fussed over her.

"Aren't you ready yet?" Szalny paced around the lab, clearly looking out of place.

"Wait a minute," Lin snapped. She glared at the slender, bald man. "Or do you want her waking up too soon?"

"Calm down, Szalny," interjected Forrest. "We don't want any mistakes." He grinned toothily at Lin. "Take your time. Don't pay any attention to my buddy, here."

"Tell your buddy to mind his manners." Lin continued straightening Li-Shin.

"That's enough out of you, you worthless piece of trash—" Szalny moved toward her.

Lin tensed, keeping Li-Shin between herself and Szalny.

Forrest gripped his partner's arm, jerking him to a halt. "Let her work, Szalny."

Szalny shrugged out of the grip but held his peace. He turned his back on Lin.

"So what's this?" Forrest walked over to where the ruby comm laser emanated from the computer bank.

"Don't touch that!" Lin blurted.

"Hey!" Forrest held his arms wide. "Wasn't going to."

Lin rubbed her head, feeling a dull ache radiate from her neck.

Just finish and get these two jerks out!

The work with the clones made her irritable. Despite Maranan's reassurances, Lin wished this part was over. Why had she ever let him talk her into taking over this project when Farrer died?

"That's the memory input," she said tiredly. "Combined with a low-power sleep field."

"Pretty slick."

"Once I turn off the field, the hypneum in the patch will take over." She looked at Szalny's back and returned her attention to Forrest. "The patch will last for two days—forty-eight hours from now, precisely—so you'd better make sure you've done whatever you're going to before then. Once it wears off, she won't respond to control."

"Just like the real thing, huh?"

Lin winced. She pressed another patch into Forrest's hand. "Here's a spare. Just in case."

Forrest transferred it to a pocket. "We won't need it."

Lin ignored him.

She ran her fingers over the control console. The glow of the laser faded. Li-Shin slumped on her couch. Lin raised the helmet and brushed the luxurious dark hair, enjoying its softness. With the touch of another control, the restraints retracted.

After checking the vital signs a final time, she removed the monitors.

"She's all yours."

"Thanks," said Forrest. "Would you like to do the honors?" he asked Szalny.

"No."

Forrest shrugged. "Come on, dear," he instructed the recumbent figure. "On your feet, Sue."

Jerking like a marionette, Li-Shin rose.

"Muscle control will be sluggish at first," Lin pointed out. "If you get a chance to move her around, that would help."

"Got it," Forrest replied. "Let's go, Sue. Follow me."

Szalny stalked out, followed by Forrest and Li-Shin—a bizarre parade.

Lin watched the procession pass down the corridor. She made sure the door of the lab closed and leaned against it, closing her eyes.

Earthdate: November 5, 2166
In transit, Mars approach

The wind whistled and shrieked past the narrow windows, the surface an ochre blur. The leading edges of the Sangerra ground-to-orbit shuttle's wings glowed cherry red with radiated heat.

"The pilot must be in a hurry," Carolyn remarked, looking up from the book she was reading, "judging by the speed of reentry."

"Either that or he knows I am."

The long gash of Valles Marineris passed below, a huge, congealed wound on the skin of the planet. Mars seemed to specialize in size to compensate for an otherwise planetary sense of inadequacy.

Chin pillowed in his hand, Duchesne kept his eyes fixed on the landscape. Olympus Mons. The towering volcano, three times as high as Earth's Mount Everest, rose starkly above the ochre plains. He thought he could almost see signs of the settlement—Mars' second largest city—but that may have been no more than an optical illusion.

"Am I crazy?" he asked.

"Huh? No. Shouldn't think so. Why?"

"It feels like home. I'm just wondering if I'm crazy to prefer a dry, cold planet with an unbreathable atmosphere to Earth."

"Where were you born?" Carolyn retorted.

"Here, of course."

"Well then. So was I. I like it better too."

Duchesne's lips twitched. "Good."

Little additional information had been received about the situation on Mars. Earth's Newsnet broadcasts had been unenlightening, the story fading after a couple of days. What occurred on Mars, with its million and a half population, was of little interest to the average Earthling. Other news, of more significance to the fifteen billion of Earth, had claimed the headlines.

Marsnews had been similarly uninstructive. The government appeared to have put a clamp on news releases, restricting what was disseminated to the public. The little that leaked out merely rehashed the obvious.

Duchesne had perused all the information he could gather about the Revitalists. Mikhaelovitch's last update contained nothing confidential, just what anybody could access from their library terminal.

Carolyn jostled him as she switched off her reader.

"All done?" he asked.

"Finally. Turgid prose and obscure meandering are the nicest things I can say."

"Maranan hasn't become your favorite author?"

"It's given me the most awful headache. The man has some strange ideas. He doesn't strike me as being your average crank, but I'm at a loss what to make of him. I think he firmly believes in what he's written, but it's hard to get at the underlying meaning. It's like he's trying to be deliberately obscure, and only if you have the key can you understand what he's trying to say."

Carolyn yanked out the reader again. "Listen to this quote from *The New Gaia*, one of the more readable ones, although it runs to nearly a thousand pages." She cleared her throat. "'How can we persuade the obstinate, long secure in her realm of inviolable isolation, to reverse the mind-set of millenia; relinquishing her self-imposed path to follow the more harmonious way of her sun-ward sister; embracing life not as an evil, but as a good; encountering the organic not as a parasite or a competitor but as a partner, a companion on the long and difficult road to cosmic unity?' Aaagh!" She switched off the book.

Duchesne snickered.

Carolyn favored him with a violet glare. "Maybe you should try reading it." She waved the reader in his direction.

He held up a hand. "Rank has its privileges. It's either you or Boris, and I don't think he'd make it past the first page. And can you imagine Nancy Cohen reading it?"

Carolyn was forced to chuckle. "She'd be more inclined to incinerate it. One shot, straight from the hip."

"Seriously," said Duchesne, "were they worth reading in spite of the headache?"

"I wouldn't do it again. Perhaps they'll provide an insight into the man's thought processes that might prove helpful." Carolyn frowned. "There's something here, but I don't know what it is."

"Give your mind a rest. It might come to you."

"If it does, you'll be the first to know."

Duchesne looked out the window again. "We're almost there."

The red blur had mutated to green; the large enclosed fields of GenAg, where plants tailor-made to survive on the inhospitable surface were being developed. Bringing life to Mars comprised only one part of the long-range strategy.

The real secret to terraforming lay in warming the cold planet, releasing it from its icy prison. Only when warm could Mars be made suitable for humanity. Massive solar reflectors hung in space, focusing the sun's rays on the polar caps, melting the ice and permafrost. Tons of chlorofluorocarbons—the same gases that had done so much damage to Earth's ozone layer—were released into the atmosphere, acting as a greenhouse lid to retain heat. Mars was not warm, by any means, but not as cold as it had been.

Eventually the atmosphere would be dense enough. Already it had been thickened to where it equalled Earth's atmosphere at an altitude of 80,000 feet, easing the burden on aircraft designers.

Eventually Mars would be warm enough.

Eventually . . .

"What's the shiver for?" Carolyn asked.

"Just imagining Ganymede. How could you terraform a ball of ice and dirt?"

"No way."

Minutes later the huge Lowell City dome flashed into view, a jewel in the midst of the flat plain of Syrtis Major. The bright sunshine gleamed off the dome and the tracery of metal supports.

The Sangerra screamed in for a landing on the reinforced thermocrete expanse of Lowell Spaceport five kilometers west of the city, raising a cloud of dust. The pilot taxied over to the squat, blocky spaceport complex. The shuttle trembled slightly as a connecting tube snaked out and attached itself to the forward airlock. The noise of the engines died away, replaced by the sound of cooling and contracting metal. Duchesne and Carolyn unfastened their restraints.

The slightly flat odor of recycled air greeted their nostrils. Funny how recycled air—or even air straight from the oxygen plant—smelled like home, while the air of Earth could be so different.

A sergeant in Security black and gray strode over to greet them. He paused at attention and saluted. "Welcome back, sir. Lieutenant Mikhaelovitch was unable to meet you, but he sent me to accompany you."

"Thank you, Jacland." Duchesne recognized the sergeant as being attached to headquarters staff. "Where is the lieutenant?"

"At headquarters, sir."

"I'll go directly there. Do you want to take the baggage home, Carolyn?"

"If it's all the same to you, I'll come to HQ too. Might as

well see what's happened in my absence."

"Very well," Duchesne acceded. "On second thought, it'll only take a few minutes. Let's stop and change first. I want to get out of this grungy stuff. Lead on, Jacland."

A line of arrivals chafed at the civilian entry port from a commercial shuttle that had touched down. Customs, an archaic if still occasionally encountered institution on one-government Earth, was a necessary evil here. The guard at the military entrance saluted as Duchesne flashed his ID, allowing them to pass through unimpeded.

"I have a flitter waiting, sir," said Jacland.

"A flitter?"

"The lieutenant thought you might not want to wait for the monorail."

"Sounds like Boris has learned how to read your mind," Carolyn remarked dryly.

"Hmmm. Perhaps he's been doing too well."

Jacland stowed their bags in the storage compartment at the rear of the flitter and made sure the canopy was sealed before taking off.

Duchesne could imagine the grumbling occuring at the monorail terminal; those newly arrived from Earth learned quickly that you could take no risks on Mars—everything had to be double-checked before venturing outside. Many Earthers had trouble adjusting to the need for caution. At least the long awaited monorail had been finally completed; otherwise, it would have been crawler travel across the sands.

At Lowell City Security air lock, they exchanged the flitter for a groundcar. Jacland drove to the apartment. Duchesne could have taken over Garcia's larger apartment after the major's departure, but he preferred to keep his own. It was smaller, especially for two, but at least it had a window, which Garcia's lacked. Carolyn still found living in an apartment with a window a novelty.

Jacland waited with the car while the two senior officers went inside to change. Conscious of appearance, Duchesne hated to be seen out of uniform.

"How does it feel?" Carolyn deposited her travel-worn clothes in a heap at the foot of the bed.

"What's that?" Duchesne followed suit. He wished there

was time to take a shower.

"The uniform, silly. Getting back into the routine."

"It beats riding cargo on a transport." Duchesne adjusted his collar. "I'll be glad to get back to work, I think. I'll defer a final decision until I've had time to talk to Boris."

"Toss me my other boot, would you?" Carolyn eased her foot in. "How do I look?"

"Charming and thoroughly professional."

"Flatterer. Are you ready?"

"All set. Let's go."

Jacland was humming along to a program on the car's small telescreen. They rode in silence until the bulk of Security HQ rose up before them. One of Lowell's more impressive surface structures, HQ was neither the tallest nor largest, but exuded an air of solid authority.

Parting company from Carolyn inside the entrance, Duchesne headed to his own office several floors above. His aide sprang to his feet. "Welcome home, sir. I wasn't expecting to see you back quite so soon."

"Thanks, Lofter. I wasn't expecting to be back so soon either. Where's Lieutenant Mikhaelovitch?"

"In his office, I believe, Major."

"Have him come up."

"Sir." Lofter bent to his screen.

Duchesne sat down behind his desk, eyeing the clutter. On one corner rested a holophoto of his and Carolyn's wedding. Papers, printouts, and computer wafers, all doubtless requiring his attention, submerged the remainder of his desktop. Incredible the backlog that could accumulate during a few weeks' leave.

He was debating where to begin, when Lofter's voice came on.

"Lieutenant Mikhaelovitch to see you, sir."

"Send him in."

The door parted to allow the entrance of a giant of a man. Martians were tall by nature, a consequence of the low gravity. Duchesne peaked at 2.3 meters, but the Russian topped him by a good head. Short cropped, blonde hair surmounted a rectangular face composed of vertical planes and straight lines. The lieutenant's facial expression, as usual, was somber. Rumor had it that Mikhaelovitch had never been seen to smile. Presumably his consort knew, but she wouldn't say.

"Come on in, Boris." Duchesne waved him to a seat.

"Welcome home, sir." Mikhaelovitch lowered his bulk into a chair. "Are you glad to be back?"

"Yes and no. Glad to escape the gravity, but not sure what I'm walking into." Duchesne indicated the stack of printouts. "Looks like things were busy."

"Nothing major. Most of that is merely routine, to sign or review. It can wait."

"Any further word on the crisis?"

"Very little, unfortunately. I made an appointment for you to meet with Colonial Administrator Thorston in the morning, as you requested."

"Any problem with the administrator?"

"No. He sounded relieved that you wanted to see him. I expect he'll be grateful for any support. It doesn't seem as if he's getting much."

Duchesne frowned. "I hope his expectations aren't too high. I don't know what Forbes promised him, but it's really not our position to be interfering in politics or religion."

"If they're legal."

Duchesne cast a sharp glance at his subordinate. "Meaning?"

Mikhaelovitch shrugged, his deep blue eyes expressionless. "All may not be as it appears."

"Agreed." Duchesne pursed his lips. "You have a suspicious mind, Boris. But I suppose we'll have to wait and see what Thorston says."

FOUR

The driver pulled the car to the curb and stopped in the "Authorized Vehicles—Waiting Only" space outside the Administration Complex. A trickle of people entered and left the building, but no more or no less than would be expected. Certainly nothing to indicate an acute crisis.

"Find somewhere to park and wait for me," Duchesne instructed, climbing out of the back seat. "I don't expect to be overlong."

"Yes, sir."

Duchesne closed the door. The car pulled away and circled behind the building.

The Administration Complex, contructed of the same dull pink thermocrete as Security Headquarters—and apparently designed by the same inspiration-deprived architect—functioned as a multipurpose facility, housing Colonial Administration, Lowell City Offices, and Marspolice.

The guard at the entrance saluted, Duchesne's uniform all the identification he needed. Society was more relaxed on Mars than on Earth; undesirables were usually weeded out in Customs. Exceptions occurred, of course—Lowell had its seamy side, the same as any major city—but in general the citizens of Lowell prided themselves on their law-abiding nature.

Duchesne entered the foyer, its floor contructed of hexagonal slabs of heat-fused polished stone to resemble marble, and crossed over to the banks of lifters.

Another guard, as nonchalent as the first, patrolled outside the Colonial Administration offices.

"Major Duchesne." The receptionist, a pretty brunette,

greeted him. "Administrator Thorston is expecting you. I'll tell him you're here."

"Thank you."

Duchesne settled himself in a seat and picked up a reader from off a table. He flipped through the latest issue of *Interworld Geographic*. An advertisement at the end encouraged the adventurous to emigrate to the "new frontier"—the Outer Worlds; promising excitement, opportunity, and the chance to be on the cutting edge of humanity's next great venture. Duchesne snorted and silently wished them luck.

After a few moments' wait, an inner door opened. The administrator poked his head out. "Duchesne. Good to see you, m'boy. Come on in."

Duchesne shook the older man's hand and followed him into the inner office. The door slid shut behind.

"Take a seat, son."

Administrator Thorston settled behind his desk. The Administrator was no stranger to Duchesne, having met him officially and socially. In his late sixties, short and stout, Thorston's hair had turned prematurely gray. His small, neatly trimmed moustache bore no comparison to Forbes's. Normally beaming and cheerful—even avuncular—Duchesne thought the jovial greeting forced, performed more out of habit than from any real enthusiasm.

"Hear you just returned from Earth."

"Yes. Carolyn and I took a much needed vacation. Or rather, a very delayed honeymoon."

Thorston sighed, his expression becoming vacant. "I'd like to be going back myself."

Dark circles beneath eyes bloodshot and slightly swollen discolored Thorston's fleshy cheeks. A multitude of fine lines creased his forehead. If all Duchesne had heard was accurate, he couldn't blame the administrator for being tired and worried.

"S'pose you're wondering why I asked you here." Thorston's abstracted air dropped.

"You could say that. I assume it has something to do with our friends the Revitalists."

"Maybe they're your friends, but they're not mine." Thorston sat in thought for a moment. "Could have told

Mikhaelovitch, but I prefered to wait until you returned. Do you know much about the Revitalists?"

"As much as anyone else. We have a file on them of course, but it's not very detailed. They've done nothing to warrant investigation in the past."

"No. As a small, insignificant, harmless group of cranks, you wouldn't expect much from them. That's what makes the current situation so unexpected." Thorston rubbed his head. "Totally unexpected."

"What exactly is the situation?" Duchesne asked. "News broadcasts have been singularly unhelpful."

"Ah." Thorston recollected himself. "The situation, m'boy, is this. As you know, the Planetary Council is composed of fifteen members, plus assorted ex-officio individuals, all duly elected. You are probably familiar with some of them. None were members of the Revitalists."

"Were?"

"Were. Unexpectedly, eleven—a clear majority—suddenly declared themselves to be members of the Revitalists and insisted that the Council adopt a Revitalist posture."

Duchesne whistled. "You had no warning?"

"None. And there is no trace in any of the members' backgrounds of Revitalist connections. You can be sure I had my sources check that as thoroughly as we could. Since Sue Li-Shin is one of them, I don't know how far I can trust the Marspolice files."

"Sue joined them?"

"Uh-huh." Thorston nodded dourly. "She did."

"Surely something of that sensitive a nature would have come out in the elections," Duchesne protested.

"One would have thought."

Duchesne drummed his fingers on the desk.

"Can I get you a drink?" Thorston rose and went over to the synthesizer. "Very remiss of me. I don't know where my mind is these days."

"No thanks." Duchesne watched as Thorston entered his request. "You mentioned a Revitalist agenda. What exactly is that?"

"You'll love this." Thorston returned to his seat with a frosty glass of something orange and green. "An end to mining, terraforming, and all other acts that disturb the planet; independence from Earth; 'cleansing' of the planet from certain 'disruptive' elements; removal of Security;—"

The corners of Duchesne's mouth turned up. "Of course they'd want Security removed. Without us, neither the Colonial Board nor the World Council would have an enforcement arm here."

"Umm."

"But you don't have to accede to the Council's wishes," Duchesne continued. "You have the authority to overrule them."

"Let me finish, son. You know I've believed in allowing the citizens to direct their own affairs as much as possible, unless those affairs opposed the interests of Earth. I try not to overrule the Council unless it's absolutely necessary." Thorston sipped his drink. "Where was I? Oh, yes. The immediate dismissal of the current Colonial Administrator and installation of his replacement."

"Who are they wanting to replace you with?"

"Your grammar is terrible, son." Thorston took another swallow of his drink. "The Council has forwarded a recommendation to the Colonial Bureau. Since they can't overrule me, they've decided to petition the CB with their grievances. Under normal circumstances, their petition wouldn't get far. But these are not normal circumstances. My sources tell me that, unlikely as it sounds, the Bureau is expected to approve the recommendation. It appears that the Colonial Bureau has likewise developed a sudden love affair with the Revitalists."

Duchesne blinked. "Forbes didn't tell me that."

Thorston stared into the translucent depths of his glass. Without looking up, he said: "Their nomination is one Ghalji Maranan."

➤

Duchesne returned to Security HQ with his mind in a whirl. A group of protestors failed to attract his attention; his eyes passed over the banners and placards they waved.

It was inconceivable that a fringe group such as the Revitalists could assume control of a whole planet. Garcia would have had to have been incredibly remiss—or stupid—to have allowed a small sect to obtain a majority on the Council without knowing about it. There were ways an election could be manipulated by the discreet disclosure of information.

The normally sane and hard-boiled population would not vote in a fringe majority, even if the fringe was a member of the United World Church.

What about the Revitalists? Were they hopelessly naive, or conversely, amazingly cunning? And what did they hope to gain? What possible reason could they have for such a drastic action? They were fortunate to live in a society where they were tolerated, if not enthusiastically approved. Why take over the planet?

Granted, the administrator was a symbol of Earth's authority, resented by those who desired independence for the Red Planet. Did the Revitalists think Earth would concede that? And wasn't Maranan Earth-born?

It didn't make sense.

He followed the corridors to his office. Derek Lofter half rose and began to speak, but Duchesne waved him to silence.

He sat in quiet contemplation for several minutes before activating the intercom.

"Sir?" began Lofter. "I have several messages—"

"Later, Lofter. Get Mikhaelovitch and McCourt up here. What's the status of the squads?"

"Yellow Horse is here, unassigned. Cohen is on Deimos checking out a crew of students attempting to import illegal materials, but should be back shortly. Hernandez is in transit from Titan. Marlais is on leave—locally, I believe. There was little happening while you were away, and Lieutenant Mikhaelovitch approved."

"Good."

Mikhaelovitch arrived on McCourt's heels. Carolyn seated herself, while Mikhaelovitch remained standing. Tersely and concisely, Duchesne filled them in, repeating what Thorston had told him.

Mikhaelovitch's face hardened. "We had no inkling."

"Oh, I'm not blaming you, Boris. It doesn't appear that anyone had any warning."

"It would be a disaster if Thorston was removed!" said Carolyn. "Even if he's not native, he's at least spent a good part of his life here and has the interests of the planet at heart. Most of his predecessors have acted as if Mars was a prison from which to escape at the earliest opportunity with their pockets lined as much as possible."

"No argument there."

"What are you going to do?" Carolyn asked.

"For the moment there's nothing much we can do. There hasn't been any illegal activity as far as I can determine, although the situation stinks to high heaven. We have no legal basis for action."

"But you're suspicious?"

"I'm always suspicious."

"Well then?" Mikhaelovitch growled.

"We watch, and we wait."

"We must act!"

"We would be acting blindly, and that could be worse. We wait."

"But J. I.—!" Carolyn expostulated.

"And," he held up a finger, "we look. Boris, I want you to nose around, see what you can dredge up about the Revitalists. I appreciate all you've done so far, but we need more. I want to know everything about them—who they are, where they are, their resources, what influence they have, everything. Check their permits, licences, passports, credit. I know you've used all the usual channels but now use everything else. I don't much care how you do it as long as it gets done."

"Carolyn, I know you won't appreciate it, but I want you to go once again through everything of Maranan's that you can lay your hands on. I want to know what makes the man tick, and see if we can get some idea of the motives behind his agenda."

"Knowledge is power," remarked Mikhaelovitch.

"Exactly. Get to it, people."

When McCourt and Mikhaelovitch had departed on their assignments, Duchesne called through to Lofter. Better get on with it. The routine wouldn't stop, even for a crisis. "Come in and bring the messages with you."

Hellas Planitia, The Enclave

The scent of pine and freshly mown grass lay heavy in the air, like a midsummer's day. Ghalji Maranan filled his lungs with the clean, pure fragrance. Insects buzzed and chirped; small animals rustled unseen in the underbrush. Maranan let his mind empty, willing all thoughts to cease. His breathing became slow and easy, his chest rose and fell in a regular, unhurried rhythm. His eyes closed; without sight, it was easier to forget that he was not on Earth but in a chamber deep beneath the Martian surface, the sounds and smells recorded. Holographic images of his native India removed all sense of confinement.

The meditation room existed for his personal use.

He left the meadow. His feet trod the well-worn path through the forest, crushing fallen leaves underfoot. He wore only his dhoti and choga. In a few moments, when his mind was prepared, he would reach the small, sun-dappled glade at the forest's heart. Waiting there would be his spirit guide, his inner teacher, the one who gave him advice. He could almost think of this being as a messenger from outside, but he was sure that it was his subconscious, his true inner self, appearing in a tangible guise.

Maranan trusted his Guide implicitly.

Confrontations with Erik Klassen always left him tired and drained. Lately it had been one confrontation after another.

Thankfully, the traitor Hannik had been caught and killed. Maranan had applauded the successful men before sending them on their next assignment.

Why had his Guide not warned him of Hannik? He would have to ask.

"See, Erik," he had said. "They were successful. You should not worry so."

"It was my orders they followed. If not for my action the man would have gotten clean away. And then where would we be?"

Now they had declared themselves in the Mars Council, assuming the reins of government. One would have thought that Klassen's impatience would have been assuaged. But no.

"I still think you should have dealt with Security," he'd complained. "They may cause trouble."

"We have discussed this before, Erik. It could not be done. Security is too tight on Earth, and while we were able to replace some people, we could not get at Forbes himself. There was not time to complete a replacement for Duchesne. Besides, Security will not involve themselves in politics."

"You're a fool if you count on that."

"Garcia's dismissal was an inconvenience, no more. The Plan will succeed. I am confident the World Council will order Security recalled."

The forest wavered. Maranan willed himself to relax, stabilizing the scene. This was not a time to be thinking about Klassen. Now was for waiting, until an official response from the Colonial Bureau arrived. But that shouldn't be a problem. Maranan had seen to that.

Now was time to consult with his Guide and determine the next move.

➤

Erik Klassen sneered.

His private monitor showed Maranan, relaxed in his meditation chamber. The sneer mutated into a smirk. The internal monitor system was one of the many things which Maranan didn't know about. Klassen would have liked to have a camera in the lab too, but Grainger was wary, and he dared not mess with the electronics.

"Fat slob," he muttered as a benign smile spread across Maranan's face. "Consulting the spirits again. Bah!"

He snapped off the screen.

One did not need to contact the supernatural. All one had to do was reach out and take. And if Maranan was too weak and feeble to reach out, then he, Erik Klassen, would.

"There are plenty, *Master*, who would like to see *me* as leader. Your usefulness is ending."

"Intercom," he barked. The line opened. "If Szalny is still around, get him in here."

He paced around the room, hands clasped behind his back.

Szalny ducked his bald head as he entered.

"What are you trembling for? Am I surrounded by fools and weaklings?"

"I . . . uh . . ." Szalny faltered.

"Never mind. Why are you still here?"

Szalny wiped a bead of sweat off his forehead. "Where else should I be? Grainger finished Li-Shin. One of our contacts in Lowell accessed her itinerary; Forrest and I had no trouble with the switch. It went off fine. We've been back for days." He continued, "Olympus isn't up to much. Dismal mining town. There's nothing like what you can get in Lowell—"

"All right!" Klassen smacked his desk. Szalny shut up. "Since you're done with that, I have something else for you."

Szalny leaned forwards. "Anything."

"Duchesne," said Klassen.

"The Security chief?" Szalny queried.

"Yes, the Security chief, you idiot! I want you to find out about him, Szalny, all about him. Most particularly about his weak point."

"Weak point?"

Klassen gritted his jaw, the muscles straining. "Everybody has a weak point, Szalny, everybody." He punctuated each word with a finger to Szalny's chest. "And I want to know Duchesne's."

Klassen stared deep into Szalny's eyes, his own burning. "Find it, Szalny. And don't disappoint me."

Szalny scurried out.

Klassen smiled, baring his teeth.

"If our beloved leader won't take steps to neutralize Security, then I will. Your days are numbered, Duchesne. Numbered."

FIVE

The Reverend Paul Sommers, pastor of the First Unaffiliated Christian Church of Lowell, checked his chrono.

"Would you *please* relax?" his wife pleaded. She paused from writing a letter. "You've got loads of time. And sit down."

He crossed the room and parked himself in a chair beside her.

"I can't help it, Anita. I'm nervous. 'I can do all things through Christ who strengthens me.' I believe that. But it doesn't mean I can't be nervous."

"What do you need to worry for? It was a social invitation, wasn't it? It's not like they're dragging you off in restraints to Headquarters. It was very politely worded, if memory serves."

Sommers ran a hand through his fine, brownish-gray hair, feeling how thin it was becoming. Definitely receding. Anita wanted him to have a hair rejuvenation.

"You're right, of course. But old attitudes die hard. I can still remember when an invitation from Security was tantamount to a death sentence."

His wife clucked. "That was years ago and back on Earth. Since when have we had a problem on Mars in all the years we've lived here?"

"We're not well-liked," argued Sommers. "Have you seen the propaganda appearing lately? Some of it is downright obscene."

"I have." She quoted, "Old Religion Denies New Life. Choose Mars, Not Christ. Mother Mars not Father God."

Sommers nodded. "Have you seen the one with a minister dressed as Hitler? Black uniform and crosses instead of swastikas. Two hundred years later and the monster still has power."

"I must have missed that one."

"Christians: The New Fascists. Some of them accuse us of trying to ravage Mars in the same way that Earth was ecologically ruined."

"Nobody takes them seriously," Anita protested. "There are only a few hundred committed believers on Mars. Surely this propaganda is the work of some small hate-group."

"Don't they take it seriously?" Sommers frowned. "I've been receiving strange looks lately—not only teenagers but even adults passing in the street. Store clerks ignore me, serving other people as much as they can, making me wait. And did you notice how hard it was to get a repairman for the synthesizer? And how about the new Council? I hear they're considering a new Religious Unity Act, to force us into the United World Church."

"That's never succeeded before. Sure some people will join, but the rest will continue on as always."

"Hiding in homes, worshiping in secret. Receiving unwanted invitations from Security."

Anita sighed. "In every age, God's people have been persecuted somewhere."

"I know. You don't need to remind me. 'Blessed are you when people insult you, persecute you and falsely say all kinds of evil against you,'" he quoted. "'Rejoice and be glad, because great is your reward in heaven.'"

"There you go," Anita said cheerfully. "Think of the opportunity."

"Perhaps you're right," Sommers conceded. "Maybe they really are interested."

"Let's have a time of prayer before you go out, Paul."

Mars, Hellas Planitia

Gordon Blanchard checked the readout on the spectral analyser and muttered an obscenity, inaudible over the pounding, amplitude-distorted rhythms of *Ratbane*. The instrument had nearly finished with the kilometer-long, micro-thin core the laser borer had extracted. The readings were uniformly monotonous. Iron oxides. Silicates. Garbage rock. Not one blip of interest.

The analyser beeped to signal the end of the run. Gordon stored the results on a wafer, making certain the coordinates were accurate. Not that anybody would be particularly inter-

ested in another futile boring. The results would be filed along
with thousands of others at Olympus Mining Consortium headquarters. The only possible benefit would be to ensure that no
one else wasted their time prospecting in this forsaken spot.

Gordon yawned.

Prospecting—or subsurface mineral detecting as he preferred to call it—was hardly a glamorous occupation. But at
least he received a regular paycheck from Olympus Mining,
unlike a score of freelancers he knew. They took their chances
and were more often disappointed than not, eking out an existence.

He focused his eyes on the inside of his faceplate to the dig-
its of the chrono. A couple of hours of daylight left. He had time
to move on to another location and set up camp for the night.
Although it would be too late to perform another boring, he'd
be able to get an early start in the morning. The Company set
the number of borings he had to perform. No quota, no pay.
Gordon was frequently out for as much as a month at a time and
not uncommonly two or three, traveling in long loops out from
Olympus and back.

But his luck had been poor lately, and his boss was getting
fed up with Gordon's barren reports. In desperation, Gordon
had decided upon a new tack and had set out from Lowell
instead, searching for better prospecting grounds. So here he
was, at the northern edge of Hellas Planitia, fifteen hundred or
so kilometers south of civilization. Drilling his cores. Hoping to
hit a lode that would make him and the company—particularly
him—wealthy.

He shut down the analyser and the borer, built directly into
the side of the crawler, and closed the protective shields. Gordon
took care of his equipment. He didn't want to have even a few
credits stopped from his pay to replace instruments damaged by
negligence.

About to swing himself into the cab, something caught the
corner of his eye. He turned around for a closer look, rubbing
his glove across his faceplate to remove a smear of dust.
Probably just a trick of light and shadow. He moved toward the
cab again. Or was it too regular?

It wouldn't hurt to look.

Gordon crunched across the ground to a pile of rubble

that appeared no different from a thousand others. But as he got closer, he stiffened.

There *was* something there!

He slowed his pace. Protruding from behind the pile was the unmistakable outline of a boot. He rounded the pile. The boot was attached to a body.

Gordon moved cautiously. There was no movement, no trace of life that he could detect. He laid a hand on the shoulder and rolled the body over.

There was the reason. The faceplate was shattered, a gaping hole where there should have been clear plastic. It wasn't hard to guess what had happened; the man had fallen, and his faceshield had hit a sharp-edged rock.

End of story.

Gordon rummaged through the dead man's pockets but came away empty handed. Whoever he was—or had been—he carried no identification. The generic suit could have come from anywhere. There were no distinguishing patches on the breast or sleeves.

The man had lain here a while too, although Gordon hesitated to hazard a guess. He wasn't a pathologist. It could have been anywhere from a few days to a few months for all he knew. But the body wasn't buried by dust, therefore the time probably wasn't too long.

Gordon steeled himself and looked closer at the shrunken face.

Skin shriveled into a mass of wrinkles. Dried blood from ruptured vessels, eyes, and nose covered everything. The body was already well into mummification, cold and dryness doing their work.

Gordon couldn't have identified the body if it had been his own mother.

He rocked back on his haunches.

What to do?

He couldn't recall any reports on local news updates or emergency channels about missing prospectors. And what else could the body be? There was no other good reason for anyone to be out here. Hellas Planitia wasn't on anybody's way anywhere.

Gordon stood up and scanned the horizon in a circle. No sign of any vehicle in visual range. Curiouser and curiouser.

What should he do? It wasn't likely he'd obtain any answers here. And he wasn't about to interrupt his schedule. He had a dozen more borings to perform before he could return to Lowell. Still, someone might be worrying about whoever this guy was. Had been.

He stooped down, put his arms under the corpse, and hoisted it over his shoulders. Staggering under the weight, he lugged it over to the crawler and dumped it on the ground. He then took a plastic bag out of the storage compartment and tugged it over the dead man. A thought struck him as he was reaching for the sealer, and he shivered.

What if the man had died of some disease? A mutant virus from GenAg or one of the other genetics labs? They said it couldn't happen, that their safeguards were too stringent. But Gordon knew otherwise.

Wasn't there that incident on Ganymede a couple of years back? Hushed up quickly—too quickly. Nothing was ever admitted publicly.

He ran the sealer along the opening of the sack. That was better. Nothing short of a cutting torch could get through the tough plastic—certainly no virus. He slung the bundle onto the deck of his cargo sled and tied it down. The body would come to no harm there. And when he returned to Lowell, someone else could take care of it.

Gordon rinsed his suit off with cleaning solvent.

Nothing should survive that, either.

Humming tunelessly, Gordon hoisted himself into the cab and started the motor.

Lowell City

Duchesne arrived home later than usual.

The door mechanism recognized his voice-print and slid aside. The unexpected sound of conversation met his ears. An unfamiliar figure sat on the couch.

Carolyn rose from a side chair and came over to greet him.

"Welcome home, dear," she said, kissing him lightly. "You're late."

"I stopped for a workout. Who's that?" Duchesne inclined his head toward the man on the couch.

72 *Andrew M. Seddon*

"Did you forget we were having company?"

"Not only did I forget, I never knew."

"Yes, you did. It's Reverend Sommers from the Christian church. We invited him over, remember?"

"Tonight?!" Duchesne hissed. "With all that's going on? I'm hardly in the mood for discussing—"

"Look, the man's nervous enough about being here; try to pretend like you're interested."

Carolyn turned on her heel. "Reverend, I'd like you to meet my husband, J.I. Duchesne."

The elderly, slightly stooped man stood up and crossed the room. If he'd heard the exchange, his face did not express it.

"It's a pleasure, Major," he greeted. "I've heard of you, of course."

Duchesne returned his grip. "Reverend."

"Please, call me Paul. I've never liked formality."

Duchesne gestured toward the low table in the living area, where a pair of glasses rested on coasters. "Carolyn has been taking care of you?"

"Yes, thank you."

"I'll just get a drink, and join you." Duchesne went into the synthesizer in the kitchen and ordered a large glass of fruit juice and mineral water. He rejoined the others and settled himself in a chair. He toyed idly with his glass.

"I must say, Major, this invitation caught me by surprise," Sommers said, a perceptible tremor in his voice. "Security doesn't have a reputation for being well-disposed toward Christians."

Duchesne ran a hand through the overlong, jet-black hair that curled over his collar. He pointed toward his short-sleeved blue shirt and slacks. "I'm not in uniform, Reverend."

"Paul has been telling me some of the essential differences between Christianity and the UWC," Carolyn cut in.

"Indeed?" Duchesne was noncommittal. Carolyn would try to ease him in slowly; might as well play along.

"Maybe you could tell J.I. what you said to me."

"Certainly. Perhaps the easiest way of explaining, Major, is like this." Sommers leaned forward. "The UWC embraces an astronomical number of belief systems: Goddess or Mother Earth worship, elevation of so-called ascended masters, ancestor worship, self-realization, Inner Light, you name it. I could spend all night listing the different sects. But at the heart, they all worship creation."

"Aren't all religions paths to God?" Duchesne flashed a smile to Carolyn, as if to say: *See, I can play this game.*

"In that case, we'd join the UWC willingly. No, Major. If you can believe everything, then why believe anything? Think of it this way. Imagine being set down in New York or Greater Japan with no map, no street signs, and being asked to find a specific location. It would take you a lifetime to cover all the possibilities, and you would likely die without ever reaching your destination."

"Best left to computer," Duchesne murmured.

Sommers glanced toward Carolyn. "I believe you know this; despite all your searching, you haven't found God."

Carolyn nodded.

"God has given us a very specific map of the one way to reach him." Sommers drew breath. "If I sound too preachy, tell me to stop. My wife tells me I ramble."

Duchesne signaled for him to continue.

Sommers paused and stroked his hair. "The UWC is the ultimate expression of centuries of religious confusion, the do-it-yourself church *par excellence.* And that's what all man-made religions are, Major. Do it yourself. Man attempting to reach God."

"And you say—"

"That it is impossible for us to reach God because of sin. Therefore, God has to reach us. Only through Jesus Christ, the Son of God, can we come to God."

Duchesne studied Sommers. He hadn't known what to expect from a Christian minister, never to his recollection having met one. A wild-eyed fanatic on the order of Maranan, perhaps. But Sommers didn't appear wild-eyed. As for being a fanatic—if putting yourself on the fringes of society for your beliefs was fanaticism, then Sommers certainly fit that picture.

To the contrary, the Reverend seemed quite sane. Lucid, rational, and well-educated. And, what was perhaps more important, he wasn't afraid to stand up for what he believed. Duchesne always had a sneaking sympathy for the underdog.

"You Christians certainly have a reputation for being exclusive and nonconformist."

"We won't compromise for the sake of appearances, Major. But we will share our beliefs with any. We aren't trying to be difficult. Neither is God. He hasn't given a multitude of ways, any of which might be dead ends, to reach Him, but one way."

"What do you think of the current situation, Rev—ah, Paul?" Duchesne asked. "The Revitalists assuming a majority on the Council?"

Sommers shook his head, taking the change of topic in stride. "It disturbs me greatly. Don't get me wrong, Major. We're used to being a minority; there has never been a Christian on the Council, to my knowledge. But the Revitalists mean harm to more than Christians—of that I'm sure. Harm to all Mars."

"Paul was telling me his views on the outbreak of anti-Christian sentiment," Carolyn spoke up.

"What about it?"

"It has been building slowly for a long time," said Sommers, "but lately seems to be peaking."

"I'd heard some rumors," Duchesne said, "but not anything particularly serious. Do you know any reason for it?"

"None."

"Or who is behind it?"

"Nor that either. But someone has been spreading vicious propaganda. Equating us with the Nazis, for example."

"I told Paul that it might be possible to look into it."

Duchesne cast a jaundiced eye toward his wife. Of all the cock-eyed promises—!

"That's hardly our jurisdiction, dear. That's a civil matter, under the jurisdiction of the Marspolice if there has been any wrong-doing. Which it doesn't sound like."

"Have you considered the possibility that it could be associated with the Revitalists?" asked Carolyn.

"What reason could there be?"

"I don't know. But isn't it strange that one religious group takes over the Council at the same time another is finding itself the butt of propaganda?"

Duchesne drummed his fingers on the couch. He didn't want to get involved in any religious disputes. But he trusted Carolyn's intuition and insight. If she felt there could be a connection. . . .

"Possibly. It may be worth checking into." He looked at Sommers. "That's all I can promise you, Reverend. If the Revitalists are connected, I'd like to know about it. Otherwise. . . ."

"We fight our own battles. Fair enough, Major. That's

more than I could have asked for," Sommers said.

"I think we've monopolized enough of your time tonight, Reverend," said Carolyn. "We don't want to get overloaded. Thank you for coming."

"My pleasure, Carolyn."

"We'd like to have you back another time, when my husband is more available."

"I'd be delighted. You have my number—feel free to call me any time."

"Good night, Reverend," said Duchesne. "Do you need an escort?"

"No thank you, Major," said Sommers, his face reflecting pleased surprise. "It's not that bad yet."

"It's too bad you forgot," said Carolyn after the door had closed behind the minister's retreating back. "We had a good discussion before you arrived. The Reverend is a very interesting man. He was excited when he found I have a Bible, and gave me some pointers as to what to study."

"I don't know if I was in the mood for it, anyway," Duchesne grumbled.

"Don't give me that. I know what your problem is."

"What's that?"

"You're afraid."

"Afraid!?"

"Yes. Mr. Self-reliant."

"I'm not—"

"Afraid you'll have to make a decision that might affect your career."

She came and laid a soft hand on his shoulder, looking into his gray eyes. "You are, aren't you."

Duchesne hated to admit it. "Don't be silly," he said, sounding unconvincing even to himself.

"Sooner or later we'll have to decide, one way or another," Carolyn continued. "And what have we found so far?"

"Just remember," Duchesne said, "that we agreed to decide together. Not one without the other."

"That's okay. But you can't keep procrastinating."

Duchesne knew when he was beaten. "Do you want to have the Reverend over again?"

"Yes," Carolyn replied. "And next time you're not to forget."

SIX

I t's official, m'boy." Colonial Administrator Arthur Thorston sprawled in his chair. The synth-leather creaked unhappily under the shifting weight. "Notification arrived last night. The Bureau has approved Maranan to succeed yours truly. Change of administration to be effective immediately."

Thorston glanced across the room. Duchesne followed the look toward a pile of storage containers, some partially filled, others awaiting their assigned contents. Thorston had already begun cleaning out his office, removing the nonessentials.

"There'll have to be a transition period, surely. You can't change the government overnight!"

"It's not like changing Earth's World Council, son. Guarantee it will be quick. This is Maranan's office now."

Somehow, Duchesne thought, Thorston looked almost relieved. The tension of the preceding days seemed to have drained away, leaving his face relaxed, his manner lighter. Perhaps just the fact that now he knew, rather than being suspended on tenterhooks, helped.

"What are you going to do? Have you formulated any plans?"

Thorston shook his head. "Don't know yet. Depends on the missus, I guess. But I have a hunch we'll be returning to Earth. Kids are all back there, and I have a hankerin' to see the little un's. Need the old grampa, you know."

Thorston's eyes moved from the storage containers to the holophoto on his desk. Three children clustered together against the background of a small stream. "Way back home in Dixie," he murmured.

"Excuse me?"

"An old song. 'I wish I was in the land of cotton, old times there are not forgotten.' This accent ain't all fake, you know."

"I would never—"

"Atlanta, Georgia. Home of peaches, Braves, and yours truly."

Duchesne nodded, at a loss for words. "We will miss you, sir," he said. "Mars has been the better for your administration."

"Don't lay it on, boy. I wasn't nothing special, and you know it. Jest a country boy tryin' to make a livin'."

"You're the furthest thing from a country boy, sir."

Thorston gazed out of his window, across the gleaming edifice of the city, twinkling in the early morning sun. Duchesne wondered what Thorston was thinking, viewing the city that for so long had been his responsibility, almost, one might say, his child. How would he, Duchesne, handle it if he were as summarily dismissed without so much as a thank you?

"Do me one favor," Thorston asked.

"Anything."

Thorston looked Duchesne squarely in the eye. The old home boy affect dropped, and Duchesne got a glimpse of the fiber behind the politician.

"Find out what happened."

Duchesne returned the gaze. "I will," he said. "I promise you that."

Duchesne declined the car waiting for him and walked back to Headquarters.

Find out what happened. Easier said than done.

The Revitalists appeared to have acted by the book, as far as their enclave went. Their construction permits were in order. The agreement for them to found an enclave was signed and sealed by the Council—possibly in a weak moment, but there it was. They proselytized quietly. Maranan wrote voluminously. The enclave received regular shipments of food and materials, purchased from local concerns.

As for the Mars Council—no law prohibited a person from changing religious or political affiliation. It looked suspicious, but members had changed affiliations before. Never, though, so many at once, enough to alter the balance of power.

Duchesne found Mikhaelovitch in conversation with Carolyn. One had to know the Russian well to be able to detect the subtle signs of excitement exuding through the stolid facade.

"Found something, Boris?" Duchesne dropped into his chair. He winked at Carolyn. "Or are you merely flirting with my wife?"

"I was leading him on, J. I. You can't blame Boris. Something about the Russian demeanor—"

"Maybe I found something." Mikhaelovitch refused to rise to the bait. "Three items." He pulled up a display on the screen. "UWC membership records for the past five years. Either Colonel Forbes was seriously misinformed, or the Revitalists have been concealing their true numbers. Far from a mere few hundred, there are two thousand full members with Enclave entrances and several thousand more loosely affiliated."

Duchesne whistled. "That's a tremendous difference and implies a lot of backing. Big money from Earth."

Mikhaelovitch nodded. He changed the display and waited as Duchesne ran his eyes up and down the columns of figures. "Consumption figures for atmosphere, power, food and water. I don't see—"

Mikhaelovitch stabbed a thick finger at the screen. "They obtain power from the orbital generators. Look at the per capita power consumption. Significantly higher than for the average citizen of Lowell."

"But out in the desert. . . ."

"Even allowing for their situation, the power consumption is excessive."

"So that means one of two things." Duchesne steepled his fingers. "Either there are still more of them than they claim—"

"In which case the food and water figures would be higher," cut in Carolyn.

"—or else they're using the power for something else. Good, Boris. What's the other thing?"

"Here. I had the computer run a search through the Enclave acquisitions scanning for anything out of the ordinary. What it came up with was this." He indicated a list of names. "Most of these are local businesses. Construction equipment, building supplies, food, etc. And then there's this one."

"ALL-Tech Inc.? Never heard of it."

"Neither had I. But I had my sources run a check. ALL-Tech is an advanced technology supply company, known for providing items that are not yet licensed for commercial distribution."

"Pirated?"

"Uh-huh."

"Hmmm. What sort of items?"

"Medical hard and software, biological engineering equipment, and possibly weapons, although my source wasn't sure."

Duchesne sucked on a tooth. "An odd combination. What
does biotechnology imply to you?"

"Genetic engineering," said Carolyn promptly.
"Recombinants, clones, that sort of thing."

"Genetics is out of my league," Mikhaelovitch said.

"Mine, too," Duchesne replied. "Remember those
October flowers we saw in Scotland, Carolyn? They were
designed to bloom later than usual. GenAg is busy creating
Martian plants, as well as our normal food stock."

"Animal cloning is done on Earth to save or recreate
endangered species," Carolyn added.

"Beyond that, I don't know. Everything else is pretty well
prohibited. I remember a couple of cases of human cloning that
came to my attention when I was assigned Earthside. Talk about
a legal nightmare!"

"There are one or two human applications," continued
Carolyn pensively. "Mostly cosmetic. Skin, eye, and hair color,
beard growth."

The Russian's eyes glanced toward Carolyn's hair.

She caught the motion. "*No*, Boris," she said coldly. "This
is real."

"Sorry," he grunted.

Duchesne smiled into his hand.

"Full screening is done prior to conception, so there are no
genetically aberrant babies born. Genetic diseases have been
eradicated," Duchesne mused. "Okay. File that one away for
future reference. One more thought comes to mind."

"If we're dealing with a heavily armed group—"
Mikhaelovitch began.

"Not only that, but if they've been able to get this kind of
stuff through on a regular basis over a period of years, then we
have a serious leak in Customs." He scratched his head. "I
think, Boris, it's time we had a look at the Enclave." He opened
the intercom. "Lofter, have Lieutenant Yellow Horse report to
me immediately. And notify his squad to assemble."

Duchesne turned back to Mikhaelovitch. An eager light
shone in his eyes.

"Now we have something to sink our teeth into."

➤

Deciding she needed a well-deserved break from research-ing the torpid writings of Ghalji Maranan, and leaving her hus-band to brief Howard Yellow Horse on the next phase of the investigation, Carolyn wandered through Lowell Central shop-ping district ("five hundred stores to serve your every need"). Although only some of Lowell's citizens chose to live on Mars, all clamored for reminders of Earth, in the form of imports. Carolyn thought the Lowell Central shops were more varied than some of the other districts.

Their second anniversary had arrived, and she had yet to find a suitable present for J.I. She had encountered her own morass of back work to wade through; shopping had been rel-egated to later. Later was here.

She paused idly before several stores but saw nothing of inter-est. Her husband was a hard man to buy for. Aside from his hob-bies of music and painting, he lived simply. He could afford more if he wanted—which he usually didn't. Frills weren't his style.

"Too many possessions clutter up life," he had remarked more than once.

With Winter Festival only a month away, the center was busier than usual. Carolyn noticed a slender, bald-headed man dodge adroitly through the throngs of people but payed him no more than a passing glance.

The window of Morrisons's Music caught her eye. *New Line of Recordings—Forgotten 20th Century Masters.* She read the display. One part of Duchesne's life that Carolyn could not share was his love of music; completely tone deaf, Mozart and Shostakovitch sounded identical. It frustated her that this part of his life was forever closed to her.

Someday, she thought she might have it checked—there might be some sort of genetic correction that could be made. But up until her marriage, it hadn't seemed important.

She entered the store and perused the racks of recordings. Some of the names—if none of the music—were familiar, but there were many composers she did not recognize.

"May I help you?" A sharp-faced clerk hovered at her elbow, a plastic smile glued to his lips.

"I'm looking for something for my husband."

"Anything in particular?"

"He likes twentieth century music. English mostly."

"Ah." The clerk drew her over to a different rack. "We have a new line on the PastMasters label. Very nice recordings, all recent. Dyson, Vaughan Williams, Bax, Moeran . . ."

"He has some of those." Carolyn ran her eyes over the labels. "How about this one?"

"Rubbra? If he likes the other composers, he should enjoy the Rubbra. The only . . . ah, complaint I would have against Rubbra is that he was reportedly a very religious man."

"Many people are religious," Carolyn said. "It's not a crime."

"Let me be more specific." The clerk's voice dropped as if he was afraid of being overheard. "I meant religious in a Christian sense."

The clerk pursed his narrow lips, affecting a look of holy horror. Carolyn's stomach turned.

"Composers with very strong religious sentiments—particularly Christian—are not especially popular at the moment, even if the music is purely orchestral." He shrugged condescendingly. "But still, one has to take the period into account, of course, and things were different back then. So many of them were influenced by the beliefs of the age."

Carolyn recollected a conversation she had had with J. I. He had been complaining because he had been unable to obtain some choral works that he wanted. Mendelssohn or Elgar? One or the other.

"What difference does it make? It's *music*. But just because the text is from the Bible, nobody wants to record it anymore. Either that or 'it's available, but we can't obtain it from our suppliers.'"

"I'm sure there are plenty of other pieces you can listen to," Carolyn had replied, trying to be soothing.

"That's not the point."

And he was right. It was an insidious form of censorship. Carolyn returned abruptly to the present, realizing that the clerk was staring at her, waiting for her to make a decision.

"It sounds just the thing," she said, discounting the clerk's opinion. She picked up the recording of the *Complete Symphonies of Edmund Rubbra (1901-1986)*, the Royal Liverpool Philharmonic Orchestra, Sir Llewellyn Bryn-Jones conducting.

The clerk nodded, all sugar at the prospect of a sale. "I'm sure he'll enjoy it," he said smoothly. "And we do have a return policy if it should not prove suitable . . ."

Carolyn slipped the recording into her pocket, left the store, and continued her progress down the street. Her eyes dismissed a man evaluating a clutch of florid sweaters in a men's shop window across the street. At length, she turned into an artists' supply store and purchased several canvasses and a selection of paints and brushes.

"It's about time he did some painting again," she said to herself. "Give him the stuff and the inspiration should follow."

She made one more stop, at a specialty food store. She was going to prepare an intimate, homemade anniversary dinner. Nothing synthesized for such a special occasion.

Satisfied with her purchases, Carolyn caught a slideway back to their apartment.

>

Evgeny Szalny followed the woman until she entered the apartment building, and then he turned away, a satisfied smile hovering on his colorless lips. Szalny—he preferred the Eastern European spelling of his name although neither he nor any of his ancestors for as far back as he'd been able to trace had been there—stuck his fingers in his mouth and whistled.

A large dog, half-shepherd, half-husky, tail stiffly erect, bounded from an alley to take station by his master's side. It had been easy, almost too easy.

Here in Lowell he had the freedom to work and act on his own. Not like in the Enclave, where fear dictated every move, under the implacable gaze of Erik Klassen. It felt good to be away!

Evgeny Szalny feared Klassen alone of all men. Maranan he respected. Klassen he feared.

The deputy would be pleased with what he had discovered.

"Well, Brutus? What say we go enjoy ourselves now, huh?"

Man and dog ambled contentedly toward the seamy side of south Lowell.

>

The last notes of the Fifth, *allegro vivo*, faded into silence.

"Pick a number from one to eleven," Carolyn had said.

"Very nice." Duchesne leaned over to plant a kiss on Carolyn, nestled next to him on the couch.

"The clerk at the store said he was too religious."

"Who? The clerk?"

"No, silly. Rubbra."

"Oh. Well it was a good choice no matter what he said. I hadn't heard any of Rubbra before. It's amazing how many composers disappear into obscurity after death. All the music broadcasts are so similar. Beethoven, Mozart, Brahms."

A chime sounded in the kitchen alcove.

"Dinner's ready," Carolyn said, rising to her feet. "You stay put. I'll get it."

She'd been unsure about the evening, wondering if J. I. would remember their anniversary. She was almost certain he would, but he was a man, after all, and perhaps the events that had occurred recently would conspire to push it out of his mind.

She needn't have worried. Her anxiety faded as soon as Duchesne came through the door with a bouquet of flowers partially concealed behind his back.

"Happy anniversary, darling," he greeted.

Carolyn flung her arms around his neck and planted a kiss on his lips. He held the flowers at arm's length so they wouldn't crush.

"You remembered!"

"Of course." He looked puzzled. "Did you think I'd forget?"

"Not for a moment," Carolyn lied.

"But there is one thing . . ." he began.

"What's that?"

"I was going to have us go to dinner at the Canalside, but that idiot Lofter messed up the reservations. He got the date mixed up and made them for next week. By the time I found out, they were booked solid."

"Don't be too hard on the corporal, dear." Carolyn grinned impishly.

"Why not?"

"I asked him not to make the reservations."

Her husband's mouth hung open. "You asked him not to? Why, for crying out loud?"

"Because I wanted an evening alone. And because I prepared dinner for us."

"You—?" He spotted the table, set with an elegant cloth, candles, and pair of wine glasses. His consternation faded away into a quirky smile. "Sneaky."

Carolyn pushed him toward the bedroom. "Go and get out of that uniform, okay?"

After he changed into a comfortable outfit, they exchanged presents.

"I hope you like it," Duchesne said as he handed her a small box. "I had to bribe a jeweler to make it for you at very short notice. He looked at me mighty strangely."

Carolyn unwrapped the box. "It's beautiful!" she breathed.

"I don't know when you'll be able to wear it, but I couldn't resist."

"There speaks my husband, the nonconformist. Have you decided something without me?"

"No. We agreed, remember?"

"I'll wear it now." Carolyn bent forwards.

Duchesne fastened the necklace around her neck.

He opened his packet of music and promised solemnly to begin painting again. They sat listening to Rubbra's Fifth while the food cooked.

"What did you make?" Duchesne asked, seating himself at the table. "It smells wonderful." With the lights dimmed, the candles cast a flickering warmth over the vase of flowers. Carolyn took the lid off a dish.

"Duck a l'orange, roast potatoes, and asparagus. All natural, nothing synthesized. For dessert, I tried one of Mrs. William's recipes. Trifle, which I hope turned out all right."

Duchesne speared a forkful of duck, dipped it in orange sauce, and raised it to his mouth. "If it's anything like the duck, I'm sure it did."

"You like?" Carolyn asked.

"Love it. You continue to amaze me."

Carolyn fingered the gold Celtic cross, inlaid with garnet, he had given her.

"And you, me," she murmured. "Especially considering the length of time it took you to get around to proposing."

"I did though, didn't I?"

Duchesne sighed when the meal was over. "That was wonderful. What did you have planned next?"

"I had thought a quiet evening of romance."

Duchesne chuckled. "Want us to keep together for another
year, do you? That suits me fine."

>

Derek Lofter's heart froze in his chest. An authoritative
voice accosted him from the empty hall, echoing in the gloom.

"Halt! Who goes there?"

Lofter pivoted, arms apart. A light impaled his face. He
squinted against the glare.

"Oh, it's you, Derek. What are you doing here at this time
of the night?"

Lofter managed a weak smile. "Hi, Molly. I came back to
finish some work I forgot to do earlier. You know what a stickler the major can be."

Molly holstered her gun. "Yeah, he can be a real tyrant. Put
your uniform on next time you decide to do night shift, all right?
Don't want to scorch you by mistake."

"Sorry, Moll. I'll remember."

"You'd better. Captain McCourt ordered extra security
until things quiet down. Some of the guards are a lot faster on
the trigger than I am."

Molly resumed her rounds. Lofter padded up to his office.
He passed no one else in the corridors, although a gleam of light
emerged from underneath the duty sergeant's door.

He brought his terminal on-line and accessed a secure comm-
channel, bypassing the communications center. Next, he tabbed in
a command, coded the transmission, and waited for a response.

"Yes?"

"This is Blackboots. Got a message for the master."

"Go ahead."

"Tell him to be prepared for a recon. Don't know the date,
but soon."

"Got it. Thanks, Blackboots."

Lofter shut down his terminal, making sure there was no
trace of his unauthorized action. He exited the way he had come.

Molly was nowhere to be seen.

SEVEN

Erik Klassen was angry with a burning, searing anger that gnawed incessantly at his vitals, eating away at his very being.

Angry at the world that had dealt him a raw hand, forcing him to carve his way to success by brute force, not caring whom he injured on the way, how many bodies he trampled.

Angry at the fools who surrounded him, plodding passively through life, not knowing what they did or where they went. Wandering around in their pajama-like robes, moaning and chanting like demented ghosts—what morons, actually believing the swill Maranan spouted!

Angry at himself, for having to play the believer, parroting back the right words so that he seemed to be a true Revitalist. How low he had stooped in his quest for power!

Angry at the brainless, spineless creatures that comprised a useless humanity. Why did he even bother himself with them?

Angry at Maranan, indecisive and slow. Maranan, who took all the beautiful women for himself so that Erik had to be content with the likes of Lin Grainger—smart, but plain-faced and cold. She hated him deeply. The thought of her hatred pleased him.

But most of all, Erik Klassen's anger burned toward one man. One man above all others. One man who did not even know how much Klassen hated him, how much he wanted to hurt him.

The rage built inside him, seething and churning; the rage that propelled him, that gave him purpose to life. He fostered the emotion, enjoying the sensation that rage gave him, the feeling of power, of invincibility. Blood coursing through his veins, heart pounding, strength—

His fist suddenly slammed through his terminal. The

screen—and the face it portrayed—exploded into a thousand needle-sharp fragments that scattered wickedly across the room. Smoke erupted from the shattered instrument, sparking and sizzling in electrical death.

Klassen snarled. He withdrew his hand from the smoldering terminal. A sharp sliver of metal gouged deep into his flesh. Blood trickled across his palm. Klassen enjoyed the pain.

"That's what I'm going to do to you, Duchesne!"

He held his fist in front of his face, the blood oozing from between the clenched fingers. "I can bear pain—can you?"

"Soon, Duchesne, soon. You don't remember Erik Klassen. Don't remember the pain you gave me. But you will. I will have you in my hands, and then. . . ."

The door slid open.

Evgeny Szalny took one step inside. In slow motion, he lowered his foot to the floor. His eyes flicked from the crumpled, smoking terminal to Klassen, standing with upraised, bloody fist, like an avenging fury.

"What do YOU want?" Klassen hissed, the words barely recognizable.

Szalny's mouth worked.

"WELL??" Klassen took a step forward. Szalny remained mute.

"SPEAK!!" Klassen howled.

"Duchesne," gasped the terrified Szalny, cowering before the force of Klassen's rage. "His weakness. . . ."

"Yes?"

"I found it!" Szalny blurted, eyes locked on Klassen's raised fist.

Klassen's face changed. The expression of rage faded to be replaced by an expression even more evil. He lowered his hand.

He smiled, feral, baring his teeth. Szalny flinched as Klassen laid his bloody hand on his shoulder, fingers grinding into the muscles.

"Very good, Szalny," Klassen purred. "Come and tell me."

➤

Erik Klassen stalked down the hall, his robe billowing, responding to a summons from Maranan. One day, the fool would be answering *his* summons. Rounding a corner, he almost collided with a pair of adepts wheeling a dolly.

"Watch where you're going!" He halted in the nick of time.

"Sorry, but you—"

The woman saw the look in Klassen's eye and hushed her companion.

"Where are you going with that?" Klassen barked.

"It's the new terminal for your office."

Klassen glared. "See that's it's put in right. I don't want any more accidents like the last one blowing up on me."

The adepts nodded and wheeled the dolly past him, continuing on their way.

"Clumsy idiots."

Klassen didn't let the encounter with the adepts irritate him for long. He was too satisfied. Szalny had brought him valuable information, information that he could use if and when the right opportunity presented itself. More than that, it gave him the ability to act on his own, to take matters into his own hands if Maranan proved incapable. It was a winning card—an ace.

>

Marannan noticed the smug expression on Klassen's face, and wondered what had caused it. But he made no comment.

"It's official, Erik. Confirmation arrived from the Colonial Bureau. You are looking at the new Colonial Administrator of Mars."

Klassen blinked.

"You didn't expect me to pull it off, did you?" Maranan said. "You didn't believe that the Red Planet would rise to throw off those who oppress her."

"What do you propose to do?" Klassen countered.

"I'll be leaving for Lowell shortly to assume my new duties. You will remain here, to continue work in the Enclave." Maranan rubbed his chin. "There is much that needs to be accomplished." He fixed his cat-like eyes on Klassen. "And I would like you to leave Lin Grainger alone."

Klassen gritted his teeth. "What has the little rat been saying?"

"Her work is very important," Maranan continued. "She

needs to be free from distractions. I cannot afford for her to make any mistakes because her mind is not concentrated on her work."

Klassen opened his mouth, but Maranan forestalled his reply. "There is, of course, my harem. . . ."

"You'll need someone with you," Klassen said, suppressing a leer, "to do any dirty work that needs doing. You won't be winning any popularity contests. There may be certain things that you won't want to be seen as being connected with."

Maranan thought for a moment.

His Guide had warned him that the younger man was following his own agenda.

"It would be as well if you did not trust Klassen completely."
"Should he be removed?"
"No. That is not necessary. Merely exercise caution."
"But what if—"
"Klassen is an irrelevancy. The Plan will succeed regardless. A favorable outcome is ordained."

If his lieutenant wanted someone to accompany him, there had to be a reason. Channels of information could, however, be made to flow both ways. A link to Klassen, which Klassen did not know he knew about, could prove useful.

"Who would you recommend?"

Klassen answered without hesitation. "Szalny. He caught Hannik, remember? He's a good man."

He's also YOUR man, thought Maranan, *in a position to keep his eyes open for you.*

"Szalny is acceptable," his Guide had said.

Maranan nodded. "Agreed. One of my first activities, I suppose," Maranan scrutinized Klassen for his response, "will be to pay a visit to the chief of Security."

Klassen frowned. "Is that necessary?"

"Not necessary, perhaps, but advisable. It will give me a chance to sound out Duchesne, perhaps even convert him, or at least assure his nonintervention."

"Duchesne will never become one of us!"

"Not likely. But meeting with him will be expected of me."

Maranan consulted a memo on his screen. "Did I tell you I received a coded message from Security HQ last night?"

Klassen's eyebrows parted. "What is it?" he asked flatly.

"Blackboots says Duchesne is sending a team to snoop

around the Enclave. He thinks they may trump up a reason for an inspection."

Maranan flicked off the memo, seeing the play of emotions on Klassen's scarred face.

"I didn't know you had a contact in Security HQ."

Maranan's eyes gleamed. "You do not know everything, Erik."

"Worried?"

"No, Erik. We are all nice and legal. I made sure of that."

"There are places that Security shouldn't see."

"Then make sure they don't see them. I'm leaving it up to you."

"Don't worry, I'll make sure Duchesne's pawn sees exactly what we want him to. No more." Klassen couldn't keep the malice from his voice.

"What do you have against Duchesne?" Maranan asked. "Why do you hate him so?"

"You don't know, do you?" Klassen's jaw muscles worked. "No, you wouldn't. Do you want to know why I hate him? Because of what he took from me."

Maranan waited.

"I had a brother," Klassen began. "Don't look so surprised. Five years ago, Duchesne led a raid on Habitat 4. Went in with guns blazing, cutting down everyone in his path."

"And your brother was killed?"

"No! He should have been! Given the opportunity for a clean death. No, Duchesne took prisoners," Klassen spat. "Dragged them back like so much meat. You wouldn't know that either, sitting here writing your books, you wouldn't hear about it."

Maranan ignored the insult. "And?"

"Carl was a Luna citizen, so they shipped him there. And do you know what they did? They interrogated him. *Interrogated* him! I was there. A guard who was one of ours let me in to the prison block. I heard my brother's screams, heard them torture him." Klassen's voice grew thinner, tauter. The scar on his cheek throbbed red. "And there was nothing I could do! Nothing!"

"Eventually he told them what they wanted to hear. They turned him loose, what was left of him. A shattered, mindless wreck, wetting his pants from fear—that's what they left."

"I am sorry," Maranan said softly.

Klassen glared. "What do you care? When have you ever cared?"

Oh, I care, Maranan thought. *I care about the Plan. Nothing is going to stop me, Erik, not even you.*

"Do you know what I did?" Klassen continued.

Maranan shook his head.

"I killed him."

Maranan started. "Your own brother?"

"He asked me to. I couldn't refuse. What was there left for him, a gibbering, pitiful hulk? I killed him with my own hands."

Klassen held them up, in front of Maranan's face. "And I swore, there and then, that I would take my revenge on the scumrats that destroyed my brother. On the whole, stinking lot of them. And most of all, on Duchesne."

"Duchesne didn't kill your brother. In fact, I hear that he has a reputation for being humane."

"Don't defend him! He could have," Klassen ground out. "He could have killed my brother and spared him the agony he went through. But no, your nice guy had to take prisoners."

"You cannot kill Duchesne," Maranan protested. "Such an irresponsible action would destroy the Plan, all that you and I have worked for."

"I won't kill him." Klassen shook his head, emphasizing his words. "Killing would be too good for him. I want him to suffer, to suffer as I did, hearing my brother's screams. I won't kill him. But I will strip him of what he loves the most."

"Don't underestimate Duchesne, Erik. He's smart, and he's tough."

"I won't."

Maranan looked at him narrowly. "What do you know?" he asked. "What hold do you have—or think you have—on him?"

Klassen grinned.

"Be careful, Erik, I'm warning you. I won't tolerate any interference—or private vendetta—that could damage the Plan."

"Don't worry about your precious Plan." Klassen rose. "Isn't your Guide in control?" he said from the door.

Maranan sat in thought after Klassen had left. He would have to be very careful, or the younger man could upset everything. Now that he thought about it, Erik had changed over the past five years. He had always been ruthless and ambitious, but now he was full of hate.

Maranan knew what hate did to a man, gnawing at the soul, stripping the mind of reason. *Your hatred is not for destruction*, whispered the voice of his Guide. *You have a purpose.*

He shrugged. What did Duchesne matter, after all? Perhaps Erik had a point. As long as the Plan succeeded, Erik could do what he liked with Duchesne. If eliminating Duchesne was that important to Klassen, then perhaps it would be possible to work something out.

That was always Maranan's way—to work things out, seek a compromise, do everything possible to ensure that matters went smoothly. It would certainly be preferable to keep Klassen happy than to train a replacement.

He would have to find out what Klassen's plans were.

Feeling comfortable that he was dealing with the situation appropriately, Maranan sent for Szalny.

>

"Yes, Captain, that's an order. Fifteen minutes."

Carolyn sighed. "Yes, sir." She signed off.

Sometimes, J. I. . . .

Sometimes, having your husband as your commanding officer was a royal pain. There were times when Carolyn wanted to tell her husband the major where to get off. But, on duty, one had to be respectful and follow orders. Years of life in the service had drilled that into her.

Wait until she got home.

Anniversary or no anniversary.

Carolyn snagged her pistol onto her belt and strode out of her office.

He knows you hate the rifle range. That's probably why he wants you for a practice session.

Duchesne was lounging outside the range. The facility, which occupied a good portion of one of the lower levels of HQ, had been constructed to Duchesne's specifications. Always a stickler for reality, he had not been satisfied with the virtual reality simulator.

"Good morning, Major, *sir*." Carolyn gave him an exaggerated salute.

Duchesne grinned, not looking in the least put off. "Good morning."

"Is there a reason behind this somewhat imperious summons?"

"My, we are formal, aren't we? Need I be forced to remind you of your last scores? If memory serves me, your percentage—"

"I know my percentage." Carolyn unslung her gun. "After you, fearless leader. We'll see who gets the best scores today. One of these times, J.I. . . ."

Duchesne was a crack shot; she was average at best.

Holding his laser, an Enerweap 2000, in a two-fisted grip, Duchesne nudged open the door. Carolyn carried the lighter 1000 Security issue; she didn't think the greater stopping power and increased range of his weapon worth the increased weight.

She followed on his heels.

"Alternates." He whirled and loosed a shot at a figure springing from behind a pile of packing crates. The cutout lurched, a neat hole burned through its chest.

The current range boasted a warehouse scene, modeled after that at the spaceport, with plenty of concealed hiding places.

Carolyn fired overhead at a figure in a window. Pieces of charred cutout rained down.

"Good," Duchesne encouraged.

"Oh, shut up!"

A menacing figure popped out of the ground. Duchesne dived, rolled, and fired as he came up, decapitating the assailant.

"Show-off." Carolyn edged forward. "This is no job for a woman."

"You chose it."

She poked her nose around a corner and ducked back as a volley of laser fire skimmed past her.

"By Olympus!"

"Neat, eh? It's all right, it won't hurt. It's a holographic illusion. Gives an air of reality. Get hit and you lose."

"Thanks for warning me. Any more surprises?"

Carolyn leaned around the corner and destroyed a target with a pair of shots.

"Wasteful."

Duchesne spun past her to the security of a barrel. He spotted a narrow opening between a wall and a transfer crate and put a shot through into the shadows even as another bolt winged off the wall beside him.

Carolyn dived in behind him.

She whipped around the barrel. Another figure appeared. She held her shot in the nick of time.

"Noncombatant," she said dryly, scowling at the image of a small boy in jeans and tee-shirt.

Duchesne potted a target lurking on a rooftop and dodged as debris splattered around him.

Bent double, Carolyn sneaked in the shadow of a low wall, spinning at a noise behind. Her shot took off an arm.

"You're supposed to take off the arm with the gun, dear." Duchesne amputated the other limb with a well-placed shot.

"You seen any one-armed assassins lately?"

She fired past him, eliminating a burly, rifle-toting freight handler.

"That was mine."

"You had half of the last one," Carolyn retorted, laughing in spite of herself. "You satisfied?"

"Yeah," Duchesne laughed too. "You pass."

"So we can be friends again?"

"Sure. I know you don't like this, but I want us both to be on our toes."

"Just in case?"

"Just in case."

Earthdate: November 16, 2166

"Sir," said Corporal Derek Lofter, entering Duchesne's office. His voice hung, waiting for a response. After a moment's hesitation he repeated himself louder.

"Yes, Lofter."

Duchesne was immersed in field reports from his Operations Squads. He liked to keep a firm finger on the pulse of activity centered in and around Mars. His lieutenants, good as they were, saw only a part of the picture. Duchesne considered it his responsibility to maintain an overview. Occasionally a pattern presented itself out of what might seem a mixture of unrelated events. At the moment he was trying to determine if a series of slow-downs at an oxygen processing facility could have any bearing on the current affair. Probably not.

"The Colonial Administrator's office is on the line, sir. He requests a meeting with you."

Duchesne removed his attention from his workscreen. "I'd be happy to meet with Administrator Thorston."

"Uh, it's not Thorston, sir. It's Administrator Maranan."

"Ah. That's right, he's installed himself, hasn't he? Very well. Check my schedule and give him a time he can come over."

Lofter looked unhappy. "You're not going over to his office, sir?"

Duchesne's eyes were cold. "That's right, Corporal. If Maranan wants to meet me, he can come here. Any questions?"

"No, sir." Lofter retreated.

Duchesne toyed with his stylus. So Maranan wanted to meet with him. That was interesting. To sound him out? Pump him for information? Perhaps Maranan was uneasy, unsure of Security's position. If so, forcing him to Security H.Q. might increase any latent insecurity.

Yes, indeed. A meeting with Maranan could be helpful. He would like to get a better feel for his opponent.

He called Carolyn's office.

"Carolyn, come along to my office, would you? And bring the file on Maranan."

"Be right there."

He had been accused by certain individuals of nepotism for keeping Carolyn under his command. Your wife as your chief of staff? Not done. Not technically against regs but not done. He ignored the charges of nepotism. Carolyn could read him like a book, anticipating his requests often before he had even formulated them. He couldn't imagine functioning without her.

"What's up?"

Duchesne realized Carolyn was standing over him.

"You look deep in thought," she continued. "Brain working hard?"

He pulled his mind together. "Yeah. Pull up a seat. Guess who wants me to meet with him?"

Carolyn settled herself. "Too easy. Maranan."

"Right in one. So before I see him, how about filling me in and refreshing my memory?"

"Got it." Carolyn took a breath. "Background first, to set the stage. Ghalji Maranan, age sixty-two, born 2104 at Delhi-Agra in the India district of Earth. Educated at the University of New Delhi and later at the Sorbonne. Degrees in social anthropology and ecology."

"Interesting combination."

"Minor in genetics."

"Busy man."

"A genius, reportedly. After graduation he taught briefly at his alma mater, and there's little info on him until 2136. That was the year he founded the Revitalists. He promoted them actively for several years but eventually fell afoul of local authorities and decided to leave Earth. He moved to Mars in 2141—"

"What did he do?" Duchesne interrupted, "to come into confrontation with the law?"

"The Revitalists propounded an almost insane reverence for the Earth, far beyond the norm of the United World Church. They were denied permission to found a wilderness enclave but began construction anyway. Maranan was arrested, underwent a year's rehabilitation for crimes against ecology, and then packed up and emigrated."

"That must have made him furious, for an ecologist to be convicted of an ecological crime," Duchesne mused. "I wonder why he wanted to be out in the wilderness so much. So he comes here and the Mars Council allows him to start an enclave off in the back of beyond."

"Correct. Nobody objected at the time. Colonists were in demand. Besides, the Revitalists had money, and money talks. It was a small operation at first, until they went through a phase of aggressive expansion beginning in 2151 and lasting until 2158. From then until now they have been fairly quiescent, with only sporadic outbursts of enthusiasm."

"How about his personal life?"

"Maranan was briefly married in 2125. His wife died under suspicious circumstances. It's a very murky business. References are obscure."

"He never remarried?"

"No, although reports of liaisons are legion. I think—and

Boris may be able to confirm this—that Maranan has his own private harem at the Enclave."

Duchesne frowned. "Polygamy?"

"It's not illegal. Besides, who said he was married to them? There's no law restricting the number of partners you can have."

Duchesne sighed. On Mars, as on Earth, anything went. "I suppose not. What can you tell me about his personality?"

"Judging by the ease with which he picks up adherents when he chooses to exert himself, he must have a very forceful, even magnetic, personality. His writings—as I told you before—are devious and detailed. I think you would be wise to consider him very smart, very cunning, and almost monomanic in what he pursues. He's a dangerous man, J.I."

Carolyn regarded him seriously with her violet eyes. "Don't underestimate him."

"Oh, I won't do that, believe me. But you left out one thing."

"What may that be?"

"He's desperate. Maybe he doesn't recognize it, but he's at a crisis time in terms of his plans. He is putting into operation something he has been planning for decades. He is desperate that it not fail. And that's good. Desperate men make mistakes. And when he does, I'll be waiting."

>

If Paul Sommers had felt anxious when he visited the Duchesnes at home, he was even more so when he presented himself at Security HQ. His fingers and the tip of his nose tingled. He resisted an impulse to use the former to scratch the latter. His feet seemed unwilling to carry him into the frowning edifice.

Anita, as usual, had reassured him. He was glad that he had her to reinforce what he knew already.

"Go in faith," the female Barnabas said.

The request to present himself at Security had emanated from the major's office. Sommers was loathe to go, but thought it prudent to do so.

The guard at the entrance, a stony-faced young man, regarded him with hostility, as if unable to believe that a minister would be so foolish as to seek an audience in such a place.

Sommers felt a new sympathy for the prophet Daniel.

Finally convinced that Sommers was present by invitation, the guard pointed toward the lifters.

"Twenty," he said.

"Thank you."

The guard watched him until the lifter door cut off his view.

Duchesne welcomed him with a certain coolness; once again, Sommers thought that Carolyn provided the motivating force behind his invitation. He was relieved by her presence. Overfilling another chair was a giant, morose man whom Duchesne introduced as Lieutenant Mikhaelovitch.

"I asked you to come," said Duchesne, regarding his fingernails, "in the hopes that you would act as a kind of consultant for us in matters religious." He paused and raised his eyes to Sommers's. "I need hardly say that your assistance is not entirely appreciated by all members of this department."

Sommers thought he caught a flicker of Duchesne's gray eyes in Mikhaelovitch's direction.

"Your cooperation is entirely voluntary," Duchesne continued. "If you would rather not help, you are free to go."

He stopped, waiting for Sommers's response.

"I would be glad to help in any way I can," Sommers replied. He sensed Carolyn's approval.

"Good. In that case, you are undoubtedly aware that Ghalji Maranan is the new Colonial Administrator. The views of the Revitalists are somewhat obscure, to say the least. We thought that perhaps an opposing viewpoint, one not affiliated with the UWC, would be helpful; in short, do you have any insights into the Revitalists' mind-set?"

Sommers wondered where to begin. He settled himself in the chair, in what Anita called his "preaching pose."

"For example," Carolyn broke in, "take a quote like this, from *The New Gaia*: 'Life is inevitable. Think not of a supernatural property imposed on the unwilling and insensate, but of the inevitable outcome of matter; the ultimate expression of being. All is alive, from the smallest subatomic particle in its unmeasurable dance to the glowing orb of the largest sun; but most alive is Gaia herself, Mother and nurturer of all.'"

"Realize that I am not an expert in cults and sects," said Sommers. "I've read *The New Gaia*—last week, as a matter of fact—but only Maranan himself knows what he is truly saying."

"I told you he couldn't help," Mikhaelovitch complained. "Inviting a Christian was a stupid idea."

"Now, Boris," said Carolyn, "we can't all be atheists."

"Why not?"

"The Gaia hypothesis," Sommers continued, "was given pseudo-scientific stature in the Twentieth century by a scientist named James Lovelock. Basically, the idea is that the Earth—Gaia—is not an inanimate ball of rock but a living being incorporating all life forms. Earth is not a thing, but a who. And as a who, Maranan worships the Earth, or the life-potential which it represents."

"Rubbish," said Mikhaelovitch. "Like all religion."

"Okay, Boris," Duchesne said. "The point is not whether it's believable or not but that Maranan believes it."

"Respect for the Earth is one thing," Sommers continued, "but worship is another. Humanity has dealt badly with the Earth, and we Christians have to accept our share of blame. We have treated Earth more as an object to be exploited, not a gift to be treasured.

"But Maranan has moved beyond mere worship of the Earth to the point where Earth is everything and humanity is nothing. You see this often in religions that worship creation. Human life is unimportant. Almost any endangered species is considered of more value."

"What has this to do with Mars?" Mikhaelovitch asked.

"By extension," said Sommers, "Maranan seems to regard Mars as another Gaia. Perhaps he sees all planets as living beings—I don't know."

"That's absurd!" Carolyn interjected. "What few traces of life have been found on Mars have been proven to have come from Earth. Viruses carried on the solar wind."

"I think you'll find that what Maranan believes is this: Once, billions of years ago, Mars developed life. But for some reason, she—Mother Mars, as he calls her—shed that image, turning her back on life, becoming a sterile planet. Earth, of course, flourished with life. What the Revitalists hope to do is convince Mars to support life again."

"That is the most ridiculous thing I've ever heard!" Duchesne half-rose.

"It's a logical extension of the Gaia hypothesis," said

Sommers. "Why should it be confined to just one world? If you choose to believe that life is nothing special, an innate property of matter, then why not make all alive?

"I agree that it is absolutely absurd to worship a rock," said Sommers, shooting a glance at Mikhaelovitch, "although Maranan is not the first. Nor will he be the last. It is simply another alternative in the human saga of trying to find something to worship other than God."

"Don't forget," put in Carolyn, "that there are those who believe that life may be found elsewhere in the system, like the atmosphere of Jupiter."

"Another completely unproven hypothesis," said Mikhaelovitch. "Pseudo-scientific bunk."

"Very well." Duchesne rose to his feet to signal the meeting was over. He extended his hand. "Thank you, Reverend, you've given us something to think about."

"Glad I could help," Sommers replied, returning the grip.

He shook Carolyn's hand also; Mikhaelovitch made no move to extend his.

Sommers heard the conversation resume as he left the office.

"Now we have an idea of Maranan's thought processes," came Duchesne's voice. "But how does he mean to bring about this 'revitalization' of Mars?"

Sommers heard no response. But neither did he have one.

EIGHT

The hoverjets descended out of the rosy sky in a blinding swirl of dust, landing on rock blasted clear by sweeping downdrafts. As the blades of the wing-mounted fans slowed, the turbulence diminished and the dust began to settle. Touching down on the rocky plain, ports opened in the side of each hoverjet. Ramps snaked out and groundward. A file of black-clad troopers, armed and suited, emerged from each plane.

Lt. (jg) Howard Yellow Horse, from his position in the passenger section of the lead plane, opened a commlink to both pilots.

"MacKinnon and Solveg stay with the planes. Keep the engines warmed and be ready to take off at a moment's notice. I'm not expecting trouble but be prepared anyway. If you don't hear from us, or the Revitalists make any threatening moves, then get the planes aloft. Don't wait for instructions."

"Acknowledged."

Yellow Horse checked the pistol at his belt and strode down the ramp to join his waiting troopers. This was his first major assignment, and he didn't want to make any mistakes. The major was counting on him.

Three days of discreet observation at long range had produced minimal results. Ground traffic to and from the Enclave had been negligible. Such vehicles as Operation Squad 3 had encountered had been examined thoroughly and found to contain either adherents traveling to and from Lowell, or supplies destined for the Enclave. Nothing that looked suspicious.

A small hoverjet had departed two days previously, only to return several hours later. In response to a request, Yellow Horse had received a report from Lowell Field that the plane contained Maranan himself. Presumably, the Revitalist leader had ventured to Lowell to assume his new post.

Finally, bored with the routine, Yellow Horse decided there was nothing to be learned from distant observation. A closer inspection was required.

Little of the Enclave protruded above ground level onto the desolate surface of Hellas Planitia. Yellow Horse wondered why the separatists had chosen a location so far from Lowell when there were plenty of locations equally forbidding much closer. Surely it caused considerable expense and inconvenience to transport supplies and materials this distance across such rugged terrain. The cargo capacity of the small hoverjet would not amount to much. The Enclave's other option was to rely on cargo flitters.

Long and low, the blocky entrance building looked like it had been dropped and left to sit. Antennas and a comm laser projector protruded. A microwave power-receiving dish sat at some distance. The remainder of the Enclave was securely underground.

Yellow Horse studied the entrance, appraising the potential for offensive measures. The solid air lock doors—heavy steel composite set in reinforced thermocrete—would be hard to force. The Enclave looked as if it had been designed to withstand a siege. Probably nothing less than a naval ship's laser batteries or a small thermonuclear bomb would penetrate the structure.

Alongside the larger vehicle entrance, a smaller door for personnel seemed equally solid. A weather-scarred vidscreen was inset in a protected niche between the entrances. Yellow Horse reached out a gloved hand to activate it.

After a prolonged pause, the screen illuminated. A sallow-faced adherent stared at him.

"Yes?"

"Lt. Howard Yellow Horse, Security. Open up."

"Wait."

The screen blanked. Yellow Horse tapped the screen, wondering what was happening inside.

Eventually the screen came to life again. The adherent's expression hadn't changed.

"Enter."

The massive doors parted.

Yellow Horse beckoned to his squad. The troopers had to

squeeze together to fit in the air lock. Yellow Horse thought fleet-
ingly that it wasn't wise to have his troops packed into one place,
but it was too late, and they were in full protective gear anyway.

The inner door slid into its recess. Yellow Horse entered
the Enclave, moving along a short, brightly lit hall. A door to
his left contained the control room for the airlock and motor
pool. Through the square window he caught a brief glimpse of
a saffron-robed figure sitting in front of a control panel before
his view was blocked.

"What is the meaning of this?"

Yellow Horse pushed back the headpiece of his e-suit.

The man fronting him was a good head taller, his bone
structure comparable to Yellow Horse's, his manner aggressive
and authoritative. No trace of friendliness emerged from the
immobility of his expression or the set of his eyes. Yellow Horse
thought the man looked out of place in a robe.

Yellow Horse considered that, if necessary, he could take
the man. What Yellow Horse lacked in height, he made up for
in bulk, built low and powerful. But it wouldn't be easy. He
would rather not try.

"Who are you?" he countered.

The man glowered. "Erik Klassen. Master Maranan's
deputy."

"Very well. I am Lt. Howard—"

"I know your name."

"—Yellow Horse, of Security. You will allow us to make
an inspection of your facility."

"On what grounds?" Klassen grated.

"Section 22-a5 of the Lowell Charter authorizes Security
to make random inspections of any non-city facility to ensure
compliance with all regulations and safety features relating to
those facilities."

"You have done your homework. That section is very
rarely utilized."

"It is still on the books."

"You will find, Lieutenant," Klassen sneered, "that we
passed our last Environmental and Safety Facilities inspection
flawlessly, just last month."

"That may be, but you will allow our inspection now."

"And if I refuse?"

"But sir," spoke up a man from Klassen's shadow, that Yellow Horse hadn't previously noticed, "the Master said—"

"SHUT UP, Forrest!" Klassen barked without turning around. "Well, Lieutenant?"

"If you refuse, then I will place you under arrest and perform the inspection regardless. Perhaps Forrest will be more accomodating." Yellow Horse allowed his hand to rest on the butt of his laser.

Sow a little dissension. . . .

Klassen stiffened. The look in his eyes grew harder.

Yellow Horse's mouth went dry. He kept his face impassive. He hoped Klassen couldn't sense his nervousness. If the Revitalists had been stockpiling weapons and decided to resist. . . . He did not want to start a bloodbath. His squad was well-armed but vastly outnumbered.

To his immeasurable relief, Klassen conceded.

"Perform your inspection, Lieutenant." Klassen turned on his heel. Before he could take more than a step, Yellow Horse halted him.

"Perhaps you will conduct us, Deputy Klassen."

For a long moment the man stood still, his back to Yellow Horse. When he turned back, the hostile expression had been replaced by a thin, humorless smile.

"Very well, Lieutenant. I would be happy to."

"Klee and Howells, stay here and watch the doors," Yellow Horse ordered.

"Nervous, Lieutenant?" Klassen mocked. "I assure you we have nothing to hide."

Yellow Horse ignored the comment. One of Major Duchesne's maxims drilled into all lieutenants' heads was to be prepared for any eventuality. Leave nothing to chance. He beckoned the remainder of the troopers to follow. The short hall terminated at a row of lifters.

"The transportation and receiving dock and communication facility are the only surface level buildings. I hope you don't mind going underground."

The lifter dropped with a stomach-wrenching jerk. To Yellow Horse the fall seemed to take forever, but that was probably just him. It wasn't all that far. At length it slowed and jolted to a stop. Corridors, hewn out of the native rock, radiated away. They were coated with a thin layer of insulation that also served to prevent atmosphere leakage. There were no signs or other identifying markings that Yellow Horse could detect. The occupants presumably had to rely on memory to find their way about.

Several adherents, all dressed in the same insipid shade of saffron, passed by, incurious.

"This is the dormitory area," Klassen said. He opened one of the doors. Yellow Horse peered inside at the tiny, square room, unadorned save for a bed and mat on the floor. It looked worse than most prison cells. Klassen slid the door shut.

"There are several hundred of these rooms, all identical. We shall move on—"

"No," said Yellow Horse. "We will inspect all the rooms."

"Lieutenant, they are all the same."

"I have time."

Klassen shrugged. "As you wish."

Room by room, they proceeded slowly down the interminable corridor.

➤

Ghalji Maranan oiled into his office so smoothly that Duchesne was half-tempted to see if he left a trail on the floor behind him. Moving as if he hadn't a care in the world, the Revitalist seated himself, adjusting his pale blue robe until he was comfortable. When he was done, he raised his head and smiled, the effect, to Duchesne's mind, like that of a snake uncoiling itself. Unimpressed, Duchesne tolerated the performance, waiting for Maranan to make the first move.

"I must say, Major," Maranan began in a silky-smooth tone, "that it is highly unusual for the Colonial Administrator to be made to wait on anyone. It is customary—and, one would have thought, courteous—to respond to an invitation to meet with the Administrator by meeting him in his office in the Colonial Building."

Duchesne found Maranan's pedantic manner and tone of voice offensive. There was something else, too. Something about the cultist that made his skin crawl, his insides knot up. Something about Maranan wasn't right.

He kept his expression neutral.

"May I remind the Administrator," he replied, "that the Commander, Outer Planets, is not under the authority of the Colonial Administrator, and in point of fact, is not under any obligation to wait on him at all?"

Maranan played with the fringe of his sleeve. "Perhaps the Commander's superior would take a different view," he suggested.

Duchesne allowed his lips to curl. Obviously Maranan didn't know Forbes if he could make such a ludicrous suggestion.

Mistake number one.

"If the Administrator would like to determine the Commander's superior's reaction, he is welcome to contact him."

Duchesne swiveled his workscreen around. "Would you like my secretary to make contact with Earth for you? Real-time is awkward, but I'm sure Colonel Forbes would be delighted to accommodate you."

He had the satisfaction of seeing Maranan look nonplussed.

"If you don't like vidscreens perhaps, we are also able to provide holographic images."

The Revitalist waved the screen away with an attempt at nonchalance. "That will not be necessary." The expression of offended dignity dropped away. "Let us not play games, Major. I am the new Administrator. You are in command of Security. It is important that we establish a working arrangement, for our mutual benefit."

"Why is that?"

Maranan's eyes widened. "For the good of Mars," he said.

"Ah." Duchesne nodded. "And what may the good of Mars be?"

"The good of Mars is what we make it," Maranan replied. "My government is putting into effect a number of actions that will impact everyone in Lowell, indeed everyone on the planet. We will remove the impediments of prior administrations. Together, we will make a better Mars. Are you with us, Major?"

Duchesne pursed his lips. "It may be," he replied, "that we have different visions of the good of Mars, Administrator."

"I do not expect you to become a Revitalist, Major—"

"Good."

"—that would be asking too much. But I do hope that

Security will remember its proper sphere of activity and not be interfering in the affairs of government?"

Now it comes down to it, Duchesne thought. *He's scared. Scared of what Security might do if we become involved. There's something he's afraid we might discover if we nose around long enough.*

Mistake number two.

A thin sheen of sweat beaded upon the older man's forehead as he waited for Duchesne's reply.

"Security will continue to uphold the Constitution," Duchesne replied, "in accordance with the laws dictated by the World Council of the Commonwealth of Earth for the functioning of same."

A muscle twitched in Maranan's cheek. "Come, Major! Don't quote bureaucratic jargon to me! I do hope that you don't think that there is anything *illegal* in our formation of the new government?"

"My sources have not confirmed any illegality," Duchesne conceded.

"Then would you tell me why one of your squads is inspecting the Enclave even as we speak?"

How does he know that? wondered Duchesne, taken aback. *I only just received word myself of Yellow Horse's action.*

"Routine."

"Previous commanders never found such an intrusion necessary."

"Precisely."

"I assure you they will not find anything, either at the Enclave or in Lowell. The government of Mars is taking a new direction, Major. I tell you seriously, so that there will be no misunderstanding. We will succeed." He pronounced the words slowly, emphasizing each one, "With or without you."

"Are you implying a threat?"

"I am implying nothing." Maranan's oily smile had returned. "Only making an observation. Do you feel threatened, Major? Perhaps there will not be a need for Security on the new Mars."

"We will see, Administrator."

"As you wish."

Maranan rose to his feet with the same dignified motion as

he had entered. His robe cascaded in shimmering folds.

"Do remember my words, Major. It would be a pity. . . ."

Leaving the sentence hanging, Maranan exited. Duchesne tapped a finger on his desk.

Maranan's parting comments left him uneasy. The administrator's tone was silky, but underneath Duchesne detected the sharp edge of naked steel.

>

Lin Grainger paced around the lab, too restless to sit. She ought to be starting the memory procedure on the latest clone. The body, blank-minded, neural circuits not as yet filled with all the thoughts, memories, and desires vital to personhood, lay supine on the couch, enveloped by the pale glow of a sleep field. The empty face, devoid of animation, reminded her of a picture she had once seen of a retarded individual.

She thought the field a little light and deepened the intensity. The clones grew in a sleep field to prevent the development of memory and personality before it was time.

This one, Lin thought, was a judge, another necessary component of the master's Plan.

Yesterday, she had removed the body from the special incubation cubicle it had occupied for so long. When animated, the face could be handsome, she supposed, young to be a judge. The physique was not particularly well developed—someone mentally active but physically lazy.

When she stopped to think about it, the process created by the late Francis Farrer amazed her. The actual cloning itself was simple: Take the complete genetic material from a single body cell and make it grow. Turn on all the dormant genes and it would produce a new individual.

Back in the old days the cell nucleus—containing the genetic material—was implanted in a human egg, where natural processes took over. Such tedium was no longer necessary. The genes were known; the factors to activate or deactivate them were known. Simple mechanics.

But a clone was like any other living organism. If you wanted a twenty-year-old clone, you had to wait twenty years for it to grow. Thirty, then thirty. And so on, until Farrer developed a process whereby, using a combination of normal growth factors, synthetic compounds, and electromagnetic fields, growth could be accelerated greatly. What had taken twenty or thirty years now took two.

All that remained was to implant the memories—derived and partly incomplete but adequate.

Still, she hesitated.

Outside, separated by the thin metal of the door, Security troops conducted a search of the Enclave. Forrest had promised to notify her when it was safe to emerge. It wasn't likely she'd be recognized, but the master had told her to remain in the lab, out of sight, in the event of a search.

Start the program.

All she had to do was open the door.

Another protest to Maranan had been rebuffed.

"No more," she had said again when the files of the judge had been delivered. "I can't do it anymore. Creating these . . . replicas is not right."

"What is right and what is not, Lin? There is no such thing as 'right' and 'wrong'; there is the necessary and the unnecessary. You must continue, Lin. There is no one else who can do it."

"Human cloning was outlawed long ago. Pantropes are one thing, but running off duplicates of people—I can't. I want out, Master." Her voice rose with the intensity of her emotion, sounding shrill.

Maranan fixed his tranquil eyes on her, unphased by the outburst. When he spoke, his voice was inflexible. "There is no out for you, Lin."

"All I have to do is walk out of here."

"No, Lin, you cannot leave."

"Then I call Marsnews, or Security—"

"Again, no." Maranan remained patient but firm. "Think, Lin, what happens if you tell the authorities? Who will be blamed? They will convict you of crimes against humanity. That will be the end of your dreams, and you will find out what true imprisonment—rehabilitation—is like. You will be a marked woman, Lin. Only if the Plan succeeds will you be free again."

Lin knew he was right. She'd committed herself deeply. She'd sold herself on the altar of her ambition. No iron bars had ever comprised a more secure prison than that which Lin

Grainger had constructed for herself out of ambition. She had accomplished what she wanted—she was indispensable.

For her, there was truly no escape.

She couldn't leave. Neither could she destroy her work and betray Maranan.

If she succeeded, if she was able to populate Mars with a new race, she would be the most famous genetic engineer in history. She would have accomplished what generations of scientists had desired to do but had been too afraid to do.

Lin turned away from the door.

Her finger trembled hesitantly over a control on the console.

MEMORY INSERTION PROGRAM: ENABLE (yes) no.

Yes.

The communication laser winked into existence.

➤

While the last Security troopers passed through the airlock and climbed antlike up the ramps, Erik Klassen remained in the control room. He stayed rooted to the monitor screen until the hoverjets roared into the sky and screamed off.

Only when the black specks had disappeared into the haze on the horizon did he expel his pent-up rage in one long, explosive roar. The adherent manning the console cringed.

It had taken every fiber of self-control he possessed for Klassen to refrain from ordering the adherents to turn on the troopers and slaughter every last one of them. He himself would have taken on the insufferable lieutenant, the compulsive idiot who insisted on examining every single wretched room in excruciating detail. It would have been a bloodbath, but they would have won. Who would have cared how many adherents were killed? They could be replaced easily enough by another crop of idealistic fools.

And now the killers of his brother were gone, beyond his reach, back to the security of their headquarters. Safe and secure in their shielded complex, protected by weapons emplacements and guards.

But not for long, that he promised himself. Not for long.

It was nearly time, he mused, to act on the information Szalny had supplied. And when he did, none of Security's facilities, technology, or weaponry could help them.

Klassen allowed himself a self-satisfied smirk. What had they seen for all their prying? Nothing! What discoveries had they made? None! What had they done besides waste their time? Nothing.

Maranan had ordered that they see nothing, and that was exactly what they had seen.

➢

Klassen whirled around. "What are *you* doing?"

Lin started. "I—I'm on my way to the motorpool to collect some supplies. If I'd known you were around, I'd have left it until later."

A look of pleased malice lighted Klassen's face. "Come here," he ordered. Lin took a step forward, careful to remain out of arms' reach. "You seem eager to please the master, Grainger."

"Of course," Lin replied. She had a sinking feeling in the pit of her stomach. "That's why I wonder how he could leave a creature like you in charge."

"Shut up! I want you to do a full sensor sweep of the Enclave. There is no telling what the Security scum may have left behind."

Lin gasped. "B-but the whole Enclave? That will take—"

"I don't care how long it takes you! Perform a full sweep of the entire Enclave! And so help me, Grainger, if you miss anything, if one listening device gets past your scan, you will regret it like you've never regretted anything before."

Lin's bile rose. "Who do you think you are, Klassen?" she raged. "I serve Maranan, not you! Get one of your flunkies to do it."

She attempted to move past him, but he angled himself and stood blocking the doorway.

"Then you can be in my quarters," he said smugly.

"No more, Klassen. No more."

"It will be easier if you come willingly. If I have to find you . . ."

Lin's eyes smoldered. *Someday . . . someday, Klassen.*

"I have work in the lab to do," she said coldly. "Or do you want to explain to the master why his next dupe isn't ready?"

He didn't resist as she pushed past him.

She exhaled. So she'd spend the night in the lab. It wouldn't be the first time.

From behind her, she could hear Klassen bellowing for Forrest.

➤

Gordon Blanchard looked up from his spectral analyser in time to see a pair of black shapes tear across the sky until the distant mountains cut them off. He could almost hear them, too. His auditory implant had malfunctioned, and he had to work without accompaniment.

"Security," he muttered sourly. "They can afford to go jetting back and forth across the planet while I have to deal with this."

He kicked one of the crawler's wheels, loosening a clump of dirt.

"Hey you!" he shouted into the sky after the contrails. "I've got a present for you! Want to come and get it?"

He turned disgustedly back to the analyser. Air transportation—due to the lack of suitable fuels on Mars—was prohibitively expensive. The hoverjets had small fusion reactors. Olympus Mining would never go that far for a mere prospector. Far more economical to use battery- and solar-powered ground transport.

So what if it was slow?

Prospectors were cheap.

"Slogging my life away on this forsaken dirtball," grumbled Blanchard. He raised his eyes to the empty sky.

"All right, be that way! You'll just have to wait for him." He laughed. "Yeah, wait."

NINE

Nearly fifteen minutes late, Howard Yellow Horse was the last of the Operations Squad lieutenants to arrive. His braids—a badge of individuality worn in defiance of official dress code and secured by beaded barettes—bobbed madly as he hurried in. Carolyn cast a not-to-be-missed look at her chrono. "You're late, Lieutenant."

"Sorry, sir—"

Yellow Horse pulled up a seat at the conference table. He looked from McCourt to Duchesne. "Sorry I'm late, sir, there was a problem with some of the recordings—"

"Nothing serious?" Duchesne asked.

"Nothing Computer Science couldn't remedy."

"Good. As I was saying, I think it's time that we had a joint discussion of the situation."

"What about Hernandez?" Nancy Cohen asked from her position at the foot of the table. Cohen's blonde hair was significantly shorter than Yellow Horse's, her features severe, her attitude more businesslike. "When will he be back?"

"Another month," Carolyn supplied. "His departure was delayed. The trip from Titan takes long enough as it is."

"We can't count on Carlos to be back in time to help, although his political acumen would be invaluable," Duchesne said. He turned to the slight man seated on his left. "I'm sorry to interrupt your leave, Reggie—"

"Can't be helped," Marlais said, fiddling with his thumbs. Marlais's well-formed and debonair, ebony features always struck Duchesne as looking more like a holographic movie star than a Security lieutenant. But Marlais wouldn't be a Security lieutenant if his abilities were flawed.

"You don't have to be back on full-time duty at the moment but be available at any time. Don't forget your comm-link if you head out into the wilds."

"Yes, sir. I don't expect to be leaving Lowell." Marlais smiled. "There's enough to do here."

"I don't need to tell you that nothing of what we say is to pass outside this room. Since Captain McCourt contacted each of you directly, no one under the rank of lieutenant knows of this meeting."

"Why the secrecy?" Cohen asked, waving her arm to indicate the heavily shielded conference room.

"It's difficult to conceive of a leak, but Maranan knew of Howard's inspection in advance." Duchesne ran his eyes around the grouping. "Letting on the existence of more knowledge than you should have is a classic error, and Maranan committed it." He focused on Yellow Horse. "Howard, why don't you begin with a report of your reconnaissance."

In his soft, monotonal drawl, Yellow Horse reiterated the details of his search. He displayed a plan of the Enclave, recorded during the inspection on the screen.

Duchesne pursed his lips. "A rabbit warren."

"The place is immense," said Yellow Horse. "There is room for thousands of people, although at a guess I'd estimate there aren't above a thousand or fifteen hundred there presently. It was hard to get an accurate count with people moving around. It's a strange mixture of bare-bones utilitarianism and state of the art design and technology."

Yellow Horse concluded, "The place is built to withstand a seige."

"We had better hope that direct action isn't needed," said Mikhaelovitch.

"A frontal assault could succeed," Cohen declared, "but it would be costly."

"What did the scans reveal?" Duchesne asked.

Yellow Horse bared a row of uneven teeth. "Maranan's deputy, Klassen, thought he was being crafty. Once I told him we wanted to see every room, he went out of his way to show us every room—closets, storage, bathrooms, recycling. Or so he wanted us to believe. I don't think he took his eyes off me for a moment, making sure I saw just what he showed me. But look at this."

Yellow Horse spoke to the computer terminal. "Display file YH-1A."

A grainy image filled the screen.

"He never suspected that one of the troopers was carrying a concealed scanner. I apologize for the quality of the pics. The place wreaks havoc with radar images. A larger unit would have given more detail but been impossible to conceal—"

"Never mind the explanations," cut in Marlais. "What do they show?"

"—inside an adapted rifle casing," Yellow Horse continued. "Most of the Enclave is just what we're meant to believe—a large complex of dormitories and support structures. But here, leading off the lower level—off Maranan's private room, in fact—is another block of rooms. It is well concealed—I was looking for traces of hidden entrances and didn't see a thing."

"What do you suppose it is?" Mikhaelovitch asked.

"Don't know. And the scans aren't detailed enough to form any guesses. But whatever it is, it's important."

"How do you figure?" Marlais asked. "Perhaps it's a worship center of some kind."

"Nope. They have a meditation room on the second level which is big enough to hold everyone. And I saw a number of adherents meditating in their rooms. Why would Maranan or Klassen hide a worship area? Like we'd be interested in that."

"Medical facility?" Carolyn supplied.

"That's more like it," Duchesne nodded, "especially as we know that Maranan has made significant purchases of biotechnology. But you don't need a big facility for that number of people, not in this day and age. One or two autodocs would be plenty."

"Research," said Cohen. "Biological weaponry."

"But that doesn't fit Maranan's profile," Carolyn objected. "According to his writings, he has a fanatical regard for the Earth and Mars. Would he risk releasing a weapon that could render the planet uninhabitable?"

"How much credence can you put in the writings of a fanatic?" Mikhaelovitch asked. "Perhaps they're designed to be misleading."

"Let's not get carried away," Duchesne said. "We can lose

ourselves in a sea of speculation. Maranan's Enclave has secret rooms, and we don't know what they're for. Perhaps they're related to biotechnology, perhaps not. Let's move on."

"There is this," Mikhaelovitch continued. "One of the names I came across while researching the Revitalists was Lin Grainger."

Duchesne shook his head. "Means nothing to me. Anybody else?"

There was a chorus of "nos."

"She's a biotechnician—apparently fairly well-known but reputed to be a maverick."

"So that may tie in with the rooms. Good, Boris. Keep at it. See what else you can find out about Ms. Grainger. Next topic."

"Wait a sec," said Marlais. "What about finding out what's in those rooms? I presume satellite scans would be useless, but how about getting a man inside?"

"Suicide," declared Yellow Horse. "That lot is as suspicious as prairie dogs in hunting season. Anyone who tried to penetrate inside would be spotted and killed immediately. They'll be looking for us to try something like that, guaranteed."

"What about one of the converts?" Cohen asked. "Is there a possibility of subverting one of them?"

"Or bringing one in for questioning?" Marlais persisted.

"Possible but doubtful," said Carolyn. "I would suspect that the adherents are pretty-well brainwashed before they're allowed clearance to join the Enclave. Deprogramming one of them well enough to extract any useful information would be very difficult, perhaps impossible."

"It's an option," said Cohen.

"I'll keep it in mind," said Duchesne. "Anything new on your end, Boris? What have you got on that deputy of Maranan's, Klassen?"

"Erik Klassen has been Maranan's right-hand man for years, as far as I can determine. Prior to that he was involved with the Mulvanni family—"

"The drug and smuggling clan?" asked Marlais.

"Yes. The self-styled Mafia family of the Inner Worlds. Klassen was a hit man, a very effective one. Implicated in several murders, convicted of none. After hooking up with

Maranan, he dropped out of sight. Incredibly, the authorities lost interest in him. He seemed to be behaving himself and restricting his activities to promoting the religious beliefs of the Revitalists."

"What about his personality?" Duchesne asked.

"Reported to have a hair-trigger temper, ruthless and unscrupulous. Said not to let anything or anyone get in his way."

"Delightful piece of news," said Yellow Horse.

"Very nasty and very dangerous."

"How about you, Carolyn, anything from your reading?" Duchesne asked.

"To start with, I'd suspect this outbreak of anti-Christian violence that you've all heard about is connected with the Revitalist agenda, whatever that may be."

"Is that important?" Cohen interrupted. "They're a bunch of nonconformist radicals too. I wouldn't waste any sympathy for them."

"Perhaps, perhaps not. What is important though, is that under their 'we love Mars' image, the Revitalists are equally intolerant. Being a member of the UWC is not good enough. One must be in sympathy with their goals and ideals."

"Do you think they may force the issue?" Duchesne asked.

"It's a definite possibility. Once they've finished with the Christians, I'd expect to see a mass program of evangelization."

"Come off it!" Marlais scoffed. "Do you really think a fringe group could take over the mind-set of a planet? Do you see lines of people waiting to join up with this bunch of weirdos? Please, let me in!"

"It's happened before," said Carolyn. "Remember Nazi Germany. One group converted the entire country—a country with a lot more people in it than we have here on Mars—to their distorted way of thinking. And then, war."

"And after that?" inquired Duchesne.

"Whatever it is, they're going to promote it for the good of Mars. That's a phrase that continually crops up in Maranan's writings."

"He used it with me," said Duchesne. "But what does it mean?"

"Nothing that the rest of us would like," Carolyn said seriously.

"What do we do, then?" Cohen jumped to her feet. "Just sit around playing amateur detective while a group of lunatics takes over the planet?"

"I'm with Nancy," Marlais agreed. "We must put an end to this. Nip it in the bud before it gets out of hand."

"We've got the firepower," said Cohen.

"I fear there is little we can do at this point," argued Mikhaelovitch, "firepower or not. At the moment, we have no evidence of law-breaking, much as we would like it."

"Unfortunately, I agree," concluded Duchesne. "But we keep on looking. Sooner or later we will find something we can act upon."

"Let's hope it isn't too long coming," said Cohen.

"Amen to that."

>

Anita Sommers paid little attention to the gang of youths as she left the store, turning right down the street.

"Corridor" would have been just—if not more—appropriate a term, in the underground complexes. But "corridor" had a narrow sound, and the streets certainly weren't narrow. Knowing the effect on the human psyche of terminology, the designers had purposely chosen the designation "streets."

Aside from the bright, overhead illumination replacing sky and the lack of aircars, the street could have passed for an outdoor thoroughfare on Earth.

The shopping complex, located not far from a school district, was a favorite hangout for students spending their lunch breaks loitering or playing in the virtual reality arcade. Used to the sight of the juveniles, Anita felt no alarm. The complex was only one level above their housing block.

She heard a stir of interest as one student pointed her out to the others.

"Look! There she is!"

"You sure?"

"'Course! Seen her comin' out of church once."

Anita looked over her shoulder and began to walk faster.

The group followed her. They narrowed the distance and then surrounded her.

"Hey lady, whatcha got?" A hand tugged on her shopping bag.

Anita jerked it away. She knocked into another body. "Please! That's mine!"

"Touchy, ain't she?" The student, much bigger than she, shoved her away. Anita staggered but maintained her balance.

"Maybe she's got a Bible in there," suggested a giggly female. She reached around Anita. "You got a Bible in there?"

"You're one of those Christians, aren't you?" a tough-looking boy demanded, his face tattooed with a grotesque death's-head.

Anita looked around for help, but she couldn't see over the tall youths. If anybody was close, she couldn't tell.

"Aren't you?" The boy grabbed her shoulder and shook roughly.

"Yes, I am," Anita said. "Please let me go." She tried to push ahead, but the students wouldn't yield.

"In a hurry?"

"Maybe she's got to go to church. That it, lady? Got to go to church?"

"It ain't Sunday!"

"Shouldn't you be in class?" the frightened woman asked.

"Class? Hey, anybody wanna be in class?"

"Noooo!"

"Check the bag!" said the giggly girl.

This time the jerk was too strong, and the bag was torn from Anita's grasp. She made a desperate grab to retrieve it.

"Please—!" The bag was gone, passed from hand to hand.

One of the girls upended it and dumped the contents on the ground. Anita bent over, trying to see between the feet to retrieve her belongings. Someone jerked her back up.

"Not so fast!"

Feet lashed out, kicking the contents of the bag away, scattering them across the ground.

"Where's the Bible?"

"Don't see one."

"Where's the Bible, lady?"

"Let me have my bag back," Anita pleaded.

"What's a Christian doing without a Bible?"

A face pushed close to hers, raw hatred distorting the features. "We don't like Christians around here. Any of you guys like Christians?"

"NAAAH!"

"Bunch of troublemakers."

One of the students, taller than the rest, slapped Anita across the face.

"Wanna turn the other cheek?"

"Help!" Anita called. "Somebody help!"

"Shut up!" A hand clapped across her mouth. Anita wrenched away, catching the student by surprise. For a moment, she was free. The students paused. Across the street, a brown-clad marspoliceman was talking to a Security trooper.

"Help!" Anita called. "Please help me!"

"We ain't doin' nuthin'," one of the boys waved his arm.

"Just helping this Christian find her Bible. She dropped her stuff," said a girl.

The policeman and the trooper exchanged a glance and then turned away.

"Wait!" Anita called. "Please!"

The men disappeared down the street. The students leered at each other.

"Looks like they ain't gonna help you, lady."

Anita nearly fell over as the student jostled her. A fist hit her lower back, and she gasped in pain.

"Why don'tcha pray? That's what you do, ain't it?"

A hand wrapped itself in the collar of her shirt, bending her neck, forcing her down to her knees.

"Pray, lady, pray."

➤

"Have you heard the latest?" Carolyn asked, depositing herself decorously in Duchesne's desk-side chair.

"What latest?" Duchesne yawned. "If it's bad news forget it. I'm not interested. It's been a long day, and I'm ready to go home."

"From the legislative session. It was on the morning news."

"No, I haven't. Our new administrator doesn't keep me as well informed as Thorston did, and I haven't had time to listen to any broadcasts."

"Here it is, then. Latest measures passed by the Council in special session. This is incredible, J.I. I can't imagine that this stuff actually passed."

"Don't keep it to yourself, then. If you're determined to tell me."

"Surface mines to be closed. Subsurface facilities to be strictly monitored and subject to production quotas. Surface building to cease immediately. Immigration prohibited. Terraforming restricted to atmosphere production."

"Are they completely crazy?"

"New governing board comprised exclusively of Revitalists appointed to oversee all GenAg facilities. Exports of all minerals and metals to Earth will stop, effective immediately."

"They'll cripple the economy!" Duchesne's lethargy vanished.

"One last item. Practice of Christian religion is prohibited. All citizens of the new Mars Republic will swear allegiance to the UWC and preferably the Revitalists."

"That one doesn't surprise me," Duchesne grumbled.

"Have you been outside today?" Carolyn asked.

Duchesne blinked at the sudden change of topic. "Are you kidding? Lofter's had me up to my eyeballs in status reports and requisitions. I've hardly left this office, let alone gone outside."

"I went for a walk at lunchtime," Carolyn explained, "and if I saw one yellow robe, I saw a hundred. There was one on just about every corner. They're out in force." She leaned forward. "What are we going to do, J. I.? We can't just sit back and let them ruin the planet."

"I know that!" Duchesne said, suddenly angry. "But what are we supposed to do? They're not doing anything illegal for pity's sake!"

Carolyn held up her hands in mock surrender. "Hey, don't come down on me. I didn't join them."

Duchesne leaned over the desk and kissed her on the lips.

"Sorry. It's just frustrating, that's all. I know, as sure as I'm sitting here, that there's something wrong, but I just can't find it."

"Maybe you need a break. Let your mind cool down."

Duchesne shook his head. "No time for that."

"J. I. . . ."

"I think what I'll do is call Forbes and see what he says. If we can get authorization from the World Council, maybe we can do more than simply sit here nibbling around the edges."

"Good idea. While you're doing that, I'm going over to Reverend Sommers's place. I wonder if he has any more insights."

"Okay. Just don't be spotted, all right?"

Carolyn laughed. "Who's going to mess with me? I'll be in uniform. Official business." She returned his kiss. "See you at home."

"I won't be too late, I hope."

"You'll probably be back before I am."

Carolyn departed on her visit.

Duchesne called the comm officer. "Raise Colonel Forbes for me. Priority real-time request and make it a secure channel to my office."

"Yes sir."

The time lag to Earth—anywhere from four minutes up, depending on the relative positions of the two planets—was just long enough to make live communication irritating.

Fifteen minutes passed before the comm officer came back on line.

"Colonel coming through, sir."

"Holo."

Duchesne's far wall flickered and dissolved into the holographic image of Colonel Gerald Forbes. Duchesne had no way of telling from the colonel's appearance what time it was on Earth.

"Duchesne," Forbes began unceremoniously, "this had better be important. I'm delaying an important meeting. What's so vital that it can't wait for a dispatch?"

The figure turned away and concentrated on something out of field. Duchesne had never become used to talking to someone who was apparently not paying attention.

"It is, sir. Sorry for the interruption. Matters on our end are taking a decidedly unpleasant turn." Duchesne described the results of his investigation, concluding with a summary of the Revitalist agenda.

"You see, sir, with no evidence of wrongdoing, my hands are tied unless the World Council or Colonial Bureau authorizes me to take more aggressive measures. We need to keep on top, because if the situation turns violent, I'm not sure we have enough manpower. I'd appreciate your input. Over."

Duchesne finished speaking and turned his attention to other matters. In just over five minutes time, Forbes sucked in his moustache and scowled. His reply came after another five minutes.

"Matters are worse than that, Duchesne, much worse. I hadn't heard of your Council's specific plans, although they fit in with rampant rumors. Should have called you sooner, I suppose. I can't give you any authorization to act directly, at least officially, much as I would like to. You're on your own on this one.

"The Colonial Board has endorsed the Revitalist government, seconded by the World Council, and inconceivably approves their agenda. It appears that several members of the Board either have Revitalist sympathies or are members themselves. How they could approve such a ludicrous set of misplaced plans only another bureaucrat would know. I've got several good officers working on the Revitalist connection at this end, but they have little to go on."

Forbes inclined his head, his presence seeming to fill Duchesne's office.

"You're stuck, Duchesne, the man on the spot. My hands are tied, more so than yours. If you act, you'll be violating the instructions of the Colonial Bureau. If you don't—then Mars falls into the hands of an irresponsible regime.

"Find a reason to act, Duchesne. Find something—anything—to enable you to get a grip on these maniacs. If I find evidence of a conspiracy here, you'll be the first to know. And locate Hannik—if he penetrated the cult, perhaps he has clues."

Forbes shrugged his shoulders. "Sorry, Duchesne. That's all I can do to help at the moment. I'll contact Commodore Washburn at Phobos Navalport and authorize him to loan you any bodies you need. Admiral Rawlings at Command is an unknown commodity at present. You have my full support, Duchesne, remember that."

Duchesne's anger rose. "What do you expect me to do, sir? My loyalties are being called into question! I'm sworn, as a Security officer, to loyalty to Earth, but Mars is my home. I can't stand by and see my home destroyed! You're placing me in an impossible situation, sir."

Duchesne fretted while waiting for the response. Forbes's words, when they came, weren't reassuring.

"We all face impossible situations, Duchesne. Not only your reputation, but mine and all of Security's is resting on what you do. Whatever you decide, you'd better be deuced sure you make the right decision.

"One other thing, Duchesne. I hear that you've become friendly with a Christian group there. Per our prior conversation on the subject, I need hardly remind you that they are a politically incorrect group. Associating with them can only be detrimental. I don't want your decision making affected by outside influences. Don't let your sympathies cloud your judgment. If it's part of your investigation, fine; disregard the previous. Just don't get in over your head."

Forbes's tone softened; he lifted a stout finger.

"Be cautious, Duchesne, be deuced cautious. I don't want to lose you."

He opened his mouth as if to say more, then shut it. "Forbes out."

The hologram faded and disappeared.

Duchesne remained staring at the wall, almost wishing he had turned down his promotion.

Find Hannik! How was he supposed to do that? One man on a whole planet.

And how, he wondered, did Forbes know about Sommers?

➤

Captain Carolyn McCourt, her mind occupied, took a wrong turn and exited the lifter a level too soon. She turned around quickly, but the doors had already closed. She'd left her Security groundcar on the main level above. At this time of the day, after working long hours in the office, she preferred to walk the short distance remaining rather than take the car down.

"I suppose I could cross the Center," she mused, watching the lifter disappear into the depths, "or take a ramp. Cross the Center."

She spotted a group of teenagers milling about—twelve or fifteen—as she entered the shopping area. She couldn't tell but thought they were clustered about something. Or someone. She strode across the intervening distance.

"What's going on here?"

The students straightened. Their air of aggression melted away at the sight of Carolyn's uniform. All except for one student, a burly young man with rugged features and hideous facial ornamentation.

"We ain't doin' nuthin'."

"Move aside. All of you," Carolyn pointed.

The student planted his feet firmly.

"You too," Carolyn said.

The boy put his hands on his hips. He smiled defiantly. "I told you. We ain't doin' nuthin'."

The other students edged apart. Carolyn caught sight of a slight woman kneeling on the ground, her face ashen.

The boy followed her glance. "She's a Christian."

"So?"

"It ain't wrong to teach a Christian her place. Or haven't you heard the news?"

"The lot of you, home, now." Carolyn stared the youth in the eyes. "You included."

"I got a right to be here."

"Your friends are leaving."

The boy looked around. The nearest student was twelve feet distant and moving down the street.

"Cowards!" he shouted after them. "We're okay! She can't do nuthin!'" His head swivelled back to Carolyn.

"Don't be an idiot," she said, still staring. "Go home without making a problem for yourself."

"I can take you. You ain't even got a gun."

The comment surprised Carolyn into laughing. The boy's cheeks flushed.

"You're dumb enough to think you can take on a trained Security officer, boy? I've landed tougher men than you in the hospital without breaking a sweat." Carolyn bounced on her toes. "Come on, tough guy. Strut your stuff."

Indecision twisted the boy's face.

Probably the last thing he expected, Carolyn thought. *Somebody to stand up to him. Typical bully mentality.*

"What are you waiting for? Afraid that somebody at HQ is watching it on the monitors?"

The boy's head jerked about. He searched for the concealed cameras that monitored all public areas. The other students had disappeared.

"I . . . uh . . ." He turned and fled down the street.

Carolyn had nearly forgotten about the woman, intent on her confrontation with the boy.

"Thank you, officer. . . ." The woman struggled to her feet. Carolyn reached out a hand to help her up. She moaned and held her side.

"McCourt. Captain Carolyn McCourt. Did they hurt you?"

"Just bruised. There was a police officer and a Security trooper . . . they . . ." She paused.

"They what?"

"They walked off. They saw what was happening and walked off."

Carolyn's eyes narrowed. "You're a Christian?"

The woman regarded her warily. "Yes."

Has it spread so far already? Carolyn wondered. "What's your name?"

"Anita Sommers."

Carolyn perked up. "Are you related to Reverend Sommers?"

"His wife."

Carolyn held out her hand again, and the other woman shook it. "What a coincidence! I was just on my way to see him." Seeing the look of puzzlement on Anita's face, she continued, "He was over at our place the other day."

"You must be Major Duchesne's wife!" Anita blurted. "I thought the name sounded familiar."

"Let me help you home," said Carolyn, embarrassed by Anita's effusiveness. "No one will bother you now. While we're walking, you can tell me all about what happened."

Carolyn's arm supporting Anita's shoulders, the two women walked down the street.

➤

That night, Carolyn pulled the sheet up to her neck and snuggled down.

"It was awful," she said. "A mob of students attacked her right in the middle of the complex. If I hadn't shown up, they might have hurt her badly. How could something like this be happening here?"

Duchesne shucked his shirt. "It's nothing new. The Revitalists' actions are no more than the same divisions and hatreds that have plagued humanity forever."

"The boy was ready to fight me!"

Duchesne's pants followed his shirt. He pulled on a pair of pajamas. "Show me a teenager who *does* respect authority."

"If I find out who that Security trooper is, he's going to be in big trouble."

"I don't envy him." Duchesne slipped into bed beside her. "If the Reverend is correct, things are only going to get worse for them."

"And for us. Confound Forbes! Is that all he could say? Good luck, it's up to you?"

"Don't be too hard on him. He's got the government breathing down his neck."

"And what have we got, J. I.?"

"Roll over," Duchesne replied. He rubbed Carolyn's back muscles, easing out the knots and tension.

"Mmmm," she purred. "You're evading the question."

"We have got a night to sleep on it. Something will break."

"As long as it's not us."

"Never us, dear. Never us." He kissed her neck. "Light out."

TEN

The crawler jolted to a stop outside the south Lowell air lock, joining a vehicle with the insignia of Lowell University Department of Physics emblazoned on its side and another from something called Marstrans which he'd never heard of before. Gordon Blanchard glanced disgustedly at his chrono; another hour to wait until the lock opened.

Except in case of emergency, the air lock schedule never varied. In order to limit passage in and out of the dome and reduce atmosphere leakage, the lock opened only at certain times. It seemed ridiculous to Gordon, since the idea was to build up the planet's atmosphere anyway. The policy dated from Lowell City's earliest days, before the oxygen-cracking plants came into full operation and had never been rescinded. Now it was tradition.

Still, better to be an hour early than late, in which case he'd have to wait five hours before the next opening. Gordon wondered what the lockkeepers would think of his unusual burden and smiled. He spent the hour correcting his report, eliminating irregularities and omissions. It was little different from dozens of other reports that he had filed.

The vehicle in front of him raised a puff of dust and jerked into motion. Gordon powered up his crawler and moved ahead. The air lock doors closed behind the three vehicles, and he watched the sensor readings climb as air flooded into the enclosure. The readout stabilized when full pressure was reached. Gordon popped the hatch on the crawler. He breathed deeply, savoring the relative freshness of the air.

"Hey, Blanchard! Put your helmet on!"

A lockkeeper approached his crawler.

"Stuff it, Orson!" Gordon grinned, jumping down to the ground. "How ya doin'?"

The lockkeeper clapped Gordon's shoulder. "You know how it goes, Blanchard. Same old routine. Trying to make sure you dirt-diggers don't bring in anything illegal."

"Hey, if I had anything that worthwhile, I wouldn't be bringing it here."

"No luck?"

"Shoot, Orson, when have I ever had any luck?"

"Too bad. Why don't you get a real job instead of mucking about in the dirt all day?"

"What, and work inside all the time, some hard-headed supervisor breathing down my neck? Forget it."

The inspection was another necessary but tiresome routine.

"What's in the bag, Gord?" Orson circled the crawler and pointed to the bag strapped down on the trailer.

"Chiller."

Orson jumped back like he'd been shot. "You're kidding!"

Gordon shook his head. "Truth."

"What happen? You run over him?"

"Ha, ha. Found him lying in a gully coupla weeks ago."

"He get caught in a storm?"

"Dunno. Figured I'd bring him back in case anybody was missing him."

"Well, take him straight to Path, will you? Don't go wandering through town with him."

"He's yours if you want him," Gordon offered.

"Forget it. Do your own paperwork." The keeper waved him on in. "See you next time, Gord."

"Yeah."

True to his word, Gordon drove straight to MedCentral. The technician who met him was less than enthusiastic. After much grumbling, she helped Gordon heave the sack off the trailer and into a storage room.

"Aren't you going to look at him now?" Gordon asked.

"No," the woman replied, brushing a lock of hair out of her face. She seemed tired, her pretty features distorted by lack of sleep. "See this room? We've got enough to do at the moment. He'll have to wait his turn."

"What happened?" Gordon tried not to look at the rank

of coolers. A good proportion had green lights illuminated. He could imagine the shrouded bodies lying within.

"Didn't you hear?"

"Just got back. You know how flaky reception can be outside. Couldn't hear the news if I wanted to half of the time."

She closed the door of the room. "There was a riot last night—"

"Here!?" Gordon gasped.

"East side, Kobald subdivision. Know it?"

"Vaguely. What brought it on?"

The woman regarded him narrowly. "You aren't a Christian, are you?"

"Heck, no! Ain't much of anything, actually."

"As long as you're not—anyway, seems like a group of them protested the Council's decision to force them to join the UWC. Started off peacefully enough, but I gather things got out of hand."

"Who started it?"

"Who can tell? All I know is that I've got more bodies here than I know what to do with. If you'll excuse me . . ."

"Yeah, thanks. . . . uh . . ." Gordon tried to read her name tag.

"Katie Mossing."

"Katie. Say, how about dinner tonight—"

"Sorry. I'm spoken for."

"See you around then."

Gordon left the MedCenter. One more stop at the Olympus Mining Consortium depot to drop off the crawler, hand in his report, and pick up his pay, then the evening was his. So what if Katie Mossing was spoken for? There were plenty of other women available, more than money could buy. Gordon licked his lips. It was good to be back in civilization.

➤

"You must believe me, Major! We had nothing to do with it, nothing whatsoever!"

Shards of burned and shattered plastic ground under Duchesne's heel. He stalked along the ruins of what had once been Mayfield Avenue, Kobald district. Paul Sommers struggled to keep pace with him, flanked on his other side by Carolyn

McCourt. A trio of Security troopers in riot gear followed a few steps behind, alert for danger—close enough to be of assistance if the need arose, yet far enough away to be out of earshot of casual conversation.

The street was a mess.

The bodies were gone, removed to the morgue. Dull, reddish-brown blotches splattered on the ground and walls showed where they had lain.

Blown-out shop windows revealed ransacked interiors. Insulation and covering hung in ragged strips from the rock walls. Debris littered the street—scraps of material and other items of rejected clothing. A child's toy lay in the center of the avenue. Duchesne kicked it aside. The pungent odor of burning stung his nostrils, mixed with the scent of fire-reducing chemicals, blood, and death.

The riot had raged for hours. The Marspolice had somehow proved inadequate, unable to quell the turmoil that threatened to spill over into residential areas. Boris Mikhaelovitch and Nancy Cohen had led squads into the riot zone. Peace had been restored—at a cost.

Duchesne was not angry; he was furious.

Furious that this should have happened in *his* city; furious at the incompetence and sluggishness of the police; furious at the moronic, idiotic policies of the Revitalists that had precipitated the riot; furious at the little man who scurried next to him, burbling in his ear.

"Please, Major—"

"SHUT UP!" Duchesne whirled on his heel. "Don't you think you've caused enough trouble for one day?"

Sommers flinched.

The major saw the pained surprise in Sommers's eyes, the look of sudden rejection and defeat.

"J.I.!" Carolyn admonished. "That was uncalled for."

Duchesne glared at Sommers for a long moment. "You're right, Carolyn. I apologize, Reverend," he said. "I shouldn't have spoken sharply."

"Accepted, Major." Sommers breathed again. "I realize the strain you're under."

"If your congregation didn't start this . . . this *atrocity*, then who did?"

Sommers shook his bandaged head. "I wish I knew, Major."

"Tell us again what happened, Reverend," asked Carolyn.

"All I know is that my congregation and one other planned on having a peaceful protest. We were going to march to City Hall to protest the enforced enrollment into the United World Church. I don't know what went wrong. . . ."

"Was it strictly your two congregations?"

"Yes, but . . . there were some people I didn't recognize. With so few of us," Sommers explained, "it's not hard." His eyes were downcast, his voice a mere whisper. "I didn't realize the animosity, the depth of the hatred . . . even after what happened to Anita." He wiped a tear from his eye. "We did not do this, Major. I'm as appalled as you are."

I doubt that, Duchesne thought sourly. But Sommers seemed genuinely affected. His words had the ring of truth.

They detoured past a fallen column where a fountain had once stood. There was no sign of life in the blackened buildings. Shopkeepers had not been allowed back in the sealed-off area.

"Had you thought that it might be a setup?" asked Carolyn.

"Stirred up by the Revitalists?"

"An excuse, you mean?"

"Deliberately provoking a riot in order to blame the Christians. It's been done before."

"Then they have a reason for whatever they want to do," said Sommers eagerly. "It fits!"

"Isn't that going a bit far?" Duchesne was skeptical. "They control the government—"

"But this puts popular approval on their side. They can do whatever they like, and people will agree with it."

"Hmmm."

"You're not convinced, are you?" said Sommers. "You still think we might have had a hand in this, despite all I've told you about our beliefs."

Duchesne's expression remained stony.

"What can I do to convince you?" Sommers mused. "Come to one of our services, Major. You and Car—the captain. Come and see."

Duchesne's eyes widened. "Are you completely mad? Go to a Christian service? A discussion at home is one thing, but—"

"It might be a good idea, J.I.," Carolyn interjected.

"You agree with him? What if we're seen?"

"So what? We can go casually and say that we were spying out the opposition."

"This isn't a game!" Duchesne snapped. "People are losing their lives over this religious nonsense!"

"Give me credit for some intelligence!" she retorted. "I know that! But don't you think you should hear both sides of the story? Goodness known we've heard enough propaganda from the Revitalists."

"Maybe you have a point."

"Please, Major?" said Sommers. "I won't tell anyone who you are, I promise."

Duchesne looked from Sommers's pleading hazel eyes to Carolyn's querying violet ones.

"Very well," he agreed reluctantly. "Once."

➤

Duchesne could tell by Carolyn's rigid posture that she was upset. Her back was stiff. She barely looked at him, fixing her gaze out the window. The car hummed quietly, leaving the scene of devastation behind.

"What's bugging you?"

"Me? What's the matter with you? It's not like you to act like that."

"Look, I'm sorry if I spoke sharply to you—"

"Not just to me, to the Reverend, too!" Carolyn's eyes bored into his own. "What's come over you, J.I.?"

"Come over me?"

"You haven't been yourself—"

"I hadn't realized it was that obvious."

"What's eating you?" She laid a hand on his knee.

"I don't know. For the past few days—I—I feel like there's a black cloud hanging over us. I know I shouldn't have snapped," he said, responding to her scrutiny, "but the sight of that street . . ."

"What about it?"

"We can be thankful it was a shopping area, three levels down; a harmless place for a riot, I suppose. But what if it had been somewhere else—next to hydroponics or environmental support or the power generators? My stars, can you imagine the catastrophe? People forget that it's not like Earth where you can just walk away from the city if something goes wrong. The Revitalists—if they were truly behind the riot—put everyone's life in jeopardy."

"You're scared, aren't you?" Carolyn asked softly. "You're used to being in control, and you're not. It frightens you."

"You can bet I'm scared. I'm scared witless. I have this feeling . . ."

"Go on."

"This feeling that we won't make it out alive."

Carolyn sucked in her breath. "You're being morbid. You're letting the situation prey on your mind too much." She gripped his shoulder. "Let's go to the Reverend's service. Maybe it will distract you."

"I already said I would, didn't I?"

Carolyn sighed. "You're incorrigible."

➤

Enshrined in the well-apportioned office that had once belonged to Arthur Thorston, Ghalji Maranan listened attentively to the Marsnews broadcast and then to Szalny's firsthand report.

"You've done well," he purred. "Very well."

"Thank you," Szalny replied. So far, he was playing his cards right. The riots had come off without a hitch, blamed on the Christians. Maranan was pleased; he knew Klassen would be equally delighted. The riots reflected badly on Security. Szalny was in a no-lose position, trusted by both Maranan and Klassen.

"You're sure no one will squeal," Maranan said. "A whisper of suspicion could—"

"Not a chance. I took care of that." Szalny flashed a wicked grin. "It was too easy. Bribe a few dolts to instigate the riot, and then make sure they were among the casualties. Piece of cake."

"Excellent. Go now, Szalny. I'll call you when we're ready for the next stage."

Back in his quarters, Szalny encoded a message to Klassen. He had an idea, one that he knew Klassen would like.

"What is it, Szalny?" Klassen grated, in a foul mood as

usual. Szalny wondered what had ticked him off this time. Klassen seemed to be becoming more and more unstable. Not a good sign. "This channel had better be secure."

"It is. I hooked it onto a Marsnews carrier. No one will suspect." Szalny spoke obliquely knowing that Klassen would not take kindly to being upstaged: "The contingency plan. There's a better way, but if you like it I'll have to act fast."

"What?" Klassen barked.

"We don't need to do it," replied Szalny. "There's a way to get it done for us." He explained quickly.

When he was done, the annoyance on Klassen's face had been replaced by a feral expression.

"I like it," Klassen smirked. "I like it a lot. Do it, Szalny."

Szalny leered back. "You got it."

It was definitely a good day.

➤

"You are sure that this is the next step?" Maranan asked

His Guide shimmered. *"Do you doubt me, Ghalji?"*

"No. But I distrust leaving Erik alone."

"He is an irrelevancy."

"And Grainger? Will she follow my instructions?"

"All is well, Ghalji. Believe that. Trust me. Trust me."

"Tell me how to proceed."

ELEVEN

Lookit that!" The monkey bounced up and down in agitation. He pointed a hairy digit toward the hill across the valley. Their small group perched on a ridge, lying in the dry, yellow grass of fall. The sun peeked over the horizon, silhouetting the next hill. Ominous figures emerged from the burgeoning orb of the sun.

"Nuts!" exlaimed his companion, a slighter, paler brown version. "Whatta we do?"

"What can we do?" the woman interjected. Her eyes were large, like a cat's, round and luminous, pupils widely dilated. "We stay here, we die. We run, we die. Either way it makes no difference."

The man checked the power cartridge on his rifle. It was the only weapon they had left. "Fight," he grunted.

The woman didn't take her eyes off the approaching figures. She wasn't surprised by his answer; he was engineered to fight; that was all he could do. Normally she would have argued, but this time. . . .

"LLLLet's run!" stuttered the monkey.

"YYYeah!" chattered the other.

"They're military," said the woman, peering into the sun. "I can see their badges. So what do we do, Carolyn?" she asked. "You're the leader."

Carolyn looked up sharply. She felt out of place here. She was a normal human, not an augment or boosted animal. She had no particular talents or abilities. She didn't even know why she was here.

The decision was taken out of her hands. A laser bolt cleaved the morning mist, leaving the sharp tang of ionized air in its wake.

A stream of solid projectiles snickered through the foliage.

"There they are!" shouted a voice. "Get 'em!"

The monkeys bolted up a tree.

Soldier unlimbered his rifle and loosed off a shot.

Carolyn ducked as another volley seared overhead. She willed her legs to move, heading for the ravine she knew—some-how—was just through the trees.

"You lead!" she gasped to Recon, knowing the other woman's vision was much better.

"Take 'em out!"

A storm of laser fire erupted from the advancing troops, shattering the dawn. The tree where the monkeys hid burst into flame. A furry figure, enveloped in fire, ran past Carolyn, screaming pitifully.

Her legs were moving so slowly. Why wouldn't they go faster? They felt like lead.

She cast a glance over her shoulder. Incredibly, Soldier was still standing, seemingly impervious to the barrage of firepower, feeling nothing as projectiles slammed into him. Each shot he loosed dropped a trooper.

"Filthy augments!" someone cursed.

The glade where they had been resting burst into light as a grenade exploded. When her eyes cleared, Soldier had dis-appeared.

She almost tripped over the woman, who had taken a laser bolt in the back, and lay unmoving, eyes sightless.

She was the last.

The troops concentrated their fire on her, bolts singeing her hair, her skin. . . .

Why wouldn't her legs move?

Pain. . . .

➤

"Carol, what's the matter?"

"No! Not me! Not me!" A hand shook her shoulder. She squirmed.

"Carolyn, wake up!"

Her fist hit solid muscle, evoking a grunt. She came to, bathed in sweat, struggling.

"Hey, slow down! It's me!"

The light illuminated. Exhausted, she rolled into her husband's arms. Duchesne held her tightly for a long moment, waiting for the shivering to cease, feeling the frantic pounding of her heart against his chest.

"What's the matter?" he asked again, stroking her hair.

Carolyn laughed nervously. "Oh, J. I.! It was . . . just a dream."

"Must have been some dream." He studied her pale face. "You don't frighten easily. Care to tell me about it?"

"No . . . I. . . ."

"Come on," he prompted. "It's the least you can do to apologize for hitting me."

"Sorry. It was from an old movie," she confessed. "About the Clone Wars."

"The *Clone Wars?*"

"A long time ago. Before . . . oh, when I was in school, I suppose. It was a poor movie, one of those grade-B jobs. I had nightmares for days afterwards. Thought I'd forgotten about it. Don't know why I should dream about it now."

She shivered again. "It was horrible, J. I. They were killing all the augments, and somehow I was with them, and they were after me too, and I couldn't get away . . ."

He kissed the top of her head. "It's okay. It was only a dream."

"I know it." She laughed again, tearfully. "I feel so stupid."

"Go back to sleep. And try not to dream anymore, huh?"

"I'll try." Carolyn lay back down.

Duchesne laid awake, unable to follow his own advice. Carolyn's explanation sounded reasonable, but there had to be some reason why she would dream about this now.

The Clone Wars. That was funny. The so-called Clone Wars had occurred well before they were born, back in the mid-21st century.

Genetic engineering at the turn of the millenium had gone mad. Not content with experimenting on bacteria, geneticists had turned their attentions to plants, then to animals, and finally to humans. They embarked on a quest for the next generation human, an improved version, the next step in evolution.

Some scientists, some countries, had gone further than others, producing augments—humans and animals with improved senses, bred for specific tasks, more fitted to survive in the envisioned world of the future.

Taken in combination with the immunomodulators, which eliminated disease and extended the human life span, it seemed humanity was on the verge of a new era.

Until word of the disasters leaked out.

The unsuccessful tests.

The mutants.

The hideously deformed who died in pain. Young, if they were lucky.

The bodies grown for spare parts. Fetal tissue banks.

The spate of clones. Human duplicates, virtually indistinguishable from the originals.

An enraged populace revolted. There was no active war per se, but the augments were hunted down and destroyed. Mobs massacred the scientists who produced them. The Health Police took firm control over matters medical. The Clone Wars dealt human genetic engineering a blow from which it never recovered.

He felt Carolyn shift beside him.

"I know you don't like it, but I'm going to put the sleep field on, okay?"

He took silence as assent. "Low-strength field, disengage 0600."

The drowsiness of the sleep field flowed across his mind. In a moment he was adrift in a world of dreamless sleep.

➤

She was . . .

Was . . .

She was drifting through space, through the infinite blackness of the void, beneath the pallid light of the distant stars. Drifting, with the coolness of space all around her, flowing past her, bathing her in illimitable stillness . . .

Content . . . Peaceful . . .

And then . . .

A crawling on her skin. Nagging. Irritating.

Her nerve endings revolted at the contact, withdrawing from the source of the discomfort.

She tried but could not shake it off.
The crawling persisted, spreading . . .
Deeper, into her skin . . .
It hurt. . . .
It hurt. . . .
She was. . . .
She recognized herself.
She was Mars.
She was . . . *CAROLYN.*

➣

The sleep field prevented her from coming completely awake. But in a muzzy-headed way, she recognized she had been dreaming. More importantly, she knew why she had been dreaming.

A single word seeped into her mind.

Maranan.

➣

"You're sure you want to do this?" Duchesne asked.

He and Carolyn strolled arm in arm along the street. Dressed in comfortable blouses and trousers, they could have passed for any other couple out for a morning stroll. Today was Weekend-3, the last day of rest for most people.

The Christians still called it Sunday.

The morning headlines were vivid in Duchesne's mind:

RELIGIOUS SECT OPPOSES REFORM.

CHRISTIANS RESPONSIBLE FOR KOBALD RIOT.

"Positively," Carolyn replied. "For several reasons."

"Do you feel up to it? After the night you had?"

"Of course. I slept okay after you put the field on."

They passed a small park where several children played on the jungle gym. Laughing and carefree, how far removed they seemed from violence! A small boy ran up to them and stuck his tongue out, then raced back to the safety of his companions hiding behind a tree.

The park plants had been designed to grow well in artificial light. And that brought another thought to Duchesne's mind.

"Did you think any more about your dreams?"

Carolyn wrinkled her face. "It must have been from what I've read."

"Such as?"

"'To reach its full potential the human race must change and adapt,'" Carolyn quoted. "'Only a new breed of human will be fit to live on a regenerated Earth, in harmony with all life.' That's one. The other goes something like this: 'The good of Mars is what we make it; what we make ourselves to be. Mars is our mother, no less than Earth. What kind of human can live in accord with her?'"

Duchesne said nothing.

"I thought he was referring to spiritual harmony, the unity of all life, monism. Now I'm not so sure."

"Did he say anything about engineering humans?"

"No. At least not in so many words. So I don't know if the connection is real, or if it's a product of my imagination."

Duchesne's mind fled two-thousand kilometers away, to concealed rooms at the Revitalist Enclave.

Biogenetic technology.

Lin Grainger.

"This looks like the place." Carolyn halted and pointed across the street.

Duchesne followed her finger. "Last chance."

She tugged his arm.

The Christians met in a warehouse. Rental space was obviously not available. There was not room for them alongside the Temple of Isis, the Church of the Great Goddess, the Sanctuary of Gaia, the Crafthall.

Duchesne scanned the street. He saw only one figure, a bald-headed man walking his dog in the opposite direction. He seemed not to be paying them any attention.

Sommers greeted them inside the entrance. He appeared lively enough, although discolored bags hung beneath his eyes.

"Welcome, Carolyn. And, may I call you J.I.? At least for the day?"

Duchesne nodded.

"I wasn't sure you'd come."

"I made him," Carolyn confessed.

"Our people are very nervous, as you may well understand. So if you don't mind, I'll give you seats near the back, next to Anita. We don't ask you to do anything, just listen."

"Thank you," Carolyn replied.

A pile of packing crates, shifted to make room in the functional warehouse, stood off to one side. A table had been fitted out as an altar, draped with a white sheet. A pair of flickering candles flanked a cross. Several brightly colored banners decorated the walls, proclaiming Bible quotations:

> *Faith, hope and love abide, but the greatest of these is love.*
> *Come quickly, Lord Jesus.*
> *Faith without works is dead.*

Carolyn and Duchesne seated themselves in two of the hard chairs. A middle-aged couple in the row in front of them leaned back to greet them. Close to one hundred people filled the room. Duchesne was mildly surprised both by the number certainly and also the mix—every age from babes in arms to the elderly.

"Hello. Glad you could make it." Anita dropped into the end seat beside them and nodded to Carolyn. "I'm Anita Sommers," she said to Duchesne.

Carolyn said: "You're looking better."

Anita touched her cheek. "The bruises are fading."

"There's a lot of people present," Duchesne observed. "I hadn't expected to see so many."

"There are usually more," Anita replied sadly, "but I expect some have chosen not to come today in the wake of . . . Monday's unpleasantness." She continued: "Most of the congregations are small, with part-time pastors. Paul used to be an analyst for the Department of Recreation before he retired."

"Is this congregation the same as the others?" Carolyn asked.

"Essentially. There used to be different denominations," Anita replied.

"Different what?"

"Denominations. Varieties of expressing or understanding Christian belief. Over time, many became indistinguishable from neo-pagan groups and joined the UWC."

"And the rest?"

"The rest found that despite the differences and faced with

growing persecution and shrinking numbers, unity in the body of Christ was also important. Eventually denominations were abandoned, and the nonaffiliated churches banded together."

"Let us begin with hymn 214." Sommers reemerged at the front of the room.

The congregation sang vigorously. Anita offered her music reader to Carolyn, who declined with a shake of her head. Duchesne listened intently. The music was old, eighteenth or nineteenth century. There were none of the current microtonal inflections that made modern music so jarring. Following the hymn Sommers led the congregation in a prayer, more hymns, and several readings from the Bible, one or two of which Duchesne dimly recognized from readings he and Carolyn had done together.

So far, he thought, *all right*. There was nothing objectionable, radical, or political. No rabble rousing. He scanned the faces of the assembly as well as he could from the location of his seat. He saw smiles and felt a sense of community. Here and there, however, a face reflected sorrow or grief.

Eventually, Reverend Sommers rose to speak.

"We are all saddened by the loss," he began, his voice quiet but carrying, "of several of our members—our friends and relatives. We are a family, and the loss of one affects us all. But let us not forget that they have earned their reward. They were faithful, as must we be. Let's pause a moment in silent prayer and remember those who are no longer with us."

After a moment's silence, Sommers began his sermon.

He spoke simply, employing the same, clear reasoning he had evidenced when at Duchesne's apartment.

Duchesne waited. Waited for some criticism of the Revitalists, a call for action, a cry for revenge.

There was none.

"'Bless those who persecute you,'" quoted Sommers. "'Bless and do not curse.' This is not a time for bitterness or division. It is a time for prayer. God has blessed us during our time on Mars. Shall He withdraw His blessing now? What do the scriptures tell us about persecution? . . ."

Could these people have staged a riot? Duchesne asked himself. Unless this service was a performance put on for his and Carolyn's benefit, but he didn't think so.

144 Andrew M. Seddon

"'For rulers hold no terror for those who do right, but for those who do wrong,' wrote Paul. My friends, love is the fulfillment of the law. . . ."

Perhaps Carolyn was right. Maybe it was a setup—the Christians being framed.

If so, what would the Revitalists' next step be?

What would he do if he were them?

He missed the end of the sermon.

Anita interrupted his thoughts. "I have to go up and help." She eased out of her seat and approached the altar.

"What's this part?" Duchesne whispered to Carolyn.

"I'm not sure."

The congregation stood and began to recite in unison.

"We believe in one God, the Father Almighty, maker of heaven and earth . . ."

Duchesne's commlink sounded softly. He raised his arm and answered.

"Duchesne."

"Get out of there. Get out now!"

"What's up?"

"Just get out."

Duchesne laid a hand on Carolyn's shoulder. "Boris says to get out."

"What—?"

"Come on." They slipped away unnoticed, the assembly still reciting.

" . . . one holy eternal and apostolic church . . ."

They exited the warehouse and walked casually to the opposite side of the street.

"What did he say?" Carolyn asked.

"Nothing."

"Shhh. Listen."

A high-pitched whine increased in intensity, accompanied by a sudden change in air pressure. A file of groundcars swept around a corner and pulled to a halt in front of the warehouse. Each vehicle displayed the planet and shield of the Marspolice.

The cars disgorged a cluster of police who drew neural stunners and trotted into the warehouse.

A crowd of onlookers gathered. Carolyn and Duchesne melted in.

"What's in there?" someone asked.

"Christian church."

"Serves them right!"

"Yeah. 'Bout time the police did something."

"In our neighborhood, too."

Carolyn gripped Duchesne's hand.

➤

The brown-clad Marspolice burst into the warehouse. Paul Sommers stopped in mid-sentence.

"Awright! Everybody stay where you are!"

The police leveled their guns.

"Nobody move a muscle."

The officer in charge strode to the front of the room. He swept off the altar with a hand. The cross fell with a crash. Wafers of bread flew in all directions; the rich red of wine seeped across the floor.

"Lieutenant!" expostulated Sommers. "What is the meaning of this outrage?"

"Shut up!" A backhand to the face smashed Sommers to the ground.

"NO!" shouted Anita, trying to interpose herself.

A trooper fired.

She crumpled beside her husband.

"Anybody else want to try anything?" The lieutenant glared around the room.

The assembly made no move. A baby began to cry. Its mother tried to shush it.

"Line up by the door! And keep it quiet!"

Sommers picked himself up. A trickle of blood crept from the corner of his mouth. He swayed.

"You too." The lieutenant gestured with his pistol.

Sommers put an arm around his unconscious wife and heaved her up. Helped by another member, they joined the line shuffling toward the door.

Sommers cast an anxious glance toward where Carolyn and Duchesne had been sitting. He looked around the room. They were nowhere to be seen.

➤

Carolyn and Duchesne watched as the first Christians were led out of the warehouse and into waiting vans. A swarm of police cordoned off the area.

"This was no spur of the moment raid," Duchesne whispered. "Too well-planned and executed."

"Those two! I saw them enter!"

Duchesne searched for the source of the voice. His eyes lit on a man a short distance away, finger upraised. The bald-headed man who had been walking his dog.

"You!" shouted a policeman striding over. "Halt there!"

The crowd melted back from them, leaving them exposed.

Pariahs.

Diseased.

Duchesne bolted, nearly yanking Carolyn off her feet. She needed no urging. The policeman fumbled with his weapon, giving them a start.

A stunner bolt flared overhead. Duchesne ducked. He expected another shot, but stray members of the crowd interfered with the policeman's aim. The man held the shot and circled the crowd, trying for a better position.

"What are you doing?" Carolyn gasped.

"Think they care who we are?"

They bent low behind a groundcar, avoiding more fire. Several police took off in pursuit. A stunner bolt edged Carolyn's right arm. She flinched.

"You okay?" Duchesne asked.

"Yeah, my arm . . ." she slurred.

Duchesne helped support her. Carolyn's arm hung limply by her side.

A side street presented itself. They cut left, out of the line of fire. Duchesne's sense of direction and intimate knowledge of Lowell's layout proved its value. Carolyn wavered and stumbled.

"Hang on, we're almost there!"

Duchesne kept his feet moving. He could understand how the Christians felt. It wasn't pleasant being the hunted.

"Down here!" shouted a voice.

A few more steps and they were at a lifter bank.

Locked.

The police had been thorough.

"Security Override!" Duchesne jerked. "Code D1-A-1D."

The door slid open.

Duchesne lugged Carolyn inside. She slumped against a wall, unable to remain upright.

"Halt!"

The door closed on a barrage of stunner fire.

➤

Ensconced in the impregnable confines of Security Headquarters, Duchesne accessed the monitor files of the raid on the Christian church. Virtually the whole city complex was— or could be—covered by the monitors. Installed during earlier regimes when the close monitoring of every aspect of every citizen's life was the norm, the monitors were infrequently utilized, records often filed without even a cursory review. The concept of the monitors alone helped to keep crime low. Just the thought that someone could be watching gave even the most callous and confident criminal pause.

But crime was far from nonexistent.

Duchesne thanked his lucky stars that he'd had the foresight to alert Boris Mikhaelovitch to his and Carolyn's plans. The big Russian had disapproved, convinced that they were courting trouble.

And right he had been.

Boris had been more than disapproving. Duchesne could see it reflected in his eyes. Boris thought he was going soft, falling for a load of religious malarkey, for ideas and concepts that didn't rate serious consideration by intelligent people.

Was he?

Mikhaelovitch could be very narrow-minded at times.

After fleeing the church, Duchesne had taken Carolyn directly to the Security Med unit. A tech had run her through a doc. The machine had pronounced her fit, with none of the early signs of permanent damage. Carolyn regained consciousness shortly after.

Duchesne had breathed a sigh of relief.

Groggy but uninjured, Carolyn hadn't protested when

Duchesne sent her home with Sergeant Jenna Williams of Operation Squad 4.

He studied the recordings. The monitors covering the church site had been operational.

The police cars entered the screen, pulling up outside the makeshift sanctuary. Marspolice stormed the warehouse, and the first file of captured Chistians began to emerge. Duchesne changed the image to focus on the crowd. He and Carolyn loitered like innocent bystanders, the bald man pointing them out.

"Hold screen. Enlarge left. Hold."

The man became clearer.

"Identification grid." A cluster of criss-crossing reference lines superimposed themselves over the image. A visual ID was not foolproof, but it would provide a starting point.

"Grid reference C3. Enhance and isolate."

The bald-headed man jumped out at him, face frozen in accusation.

"Identification access."

The wait was brief.

"Evgeny Szalny." The words scrolled across the bottom of the screen. "Aide to Colonial Administrator Ghalji Maranan."

So.

Duchesne smiled.

He had less luck with the files on the riot. For some reason, the most important time frame—the beginning of the riot—was not available.

"Accident," he muttered. "Or systems failure?" The old monitors had an unfortunate tendency to fail. Thorston's budget-concerned administration didn't always bother with repairs, seeing little need for the system.

Or was it something more ominous? Had the files been tampered with?

He watched the riot escalate until the screen abruptly went dark. The camera had taken a shot. Stray or deliberate?

But he had seen enough.

On several occasions he saw a bald-headed man flit amongst the swirling mass of rioters. The computer confirmed identification.

Evgeny Szalny.

It seemed that Carolyn was right.

The clues pointed to Maranan.

But how to get something to stick?

>

Duchesne returned home to find Carolyn resting on the couch, draped in a frilly lavender and turquoise gown. She raised herself to an elbow as he entered and yawned.

"Hi, honey," she said.

Duchesne tossed his pistol onto a side table. He wasn't going unarmed any longer. Not safe in Lowell? How times had changed. Once, the thought of needing protection would have been inconceivable.

"Hi yourself." He gave her a kiss. "How are you feeling?"

"Other than the most awful headache, fine."

"Where's Williams?"

"I sent her home." Carolyn responded to Duchesne's skeptical look. "I'm fine. Really."

"Yeah."

"What's new?" Carolyn made room for him on the couch.

Duchesne filled her in on his researches.

"Boris thinks we're mad," he concluded.

"Carolyn laughed. "He's probably right." She sobered. "What about the Sommers?"

Duchesne frowned. "Maranan has ordered the arrest of all Christians—into what he calls protective custody. The Sommers's church wasn't the only one targeted. The police have been conducting house arrests, too. The Sommers are being held in the police detention center."

"That's awful!" Carolyn's eyes widened. "What are they going to do to them?"

"Sources tell me they're being urged to swear allegiance to the UWC Those that comply will be released. The others. . . ." he shrugged.

"Have any complied?"

"A few, I gather. Presumably the remainder, like the Sommers, are hardcore. The measure will involve the entire population as well, you know. Even though most citizens are members already, word is that everyone will be required to sign up or file an atheists' waiver."

"But why?"

"As a pledge of loyalty. Belonging to the UWC shows that you are committed to humanity." He looked steadily into Carolyn's violet eyes. "That means us too, you know."

He got up and went over to the synthesizer. "You hungry?"

"How can you think of food" Carolyn demanded, "when those poor people are being rounded up like cattle?"

"I'm hungry."

"Don't you *care* about them?"

Duchesne turned around, puzzled by the sharp tone of her voice. "Of course I care."

"Then why don't you do something instead of standing around moaning about your belly?"

"Like what? The Revitalists haven't—"

"Haven't broken the law. Is that all you care about? What they're doing is *wrong*, J.I. Or doesn't that matter to you? Are you going to support a corrupt regime because they make themselves legal?"

"Carolyn—"

"Isn't it time you took a stand on the issues, made our position plain?"

"What *is* our position?"

"Send a message that we—Security—won't stand for the mistreatment of any group. We'll back up our words if necessary."

Duchesne stared. "That stunner must have addled your brains," he flared. "Our place is to support the government, not to dictate policy."

"Even when the government is wrong? You said yourself you saw this Szalny person at the riot scene—"

"That's not proof of anything. It could have been a coincidence."

"If you believe that you'll believe anything." She stood up. "Good night."

"Where are you going?"

"To bed. To wonder what happened to the man I married." She pointed. "There's the couch."

They had had their spats before—inevitable for two strong-willed people. But never had Duchesne seen his wife so angry about anything.

Suddenly, he was no longer hungry.

TWELVE

They WHAT?!" Klassen roared.

Szalny was glad 2000 kilometers of desert separated him from the deputy. Even so, Klassen's rage was palpable.

"They got away. The police had them dead to rights, but they escaped." Szalny carried on, trying to forestall the storm. "But I have another idea."

"You had better." Klassen oozed menace. "And it had better work."

"Do you know what I'm up against? As long as they stay cooped up in headquarters, I can't get at them—"

"I don't care about your excuses! Just do it. Or you'll be be next, Szalny."

Klassen raised a fist. "This is your last chance."

Klassen signed off. Szalny sighed.

Klassen or Maranan? A difficult choice. But perhaps one that was becoming clearer.

➤

Every day the roundup of Christians continued. Duchesne heard no word of the Sommers—presumably they were holding out. The government-imposed deadline for registering with the United World Church drew closer. Carolyn made no moves toward joining. Duchesne was in two minds. He'd been a member as a child—his fully orthodox grandparents had seen to that. But when his childhood membership had lapsed, he'd seen no sense in renewing it.

To relent would be distasteful, both intellectually and emotionally.

As well as—as well as that at this point he didn't know *what* to believe. Sommers made sense, but it went against the grain to admit you were a sinner in need of salvation, that you couldn't do it on your own.

Would it actually *hurt* anything to join?

Supposing he did. It could be viewed as offering support to the Revitalists.

And Carolyn wouldn't forgive him.

She was barely speaking to him anyway.

He felt lost without her.

He could understand her concern, but what could he do?

He lodged a formal complaint with the Colonial Administration—not that it would do any good.

Lowell City Mayor Abraham Milstein was unconcerned. "Go with the flow, Duchesne. It will blow over in a few weeks."

Adrien Bozon, primate of the UWC, confirmed the Revitalists had full church support and insisted religious unity would be good for all concerned.

Maranan refused to return his calls.

Duchesne didn't know what to make of Carolyn's two dreams. Perhaps they meant nothing.

Boris Mikhaelovitch turned up nothing new.

Nancy Cohen—for once—counseled caution. "We can do without the Christians, anyway," she commented acerbically.

Yellow Horse chafed with all the enthusiasm of youth for action. He wanted another crack at the Enclave. Duchesne refused.

Marlais recommended patience.

Carolyn read the Bible more.

"Why?" Duchesne asked. "All it's done is cause trouble."

In hopes of appeasing her, he decided to visit Sommers in jail. If nothing else, he could reassure Carolyn that the police were treating the reverend appropriately.

Chief of Marspolice Sue Li-Shin's almond eyes regarded Duchesne with barely suppressed hostility—her perfectly complected face set. Duchesne's relationship with his local counterpart was generally cordial; they tried to avoid stepping on each other's jurisdictional toes.

Today, Li-Shin was not cordial.

Remember, Duchesne told himself, *it isn't really Sue Li-Shin. At least not the Li-Shin I know.* What hold did Maranan

have over her? What would make a level-headed cop an ally of
the Revitalists? Come to that, what influence did he have over
any of the high-level people who had defected to his fold?

"Your request is highly irregular," she said. The badges on
her brown uniform shifted as she inhaled. "In fact, I'm not sure
I can grant it."

"You can't refuse," he replied. "Not even the
Administrator himself can deny me the right to interview a prisoner in regards to an ongoing Security investigation. And the
riot is a Security concern since your troops proved incapable of
handling it."

A flicker of irritation passed across Li-Shin's face at the
mention of her department's failure. "We can perform the interrogation for you."

"That will not suffice."

"Sommers is under arrest for treason. I will not allow him
to be released from custody."

"I will conduct the interrogation there."

A faint smile played around Li-Shin's shapely lips.
"Security may not be a force on Mars much longer."

"Colonel Forbes is a powerful opponent."

"Even he cannot hold out indefinitely."

"That is immaterial. The investigation proceeds until—if
ever—we are recalled."

"Oh, very well, then," Li-Shin snapped. "I will notify the
detention officers. Waste your time."

As he drove through the town, the city seemed no different than usual, showing no trace of the hostility smoldering
beneath the surface. *A larger version of what we are as individuals*, Duchesne thought. What we are as individuals is what we
make our society to be.

Society seemed to be falling apart.

Was that an argument in favor of Sommers?

Anti-Christian slogans scrawled across a block of buildings
caught his attention.

Duchesne frowned. If he couldn't conquer the turmoil
within, how could he hope to do it planet—or even city—wide?

Impossible.

His driver pulled to a stop. Duchesne jumped from the car.
"Wait for me."

Duchesne felt a pulse-beat of apprehension. Li-Shin would surely not be stupid enough to try anything against him personally. But in these confused times he was no longer sure. The weight of his Enerweap 2000 on his hip comforted him.

The detention block adjoined the main Administration complex. The guard saluted as Duchesne entered. The duty sergeant ran his ID. Surprisingly, the man was not obstructive.

"Anderson, escort the major to interrogation room C." He looked up at Duchesne. "I'll have Sommers brought along, sir."

"Thank you."

The fully utilitarian detention center had none of the high ceilings and spacious interiors of the Administration building. Room C was a featureless cube. Whatever interrogation equipment the police possessed was hidden from sight.

Once, it had been hoped that prisons would become unnecessary. Identify criminal characteristics with early screening. Remove those individuals and weed out and breed out criminal behavior.

It hadn't worked.

Criminal elements continued to flourish. It seemed the cause ran deeper than behavioral studies or brainwaves could detect.

Duchesne studied the room. If he was placing a concealed monitor, where would he put it? He chose the most likely location and angled his chair so that his face would be as obscured as possible.

The guard shoved a man through the door. Duchesne almost didn't recognize Sommers. The minister's face was swollen, eyelids edematous, cheeks discolored by purple bruises. He looked like he hadn't slept for days.

Sommers opened his mouth to speak; instead he slumped into the other chair, eyes downcast.

"Look at me," Duchesne said.

Sommers hesitated but complied.

Duchesne raised his eyes to the ceiling.

They may be listening to us, he mouthed. *Play along.*

Sommers's neck tilted. Duchesne hoped he understood.

"Do you still maintain you had nothing to do with the riot?"

"Yes."

"And agitating against the UWC?"

Sommers passed a hand across his forehead. When he

spoke, he sounded as if he was reciting an answer that he had already given many times. "We object to a policy to which we cannot honestly consent. If you call that agitating, then yes."

"Have you agreed to join the UWC?"

"No."

"You have been charged with treason, Reverend. Do you know what the penalty for treason is?"

"I am not afraid to die, Major."

"Is it worth throwing your life away?"

Sommers moistened his swollen lips. "Maybe it's hard for you to believe, Major, but there are things in life more important than its mere preservation. We must obey God rather than men. If that means incurring the enmity of the UWC, so be it."

"What about the families?"

"Nobody is forced to take a stand. It is an individual decision between each person and God."

"You won't change your mind? You'll persist in defying the UWC no matter what the cost?"

"The UWC doesn't realize that you can't compel belief."

"Joining the UWC is considered a mark of loyalty to humanity and to Mars," Duchesne suggested.

"Only in loyalty to God is there loyalty to humanity," Sommers replied. "I venture to suggest that it is the Revitalists who are being disloyal."

Duchesne shook his head. "That statement would be regarded as a sure mark of treason."

"My conscience is clear, Major. I have not been disloyal. Not to God, not to the exercise of honest, responsible government." Sommers looked at him hopefully. "What is your position in this?"

Duchesne chose his words carefully, conscious that he was probably being overheard. "Very limited. My concern is with the riot. The charge of treason takes precedence over any lesser charges Security could proffer."

"I understand. That means I remain here."

"Exactly."

Duchesne locked eyes with Sommers, willing him to understand. "But you never know. The situation could change. One must be prepared for any eventuality."

Sommers nodded, but the light in his eyes dimmed.

Duchesne resumed a harsher tone. "Our investigation will continue," he said. "If we discover any evidence that you were implicated in the riot, the consequences will be severe."

Sommers gave a ghost of a smile. "I have no doubt about it. But, as you said, the consequences of treason take precedence."

Duchesne rose. "Guard."

➤

"Let us pray."

Following his meeting with Duchesne, Paul Sommers addressed the congregation, packed sardine-like in the Marspolice detention center. There was barely enough floor space for them to lie down on the paper-thin mattresses with which they had been supplied.

"Let us pray for our deliverance, for our captors, and especially for Major Duchesne."

"Him? What has he done for us?" Anita demanded.

"Don't be harsh, Anita. I'm sure—"

"Why did they leave the service then?"

"I'm sure there was a reason."

Anita stalked away and sat down on a mat in the corner, ignoring the call to prayer. Sommers gazed after her. Anita hadn't seemed the same since being stunned. They said it was harder on the elderly. He only hoped the moodiness and personality changes would pass.

He went and stood by her. "I believe Duchesne is the key, Anita," he said gently. "Even though he's not a believer, he's like Cyrus, the Persian, who without knowing it, was God's appointed servant for a task."

"A very weak servant."

"Aren't we all? But Cyrus brought down the might of Babylon." Sommers raised his voice to the congregation. "'I will not leave you comfortless,'" says the Lord. Let us join together in prayer."

➤

By the merest coincidence, Duchesne's hand brushed the intercom switch on his desk.

"He's in a meeting," he heard his aide Derek Lofter say. "He told me not to disturb him."

His mind on the status reports he was perusing, Duchesne reached out to cut the connection. He paused. Something in Lofter's voice rang false. *What meeting?*

"Give the major a message for me." Carolyn's voice.

"Yes ma'am."

"Tell him I'm going to shop at Marplanger's before I go home. I'll see him later."

"Will do, ma'am," Lofter replied.

Duchesne expected his aide to call through. He didn't. Duchesne heard another connection being made and then Lofter speaking again, quietly.

"Is this Szalny?"

"That's what I said. Who's this?"

"Blackboots. I've got news for you. Listen, you still interested in the major's wife?"

"What's the news?"

"You've got connections, right? She's on her way to Marplanger's as we speak. If you hurry. . . ."

"Got it. Thanks, friend."

Lofter chuckled.

The leak!

Something snapped inside Duchesne. He slammed back his chair and burst into the outer office. Lofter sprang to his feet, startled. He couldn't hide his expression of guilt.

"Sir—"

Blind with rage, Duchesne grabbed his subordinate by the front of his uniform. Lofter choked as Duchesne raised him off the floor.

"Traitor! Scum! Weasel!"

A fist to Lofter's face punctuated each word. Lofter's head rocked back and forth from the force of the blows. Duchesne flung the nearly insensible corporal into a corner, where he crashed and lay moaning, bleeding from his nose and mouth.

"Comm access! McCourt!"

"Comm inactive."

"Confound him!"

Bolting to the door, Duchesne glimpsed a familiar figure passing down the hallway. "Jacland!"

The sergeant paused and turned. His worried face took in the furious Duchesne and the crumpled wreck of Lofter.

"Put that . . . *thing* in irons, Jacland, and take over until I get back."

"Yes sir!"

Duchesne stalked into the corridor. "Boris!" he yelled. "Get out here, Boris!"

➤

Carolyn used the time shopping to think. She was really giving J.I. a hard time, she knew that. And yes, she was crabby and irritable. Even recognizing the feelings as stun-effect didn't make them go away.

"Maybe it will get you moving, dear," she murmured. "When it comes to love and religion, you move as slowly as a glacier."

She made no purchases. She inherited a passion for windowshopping from her mother.

She left Marplanger's feeling relaxed.

The Marspolice accosted her from nowhere. An iron hand clamped around her arm. Three men in brown uniforms surrounded her.

"Citizen McCourt? You'll come with us."

"Do you know who I am?" Carolyn protested.

"No matter." The men herded her away under the watchful eyes of the passersby.

"What's this all about? Why are you arresting me?"

"For harboring Christian sympathies and for failing to register with the UWC."

"MOVE!" Another shoved her hard from behind. Carolyn staggered but regained her footing. The first man wrenched her shoulder.

"You can't—!"

"Shut up!"

Carolyn, even with her training, doubted she was a match for three armed officers. She didn't want to risk being stunned again. She'd recovered, more or less, from the last time, but you never knew.

"Comm access—"

"SHUT UP!" The leading officer hit her across the mouth.

A tooth gouged her lip, drawing the salty taste of blood.

Her comm unit remained dead.

They'd almost reached the police car. Carolyn couldn't see any way to escape. Something must have happened for the police to arrest her; messing with Security? The pretense about Christian sympathies was just that—pretense. Somebody wanted her out of the way.

If the officers succeeded in getting her to police HQ, could J.I. get her out? Would he even know where she was?

"Not so fast!"

The officers froze. Two men burst from the ranks of bystanders, lasers trained.

Carolyn seized the opportunity. She yanked the arm of the policeman holding her and spun around. Planting a knee in the startled man's gut she followed it with a chop to the throat. He dropped to the ground retching and gasping for air. She grabbed his stunner and turned it on the next officer.

"Bring him." Duchesne laid a hand on her arm. Carolyn held her fire.

She hauled the groaning man to his feet by his collar. She ground the gun into his ribs.

"You can't do this!" one of the policemen spluttered. "We're police! You won't get away with it!"

Duchesne relaxed his grip long enough to flash his ID. "I most certainly can. Or would you prefer I let Captain McCourt handle you?"

The man's eyes went from the white, agonized face of his subordinate to Carolyn's mask of fury.

"Get moving," Duchesne ordered.

Duchesne and Boris Mikhaelovitch, attired in plain clothes, shepherded the stunned policemen into a waiting car. Carolyn brought the third, not making his journey comfortable.

Slinging the three in the back, behind the protective screen, they crowded in front.

"That was fun," said Mikhaelovitch.

"Not enough," growled Carolyn.

Duchesne gunned the engine.

"Later, dear."

THIRTEEN

Chief pathology technician Katie Mossing peeked at her chrono. Half an hour to go and she'd be done for the day. Half an hour . . .

She had a date tonight with a young man from the Department of Environmental Support. They'd met over drinks at a concert intermission. Rafe had asked her out. He looked cute—

She fingered the array of multicolored crystals hanging around her neck. Rafe had a good aura.

Half an hour. Time for one more.

The crystals tinkled as she walked over to the bank of coolers. She picked one at random. She punched the "open" button, and the green light went off as the door slid aside. A puff of chill air wafted out, miasmatic. The tray slid forward, bearing its gruesome burden.

Another riot victim—

No.

She remembered this one. This was the guy the prospector had brought in.

What was his name? She was usually good with names.

Blanchard. That was it. Gordon Blanchard.

Creep.

His aura had been uncomfortable.

The gurney floated softly on its repulsors. Katie steered it out of the "chill room" to the scanner unit. The gurney slid inside and locked in place.

"Access. Subject number 5764. Routine scan." The man had not been wearing an implanted ID chip. It was illegal to remove them, but people did.

She sat down and watched the screen as information began to flow.

MALE ... CAUCASIAN ... AGE 45 STANDARD YEARS +/- 1.44 ... HEIGHT 1.7 M ... WEIGHT 74.3 KG ... BONE DENSITY INDICATES EARTH ORIGIN ... ACUTE FRACTURE RIGHT HUMERUS ... CAUSE(S) OF DEATH: DECOMPRESSION; OXYGEN DEPRIVATION; HYPOTHERMIA ...

In short: exposure.

BORING.

Some jerk dumb enough to get caught outside. It happened often enough, you'd think people would learn.

METALLIC FOREIGN BODY STOMACH ...

What was that? Probably nothing, but better get it out.

"Extract," she coded in.

She waited for the DNA analysis. He should have a record here. If not, she'd have to query Earth. Which meant a long wait and a cooler tied up, since she couldn't dispose of the corpse until positive ID was made.

She was in luck.

IDENTIFICATION ... GERHART HANNIK ... CITIZEN NUMBER H8895390G ...

The next words caught her attention and caused her to sit bolt upright.

... WANTED BY SECURITY ... WANTED BY SECURITY ...

So maybe it wasn't such a boring day after all.

She considered the next command.

CREMATE? (YES) NO.

Better not. If he was on a wanted list, Security could do it. She hit 'no.'

>

"This just came in." Boris Mikhaelovitch stood rigidly in front of the desk. Duchesne wished his subordinate would relax sometimes instead of posing like an advertisement for a statue in the Kremlin. "From a contact in the judicial department." The Russian's normally dark eyes were worried. "I wasn't able to tell you earlier."

Duchesne was conscious of Carolyn's gaze from her seat beside his desk. "What is it, Boris?"

"About the Christians. The goverment is going to put them on trial on charges of fostering a riot and treason." Mikhaelovitch's expression didn't change. "They face the death penalty if convicted."

"J. I.!" Carolyn blurted.

"Hold it," her husband replied. "I know what you're going to say. Li-Shin told me as much, Boris. There's more?"

"Yes. There's a warrant for the arrest of one Carolyn McCourt on charges of harboring Christian sympathies, failing to register with the UWC, and resisting arrest."

"A desperate criminal if I've ever seen one," Duchesne commented.

"Figures," Carolyn said dryly.

"I," said Duchesne, "fielded a call from Chief Li-Shin. Seems that three of her officers disappeared while attempting to arrest said woman. She wanted to know if we had any information."

"And?" Carolyn prompted.

"I told her that we knew no more than she did. Two men in plain clothes. Descriptions from eyewitnesses were hopelessly conflicting. What a pity the monitors were inactive." Duchesne couldn't resist a grin. Two could play at that game.

"Pity," echoed Mikhaelovitch lugubriously.

"Placing a warrant on a Security officer is unprecedented. They must be getting desperate. They may have been hoping we'd be recalled by now, and since we haven't, are trying to disrupt our effectiveness." He turned to his wife. "I don't want you going about alone, Carolyn. I know you can handle yourself well enough, but there'll be a whole police department after you, and you aren't exactly inconspicuous."

"If you insist," Carolyn grumbled. "I still wish you'd let me finish dealing with the arresting officers."

"I could make it an order. . . . ."

"All right."

"What are you going to do about Li-Shin?" Mikhaelovitch asked.

Duchesne shrugged. "She's firmly in the Revitalists' pocket. For the moment, we play dumb. But to return to the subject of the Christians, we can't let these people be killed. Do you agree, Boris?"

"Grudgingly. I accept the fact they're innocent of the riot at least. But I don't understand you two. Why not join the UWC or sign atheists' waivers? It would remove one complication."

Duchesne and Carolyn exchanged rueful glances.

"It's a long story, Boris," Duchesne said. "The thing is, what can we do to prevent a miscarriage of justice?"

"The high court is firmly pro-Revitalist," said Carolyn. "The Sommers will be convicted for sure."

"An appeal to the Colonial Board will take months and be rejected anyway," Duchesne said.

"How about a strike?" suggested Carolyn. "Rescue them."

"You're talking rebellion. Not even Forbes would support us on that one. The World Council would send troops from Earth, send in the Navy—"

"What if the Navy was on our side?"

"You're dreaming. Most of them are Earthborn—"

"Benson isn't."

"—And ask Commodore Washburn to aid an illegal police action? He'd laugh his head off."

"What then?" Carolyn demanded. "We don't have much time. The court will act quickly."

Duchesne's intercom beeped. "Not now, Sergeant. We're busy."

"It's important, sir," Jacland replied. "I think you'll want to hear this."

"All right," Duchesne sighed. "Go ahead."

"They've found Hannik, sir."

Duchesne snapped up. "Found him? Where?"

"A call just came from the tech at MedPath. Seems they've had his body there for a while but just got around to ID'ing him."

"At last," Mikhaelovitch murmured.

"There's more, sir," Jacland continued. "He was carrying a computer chip—"

"Where is it?" Duchesne interrupted. "Still at MedPath?"

"I was sending a man to get it."

"Good. On second thought, Jacland, take help and go yourself. And bring it straight here."

"Yes sir."

A glint of eagerness shone in Duchesne's eyes. "Now we're moving."

>

The faces clustered around the conference table that evening were grim. Duchesne had convened the top-secret meeting in the shielded room.

"End."

Duchesne stopped the playback of the chip reclaimed from Hannik's body.

Swallowing the information. The oldest trick in the book. Not as sophisticated as having it melded to DNA, but it had worked. He scanned the room, seeing faces as shocked as his had been earlier, when he, Carolyn, and Mikhaelovitch had viewed the chip.

"Reactions?"

It's absurd!" burst Nancy Cohen. "Preposterous! Maranan must be insane."

"Oh no," Carolyn replied. "He's far from being insane, by any medical definition."

"But to think he could pull this off—"

"There is a fine line between madness and genius," interposed Mikhaelovitch. "Sometimes history only makes the distinction by whether one succeeds or not."

"And he has succeeded," said Duchesne, "unless we can figure out a way to stop him."

"I don't understand," said Yellow Horse, "how he could do it so rapidly. Surely the time needed . . ."

"I don't either," Duchesne confessed, "but I'm meeting with Dr. Heidi Gunnerson from GenAg to go over it with her. She's the closest we've got to a local expert."

He paused for a moment, weighing his words. "This," he said, waving at the screen, "is the only proof we have. There is no corroboration for any of this other than what we've observed. What I am considering is highly suspect. But to my mind, the situation cannot be allowed to proceed. I can't order you to follow me. Even if we succeed, we may find ourselves sanctioned by Earth; fail and we'll be branded traitors. If anyone wants to back out, you have my blessing."

He held his breath.

"I'll stand by you," said Carolyn. "You know that."

"And I," said Mikhaelovitch.

"It would set a remarkable and very undesirable precedent if the Revitalists succeeded," said Cohen.

Yellow Horse and Marlais voiced support.

"Let's get on with this," Cohen urged. "We're all together. Step one, we must assume control of the situation. We've been playing backseat for too long. It's time to take the offensive."

"How do you suggest?" Duchesne asked.

"They have hostages," contributed Marlais, before Cohen could respond.

"Who? The Christians?" sneered Cohen. "Who cares?"

"Right." Carolyn nodded toward Marlais. "Even though not much of anyone likes them, public opinion is fickle. It could easily swing once the Revitalists' plan becomes known. If opinion shifts toward the Christians, then they could be used as bargaining chips."

"Agreed," said Duchesne. "We don't want the Revitalists to have any more playing pieces than necessary. So move number one is to remove that possibility by rescuing the Christians. Nancy, I'd like you to formulate a plan."

"We're outnumbered," interjected Yellow Horse. "We have forty-odd OS troops plus headquarters staff—"

"And there are a heck of a lot more police," concluded Duchesne. "And we don't know how many have been subverted. So whatever we do must be done well. Don't forget we have the benefit of weapons, training, and surprise. But we can't be careless or messy. The last thing we want to do is provoke a bloodbath. I'd like a plan ready for implementation tomorrow, Nancy. Boris, you can help."

"Yes sir," Cohen replied.

"Anyone who has suggestions, be sure to pass them on. Second?"

He waited.

"We go public," said Mikhaelovitch.

Five heads turned as one.

"Continue."

"We publicize selected details of the Revitalists' plot. That may well turn public sentiment against them."

Duchesne nodded. He remembered Carolyn's dreams. She wouldn't be the only one to have such a reaction. "Especially if it came from an independent, unimpeachable source. I think we can locate one."

"I know one," offered Marlais.

"Who's that?"

"Miranda Majors."

"*You* know Miranda Majors?" squeaked Yellow Horse. "How—?"

Marlais grinned. "I know a lot of people."

"Okay," said Duchesne. "Reggie's social life can wait. Go with it, Reggie."

"We don't have to leak everything," said Marlais. "But the right details could create a backlash and cause the Revitalists to lose their groundswell of support."

"They'll be forced to go on the defensive," said Carolyn.

"And then what?" asked Cohen.

Duchesne pursed his lips. "Martial law."

"Is it necessary to be that extreme?" asked Mikhaelovitch into a dead silence.

"We'll have turned the populace against the elected government and neutralized the police. We cannot let anarchy ensue."

"It's never been done," said Cohen. "The Revitalists have powerful allies and friends on Earth."

"I know," said Duchesne softly. "I know."

His eyes fastened on Carolyn's, the words unspoken: *Are you happy? I've stuck my neck out all the way now. You may be looking at the most unpopular man in the system.*

➤

The shapes of the trees were like none that Duchesne had ever seen. Weird, spindly varieties vied for space with smaller, squat species. Some bore an assortment of fruit, none fully recognizable, others did not. Duchesne touched the trunk of one giant that towered like a monarch above the rest. It felt like iron.

Dr. Heidi Gunnerson strolled beside him, her white lab coat flapping open to reveal a casual shirt and slacks. Curly hair framed a face that had the potential to be either deadly serious or utterly charming. At the moment, Gunnerson played the role of tour guide, showing off her work.

"It's incredible," Duchesne said, awed. "I've flown over this place often enough but never been inside before."

The clear dome of the greenhouse arched overhead, enclosing acres of land. Multitudes of plants of every recognized—and unrecognized—sort flourished in abundance.

"You've never visited GenAg?" Gunnerson asked.

"Never. We don't get very many alerts for terrorist plants." He pointed. "Tell me about some of these trees."

"Sure," Gunnerson replied. "Part of what we do is to design plants for immediate use—either new food varieties or to improve the functioning of the hydroponics labs. Others are intended for use outside. What we try to do is envisage what will be needed in the transformation of Mars as the planet is terraformed, so we can make it the way we want it to be. What may be useful now may be entirely different from what is needed in a hundred years."

"Advance planning."

"Exactly."

"Do you have much that will grow outside yet?"

"Not much." Gunnerson shook her head. "The conditions are too harsh. The super-oxidizing soil is pretty hostile to life. Some algae and lichen have taken hold. And we've adapted some species from Earth's desert plants that we hope to introduce soon."

They turned a corner, to be confronted by more lanes of trees. The variety of new and intriguing scents almost overwhelmed Duchesne's senses.

"Take those over there." Heidi pointed to a cluster of trees with dense, dark foliage. The leaves were small and tightly packed.

"They're designed with increased chlorophyll and greater surface area to compensate for decreased sunlight intensity. This one," she patted one of the iron-trunked behemoths, "is for sooner use. Extra heavy bark protects against lower air pressure and temperatures."

"Impressive."

"Try this." Gunnerson pulled a peculiar purple fruit from an equally odd bush.

"Is it safe?"

Heidi laughed. "Of course." She pulled off another and bit in. The juice dribbled off her chin. She wiped it on an already stained sleeve. "Although we're not sure if it's ready for commercial distribution yet."

Duchesne bit cautiously into the fruit.

It had a slightly fuzzy skin, reminiscent of a peach, but a sweet, tangy interior; pulpy, but not unpleasant.

"Pretty good. What is it?"

"A mixture of various things. We haven't named it yet. If you have a suggestion, drop it off on the way out."

Duchesne laughed. "Is everything so haphazard?"

"Hardly. There are a multitude of guidelines to which we adhere." Gunnerson stuck her hands in her pockets. "Are you really interested in fruit, or is there an ulterior motive behind your curiosity?"

"There is something else," Duchesne confessed. The greenhouse stretched forever. "What we will discuss is in the strictest confidence. Understood?"

"Yes, Major."

"What can you tell me about genetic engineering, for example?"

Gunnerson stifled a laugh, turning it into a sneeze. "I've spent my life in genetic engineering. I could talk all day. Could you narrow the field a little?"

Duchesne considered Gunnerson's forthright features, square chin, honest eyes. How far could he trust her? He had no choice.

"Humans. Just the basics."

"Okay. You asked for it. In a sense, genetic engineering has been around for millenia, if you want to consider selective breeding of plants and animals—that is, breeding the best individuals to obtain a better stock. But the principles of heredity weren't discovered until the 1800s by a monk named Gregor Mendel, who had a fascination for peas."

"Peas?"

"Peas." She held two fingers slightly apart. "Little, round green things. After DNA was discovered in the mid-twentieth century, genetic engineering really took off. Bacteria were modified to produce hormones and drugs. The genetic basis of many diseases was discovered. Once genes were identified, it became possible to change them and even create new life-forms."

"The events leading up to the Clone Wars," said Duchesne,

"when undesirable genes were removed from the population, and various scientists tried to create superhumans."

"The augments and boosted animals. All of which ended with a near-total ban on human engineering. It was a case of technical knowledge far outstripping ethical considerations. We had the knowledge but not the wisdom."

"But it's not all bad, surely," said Duchesne.

"Oh, no. But the problem was where to stop. Knowing that someone has a bad gene is one thing but to use that knowledge to discriminate against them, or to eliminate those you know are going to develop a disease or illness years down the line—that's where it becomes tainted."

"To kill rather than to cure."

"Yep. It's the same with all new technology. Technology itself isn't bad, but you've got to have the wisdom, the ethical underpinnings to deal with it. Science is neutral. The applications are not."

"A dark side."

"Yeah. Fusion technology brought us power as well as bombs: mass communications, information and education as well as a means of brainwashing and manipulation. In agriculture you have to balance the growth of food against the destruction of land."

Duchesne fingered the silky leaves of a strange, spider-like tree. "Genetic engineering brought freedom from illness, but when scientists went too far, we had the Clone Wars."

"Yep." Gunnerson waited for him to continue.

"What about today, Doc?" Duchesne asked. "In terms of cloning."

"Plants and animals, sure. You mean people?"

Duchesne nodded.

"Human cloning was first accomplished when? The 1990s, I think. Maybe 1993, although it was decades later before the first adult clone was raised. But sure. The technology's no different. It could be done by any competent biotech. And it's done on Earth, even though it's illegal. Covert medlabs, where you can have yourself cloned for the right price. On Mars, I doubt it. Medlabs are few and far between."

"Can you tell them apart?" he asked. "The clone from the original?"

Gunnerson's eyes narrowed. She jammed her hands in her pockets. "A clone is an exact genetic copy. Exact. Practically, there is no way to distinguish—if the clone is good enough—except by age. If you're dealing with humans, then obviously it takes years for your clone to grow up. A scar or something on the original can be duplicated. About the only other way besides age would be memories—deep interrogation."

They had reached the end of the greenhouse, where the red sands of the desert brushed against the transparent walls. They turned around and retraced their steps past several rows of trees.

"You said any competent biotech?" Duchesne asked.

"Sure."

"Have you ever heard of a Grainger?"

"Lin Grainger? Yeah. In fact, we worked Earthside at GenAg R&D. Lin's the one who reconstructed the giant panda. Good piece of work."

"I didn't know."

"Is Lin involved in something?" Gunnerson asked cautiously.

"Her name was mentioned."

"Lin's smart all right," said Gunnerson. "Brilliant, in fact. But a little strange."

"How so?"

"She was never content with doing the same as everyone else. It was like she always had something to prove to everyone, to outdo the competition. And she hated plants—always wanted to work on higher organisms. Could Lin clone a human?—you bet. And a lot more besides."

"Hmmm."

"If Lin went off the deep end, there's no telling what you could be dealing with."

They reached the greenhouse control center.

"Thanks for the tour, Doc," said Duchesne. "You've been a big help."

"Anytime, Major. Say, maybe we could do dinner?"

"Thanks, but I'm spoken for."

"The good ones always are. Change your mind. . . ."

"Thanks, Doc."

FOURTEEN

Szalny didn't report the latest failure to Klassen.

He wouldn't admit it to anyone, but he was afraid to face Klassen's wrath again. Maranan, had he been aware of the plot, wouldn't have blamed Szalny personally for the police failure—his patience extended further. But Szalny had no doubt Klassen would order him killed. He shrugged. Confident in his own ability, Szalny was worried, but not unduly so. No one Klassen was likely to send after him was a match for him. His only fear was that Klassen would come himself, taking his revenge with his own massive hands. Unlikely, but possible.

I'll have to do the job myself, thought Szalny, *since nobody else seems to be able to.*

He preferred to leave the dirty work to others as much as possible. To others who were expendable.

But sometimes a more personal approach became unavoidable.

He thought hard as he strolled the tree-lined street behind the Administration Complex. The waning sunlight slanted down, dappling the street with gentle shadows. His shepherd-husky mix ambled alongside, darting off whenever an intriguing scent caught his attention.

Trying to walk a tightrope between Maranan and Klassen was a demanding exercise. He wondered how they had ever become partners. Perhaps they had been different once. Certainly the unstable and demanding Klassen had changed.

Szalny wasn't like that. He prided himself on his coolness, his emotional control. Outbursts of anger were signs of weakness. Neither love nor hatred stirred within Szalny's breast. He did what he did just to do it, to further the benefit of Evgeny Szalny. His only loyalty was toward himself.

But he couldn't distance himself too far from Klassen. The only escape from Klassen would be to kill him. Szalny wasn't ready for that, yet.

He checked the street signs. Intersection of Heyward and Floral. Heyward. That was where Duchesne lived—an exclusive apartment complex several blocks along. Szalny turned right on Floral, heading away.

That was a thought.

If it couldn't be done in public, then perhaps in private. . . .

He picked up his steps.

It wouldn't be easy.

He'd have to see the police were called off. He didn't want the bumblers getting in his way. Maranan could do that.

The idea had definite possibilities.

The husky too, caught his master's mood. Tail erect, he trotted down the street.

Szalny headed for a bar he knew.

The megadecibel noise would help him think.

➤

Ghalji Maranan, Colonial Administrator of the planet Mars, posed before his window, hands clasped behind his back. His eyes fixed on the retreating figure of Evgeny Szalny, disappearing down the shady street. The grounds around the Administrative complex were among the most attractively landscaped in the city, always arousing comment from off-world visitors.

But his thoughts were not on trees or landscaping—and only marginally on Evgeny Szalny.

He wondered about Derek Lofter.

There had been no word from him, and that was unusual. Maranan wondered what was happening inside the closely guarded walls of Security HQ. Had Lofter been discovered and silenced? Or was there another, more innocent reason?

Lofter had provided a constant flow of information, a pipeline to Duchesne's plans and actions.

And now the pipeline had dried up.

It had been a stroke of luck that Lofter had been appointed as Duchesne's aide. The idea of placing a spy in

Security had worked out better than he had hoped. Replacing a senior officer had not proved possible for a variety of reasons, so it had been necessary to settle for mere rank and file. But Lofter had been promoted to corporal and ended up in the major's office.

What was going on in there?

Maranan did not like being in ignorance.

He decided to consult his Guide.

He knew what was to be done with the Christians. Once they were out of the way, the last impediment to the success of the Plan would be removed.

He could feel them. Feel their presence in the detention block, feel them as they prayed to their God. They made him uneasy. They radiated a spiritual power that threatened him. But what did their God matter? What mattered was Mars, and after Mars, Gaia Earth.

He forsook his office and descended to the private garden adjoining the Complex. Arthur Thorston had planted it, but now it was his—Maranan's—to enjoy. It reminded him somehow of India, although the trees and plants were different. Nothing could compare to the beauty of the Taj Mahal; he welcomed this garden nonetheless.

Maranan grasped the trailing tendril of a weeping willow with a well-manicured hand. He breathed slowly and willed his spirit to descend. To merge with the spirit of the tree, to move along the tendril, down the trunk, into the creeping roots and beyond . . . down into the rust-red soil, into the iron-rich rocks, into the spirit that was Mars.

➤

Duchesne approved Nancy Cohen's plan.

The dome had faded into invisibility. Nighttime stars fought against the lights of the city.

The age-old battle, Duchesne mused. Light versus darkness. Could anyone know which side he was on? How many would agree that he was doing right?

"I want you to lead it," he said to Cohen, delegating assignments. "Carolyn, remain here, coordinating movements of all squads. Reginald, Howard, and Boris, lead the intracity squads, reporting to Captain McCourt at frequent intervals. Remember, this is to be a bloodless operation. We need to convince the populace that we are on their side."

"What about you?" asked Carolyn. "What are you going to do?"

"I," said Duchesne, "am going to have a talk with former administrator Thorston."

He brushed back a stray lock of hair. "If there are no questions, people, let's get to work."

Win or lose, at least they would try.

➤

"Now." Nancy Cohen whispered into her comm link.

The lights of the Administration Complex flickered and died, leaving the megalithic structures in darkness.

"Let's move!"

She beckoned her squad—augmented by members of headquarters staff—forward. They had only a few minutes with which to work.

Her troopers sprinted out of concealment, boots padding softly across the hard ground. Arrayed in full battle gear, they flitted like black ghosts up the entrance ramp of the Complex, across the quadrangle to the detention center.

The entrance to detention had locked automatically as the lights failed. Power and lights were on separate circuits. Taking the power out as well would have meant blowing the doors—noisy and messy, and posing a risk to anyone on the other side.

"Yako." Cohen hissed.

A short, stocky trooper popped the access panel and inserted an emergency override code.

The guard at the door started as the portal slid open. Confronted by a phalanx of laser rifles, he chose discretion. His gun dropped to the floor.

"Parker, stay by the door."

Cohen led her squad deeper into the detention complex. Each trooper wore a distinctive infrared ID tag and infrared visor. The police were literally in the dark.

A pair of police blundered into the corridor and were neutralized.

A trooper disabled the lifters. Anyone from the upper floors who attempted to descend would find the lifters locked at ground level and the doors refusing to open.

The guards outside the detention cells jumped to their feet, rifles pointing into the dark.

"Security!" Cohen barked. "Drop your weapons."

"What—?!"

"You're covered! Drop the guns now!"

The guards lowered their rifles to the ground. The Security squad swarmed in.

"These are prisoners against the State!" gasped one of the guards, his hands above his head.

"Never you mind," replied Cohen. "Yako, the door."

With the lighting circuits off, the detention doors had frozen. Yako unclipped a miniature power unit from his belt. He opened the access panel by the door and plugged in a lead. The power light came on. Yako made an adjustment and the room lights winked into being.

The guards blinked.

Yako punched in another code. The doors refused to open. He tried again. "Sorry, sir. The code must have changed. I can break it, but it will take a while."

Cohen spun on the guards. "What's the code?"

The guards remained mute.

She gestured. A trooper placed the end of his rifle against one of the guards' heads. His finger tightened on the trigger. A sweat broke out on the man's forehead.

"The code," repeated Cohen.

The man cast a desperate glance at his partner.

"Tell her."

He slid a hand into his breast pocket and extracted a chip.

Yako snatched it from his fingers and entered it into the locking mechanism. The door slid open.

A knot of weary people greeted the troopers' eyes.

"All of you, out." Cohen ordered. "Cuff the guards and bring them."

"I'm Reverend Sommers. What is the meaning of this?" An elderly man with a dark bruise purpling his cheek stepped to the front.

"A reprieve," Cohen grunted. She gestured with her rifle.

"Move out."

As the file of sleepy, yawning people began to move into the corridor, she asked: "How many of you are there?"

"About eight hundred, I believe," replied Sommers.

"Eight hundred? Shoot." She activated her comm link. "We're on the way out. There's about eight hundred of them. Get the vans ready. All secure, Parker?" she asked the guard at the door.

"All quiet."

"Have a separate van ready for the police prisoners. Come on Sommers, move. And tell your people to be quiet."

Sommers led the stumbling crowd along the dark corridor.

> ➤

Carolyn listened to the reports flowing in. She would rather be out on the streets participating in the action, but she couldn't. As Duchesne's chief of staff, her place was here, overseeing the operation, ready to assume command should the need arise.

She could visualize the scene taking place in hundreds of apartments across the city.

A pair of Security troopers would locate a specific apartment. Equipped with universal access overrides, they would enter each residence, surprising the bewildered occupants. The policemen and women would be taken captive without resisting, along with their families.

As long as no one escaped to sound warning, the operation should proceed flawlessly.

As long. . . .

The officers on duty, patrolling the streets, would be more difficult.

Reginald Marlais was attending to them.

Carolyn acknowledged another update from Yellow Horse. A few more hours and the hard part would be done.

No. The hard part was just beginning.

She wondered how her husband was getting on with Thorston and silently wished him well.

> ➤

"I apologize for calling on you so late at night," Duchesne said. If Thorston was surprised by the unusual late-night visit, he didn't let it show.

"Nonsense, m'boy! Come on in!" Arthur Thorston, late Colonial Administrator, moved aside to let Duchesne enter.

Duchesne had never visited Thorston's apartment before. It was modest by anyone's standards, about the same size as his own. But it felt incomplete somehow. Looking around, Duchesne saw the reason why.

Blank patches on the walls indicated where pictures had once hung. The wall-shelves were empty. Whatever objects d'art had once occupied distinguished places were packed. It was an apartment on the verge of being abandoned.

"Drink?" asked Thorston. "Don't have much left, I'm afraid. As you can see, we're living roughly."

"Just juice is fine."

"Still a teetotaler, eh? It's too late for me," Thorston continued, retrieving a single glass from the synthesizer. "Don't want to be up all night, you know."

Duchesne chuckled. Thorston seemed to be in a jovial mood. Hopefully it would last. He sipped his drink, staring into the multicolored swirls.

Thorston plopped into an overstuffed chair. "I assume from the soberness of your expression that you haven't stopped by just to say good-bye to an old politician."

"No. I wish I was. But it's something a lot more serious than that." Duchesne then told Thorston of the results of his investigation. He replayed portions of Hannik's chip.

When he was done, Thorston shook his head. "No," he said finally. "I refuse to believe it! A crazed prophet-scientist using genetic engineering to take over the planet. It's insane . . . like something out of an old—and very bad—movie."

"That's what my wife, who has seen more old and bad movies than I ever knew existed, said. And I agree. But the reality is much more frightening. Maranan doesn't want to engineer the human race, he wants to eliminate it."

"But why, if he wanted to take over so desperately, didn't he replace me? I assure you I'm the original."

"I have no doubts of that. He probably would have, but he wanted to be administrator himself." Duchesne held the chip up.

"The man who got this information did so at the cost of his life. Nothing we've discovered contradicts any of it. You know, I suppose, that he's labeled the Christians as his scapegoats?"

"I heard bits an' pieces. But I've been tryin' to avoid the news, son. We're leaving next weekend. Booked on IPCL *Planet Princess*."

"I was hoping you'd consider otherwise."

"Why?"

"Based on this information, the Revitalists didn't take over the government legitimately. The imposters they have in power—"

"But if what you're telling me is correct, son," interrupted Thorston, "there ain't no way to tell them apart."

"That's partially correct. Medical exams might help. But I can't wait for more proof, and I have no way of compelling these people to be examined. I don't know how long Forbes can hold out on Earth. We may find ourselves recalled at any time. I had to act before time ran out."

Thorston sighed. "I don't think I'm going to like what I'm about to hear."

Duchesne told him. "By now, most of the police will be in custody. In the morning, I declare martial law."

"What do you want of me?" Thorston asked.

"We need someone the people know and trust to be a fig-urehead—to tell them the truth of what's been going on. I'm Security. What I say will be suspect. But you are above reproach. I haven't got the manpower to impose order, and I can't run a planet. I need the people on my side. They trust you, Arthur."

Thorston studied him thoughtfully. "You want me to pose as the leader of a *coup d'etat*. To join in the overthrow of the government."

"Yes."

>

"You're not going to do it, are you?" asked Kerria, Thorston's second wife. Her still youthful face was anguished. When he paused, she continued, gripping his arms. "It will be political suicide to side with Duchesne! Arthur, you can't!"

"We should run away?" asked Thorston, gently removing her arms.

"Yes! Your work is done. Why should you take the part of a power-hungry Security officer?"

Thorston frowned. "Duchesne may be many things," he replied, "but power-hungry isn't one of them." He paced around the living room, marshaling his thoughts. "I've devoted my life to this place—we both have. We made it our second home. Can I stand by and see my life's work undone by a religious fanatic? One who achieved the reins of government by fraudulent means?"

"You've done your part, Arthur."

"Have I?" Thorston ceased his pacing, his mind made up. "Perhaps my part is just beginning."

FIFTEEN

Ghalji Maranan's lips moved soundlessly, repeating the words that he had heard already, the devastating import slowly sinking in. He still couldn't believe it. How could it have happened? Who had betrayed him? There were few who knew . . .

His Guide had told him nothing of this, had not warned him. . . .

Could his Guide not have known?

Or was there another reason his Guide hadn't told him? Could this still be part of the Plan?

"What are you watching for again?" demanded Szalny, hovering behind. "You've seen it three times already. You think it's going to change?"

Maranan made no answer.

Unquestionably the most popular Marsnews broadcaster, Miranda Majors's attractive features were to be seen in many places other than the news. Smart as well as beautiful, she was highly respected in the broadcasting community. In this day of tarnished integrity, Miranda shone. What she reported could be believed. *Would* be believed.

Normally, Maranan had an eye for a beautiful woman. He missed his harem, left behind at the Enclave when he took over in Lowell.

Today, he couldn't care less about her looks.

"This is a Marsnews exclusive," Majors said, her melodious voice radiating both concern and enthusiasm. She gazed toward the cameras, compelling her audience. "The information you have just heard was obtained by a Newsnet reporter on assignment from Earth. Former Colonial Administrator Arthur Thorston, arguably the most popular administrator in the history of Mars, attested to the validity of the report. To tell

you why he has taken such drastic measures, we have asked
Administrator Thorston himself to join us.

"Here he is. Administrator Thorston."

Miranda's well-proportioned face faded, to be replaced by
the homelier features of Thorston.

"Thank you, Miranda. My friends," Thorston began, speaking in the unique way that made him seem as if he was talking to
everyone confidentially, as individuals, rather than as a mass,
"what you have heard is well-nigh impossible. But it is true. We are
faced with a crisis of unbelievable proportions, unprecedented in
the history not only of Mars, but of the system.

"To deal with such a crisis, drastic measures are required.
With the assistance of Major J.I. Duchesne of System Security, I am
forming a provisional government. I urge all citizens to join with
me, repudiating the current regime formed by such a corrupt,
immoral scheme. The new Mars promised by the Revitalists is
nothing more than tyranny in new clothes, a nightmare in scientific
garb.

"I urge all citizens to comply with the edict of martial law,
remaining peaceful. Martial law will remain in effect until such
time as the crisis is resolved.

"People of Mars, we need your support; unity in this time
of crisis—"

"Shut the stupid thing off!" Szalny cursed. "If I see that
man's face one more time—!"

He grasped the back of Maranan's chair and swung it
around, forcing the older man to look at him.

"What now?" he demanded, his face distorted. "I thought
your plan was foolproof! Now listen to them!" He gestured toward
the open window. Voices could be heard ascending from street level.

"We want Thorston!"

"Maranan must go!"

"Old Mars, not new tricks!"

"Listen to them!" Szalny insisted. "They hate you! There's
a mob down there and no police to protect you! What are you
going to do now, genius?"

Maranan pulled himself together. A muscle twitched in his
face. "Not lost," he said, his voice almost inaudible.

"What are you going to do?" Szalny repeated. "Go down
there and offer yourself to them? Nobody cares about the

Revitalists! They don't care about your plans for a new Mars—they're happy with the old one."

Maranan raised his voice, looking at Szalny levelly. Szalny avoided the hypnotic gaze of the green eyes.

"Duchesne has turned the people against us. I underestimated him. But he has no proof. Szalny, we will return to the Enclave. Issue a general call to all adherents." Maranan gained his feet. "I will meet them there."

"Run," Szalny sneered. "You mean to run."

"No. Not run. Regroup."

"I am staying here. I still have work to do."

"As you wish," Maranan said, his voice flat, disinterested. "As you wish."

>

The streets were deserted, shopping centers quiet, parks and public areas barren. People seemed to be observing the restrictions placed upon them.

Which was just as well, Duchesne thought, since there wasn't the manpower to police the city. A crowd in front of Administration shouted and chanted obscene anti-Maranan epithets until Thorston showed himself and reassured them.

The roundup had gone better than Duchesne had hoped. The Marspolice and the Revitalists had been taken completely by surprise. Rousted out of bed for the most part, the police had not resisted.

Security HQ strained at the seams. Christians crammed the supply areas. Duchesne thought it prudent to keep them under guard until the city had quieted down. The Marspolice languished in detention cells.

During the day, squads combed the city for the politicians who had sided with the Revitalists. Several had been apprehended; others were in hiding. Of Maranan himself, there was no trace, but his hoverjet was gone. Most likely he had fled back to the Enclave at the first sign of trouble, leaving his adherents to face the brunt of the populace's wrath.

Lynchings and beatings had been reported. Duchesne couldn't spare the troops to investigate them. Let the adherents suffer the consequences of their actions.

He should have sent a squad after Maranan. Duchesne scolded himself for the oversight. But it had been more important to round up the police first.

Where once hundreds of yellow-robed adherents flogged their wares on every street corner and public square, now there was not one to be seen. None dared show his or her face in public. A stream of ground vehicles and air traffic headed into the desert, aiming southward. Fringe members undoubtedly remained behind, hoping to fade into anonymity, hoping their involvement would be forgotten or overlooked. Only the most hard-core believers fled. The crisis separated the sheep from the goats.

Duchesne let them go. There were too many for his thinly spread troops to stop. But he wasn't concerned. What could they get up to in the Enclave? They'd be all together where they could be kept under watch. Let them wait.

The Navy's response concerned him more. Commodore Washburn called from Phobos Navalport demanding a report. The commodore's reaction didn't surprise him. Washburn was one of them.

The commodore turned livid, his fleshy face purpling.

"You'll never get away with it, Duchesne! As of now, the planet is under naval blockade. No ships off or on. Any ships lifting off without my personal approval will be fired upon." Washburn curled his lip. "Your petty little rebellion will crumble. You're an idiot, Duchesne, you and that feeble fool Thorston."

The Navy posed a problem. Duchesne was not sure how to handle it. Watchful waiting seemed the only course.

Earth was also a problem. The Revitalists maintained a sturdy grip on the Colonial Board. What would their response be? Would they send a major force to reconquer the planet?

He didn't think it likely to happen soon. Most Earth troops were unused to working in low-gravity environments. Training would take time. Plus, a full-scale invasion would destroy the fragile civilization on Mars. Earth wouldn't risk that.

Or would they? What was control of Mars worth to them? The questions outnumbered the answers.

His groundcar slid along the deserted streets. "Return to HQ," Duchesne instructed his driver. He had seen all he needed to.

He could not continue martial law forever. He hoped Thorston could rebuild the government rapidly. Similarly, the Marspolice were being screened. The rank and file unaffected by the Revitalists, with no knowledge of their ulterior aims, would be returned to duty as soon as possible. But he would have to find replacements for Sue Li-Shin and several other high-ranking officers.

How far did the corruption spread?

And was there a way to reverse it?

>

Paul Sommers was waiting for Duchesne outside the Security chief's office. The minister looked better. Release had improved his haggard appearance, and his purple bruises had faded to yellow-green. He appeared rested, if not bursting with energy.

"Come on in, Reverend," Duchesne beckoned. "What can I do for you?"

"I hate to be a problem," said Sommers, "but I wonder when you might let us return home."

"Believe me, Reverend, just as soon as possible. Our capabilities are overstretched keeping you here."

"Then why not—?"

"It's too soon. The populace is confused and unsettled. They won't go from treating you as enemies to leaving you in peace overnight. I don't have the bodies to protect you. A few more days, perhaps."

"I suppose I'll have to be content."

"What do you think of friend Maranan?" Duchesne asked. "What will he do next?"

Sommers shook his head. "He's an evil man, Major, possessed by evil. Perhaps you laugh at the idea, but it's true. He won't accept defeat easily. I expect he's trying to find a way to reverse the situation, consulting whatever evil spirit gives him guidance."

"I think you're right. We haven't seen the last of him." Duchesne tapped on his desk. "Tell me," he asked. "Does a clone have a soul?"

Sommers looked like he'd just been told his ticket was invalid and he'd be dropped into space. His jaw dropped.

"An interesting question, Major. Referring to the news, I assume?"

Duchesne nodded.

"What do you mean by a soul, Major?"

The question took Duchesne aback. He waved a hand in a vague gesture. "You know. An immortal soul."

"Okay," Sommers said. "Two views for you. If you believe humanity to be bipartite—composed of body and mind—then I would say yes. Clones obviously have bodies. They also have a fully functioning brain and so presumably have normal minds, consciousness, and self-awareness. Maybe someone else can tell you differently, but from my knowledge of humans, a clone should be a person."

"Okay. And if not?"

"In what is frequently thought to be the Christian view—although it's really more Greek than Christian—humanity is considered tripartite—made of body, mind, and the immortal soul—meaning a spiritual part that transcends death."

"I'm with you, Reverend."

"Very well. If you mean does a clone have an immortal soul, given by God, then I can't answer for certain. I don't know. I've never—knowingly—met a clone. But either it does, or it doesn't. A scary thought, isn't it? A soul-less body waiting for something to take control."

"Reverend—"

"If you consider a 'natural clone'," Sommers said, "an identical twin, where both individuals develop from the same fertilized egg and are obviously fully human, then I suppose maybe a clone does have a soul."

"So we should consider them as real people?"

"As real as you or I. Either way you look at them. Brainwashed, malfunctioning, real people. But I think it's a mistake to talk of the soul as if it was an extra ingredient tacked on by God at some unidentified moment. We are unified beings. Holistic, if that word still has meaning."

Duchesne passed a hand across his eyes. "Considering clones in the first place is bad enough; having to consider them as real people—"

The intercom chimed. "Yes, Jacland."

"There's a naval officer to see you, sir. Glenda Wesley of SSF *Collingwood*."

"Send her in, Jacland."

"I'll be going, Major," said Sommers. "Thank you."

"Thanks for your help, Reverend."

Sommers stood aside as a tall young woman in naval uniform entered. She nodded at him.

"Welcome, Lieutenant!" Duchesne greeted her warmly. "Or Commander now, I see?"

"Yes sir," she replied. "First officer."

"And well deserved. What happened to Howard Corrin?"

"Transferred lunaside, sir. Desk job."

"Huh?"

"He and the captain didn't always see to eye to eye."

"Happens. Take a seat. Can Jacland get you anything to drink?"

"No sir. But thanks. This visit is . . . uh, off the record, so to speak."

Duchesne resumed his chair and raised his eyebrows. Glenda Wesley had changed little since he had last seen her two years ago manning a tactical console. She had been Lieutenant Wesley, serving aboard the System Security Frigate *Collingwood* when Duchesne had led a mission to Ganymede.

Outwardly, Wesley seemed no different. Her shoulder-length, brown hair bounced over her epaulets, and her trim figure filled her uniform well. But she seemed more self-confident perhaps, than previously. Probably as a result of her newfound rank.

"How so?" he asked.

"I was planetside taking a few days' leave when the . . . crisis intervened. I have to return shipboard immediately, so *Collingwood* can take part in the blockade. But Captain Benson asked me if I would visit you informally—"

"To get the facts from the top, is that it?"

Wesley nodded. "Without him being caught communicating directly with you. The commodore is said to be furious."

"He is. How is the captain?" Duchesne asked.

"Same as always," Wesley smiled. "He's quite happy there haven't been any openings for promotion. He'd be lost without a ship."

Captain Samuel Benson was a captain's captain. Duchesne felt a spark of hope. If he could enlist Benson's help . . .

He busied himself with his workscreen. He extracted a computer chip and handed it to Wesley.

"Here's a copy of our files. I think Benson will find it most interesting. But let me fill you in."

It was a serious Commander Glenda Wesley who left his office almost an hour later. Duchesne hoped he had convinced her.

He had a feeling he would be needing all the help he could get.

>

Evgeny Szalny was glad to see the last of Maranan. He preferred to be on his own. Let the sycophants and adherents go. He would work alone.

From being in a no-lose situation, he now faced Klassen's anger on one hand and Maranan's incompetence on the other. To save his own skin, Szalny would have to act.

Duchesne thought he had won.

Let him.

He would drop his guard, and then he, Szalny, would be ready. He had formed his plan.

It was no longer safe to be spotted anywhere near the Administration Complex. Szalny had plenty of other places he could hide, places that Security would never think of searching.

He would get Klassen the winning hand that he needed.

And Evgeny Szalny would come out on top.

>

Ghalji Maranan ignored the torrent of blasphemy that burst from Erik Klassen's lips. Klassen cursed and spat with the fury of an enraged tiger. Maranan waited out the storm. When Klassen subsided, Maranan said, "We will advance the Plan, Erik."

"Advance it?" Klassen's eyes bulged. "The Plan is lost!"

"No, Erik. Not lost. Duchesne has turned the population against us. Martians are different from Earthers. Earthers are complacent, indifferent, apathetic. They won't sit up and take notice until it's too late. But Martians are hard-boiled, colonial types—survivalists who won't fall for subterfuge or clever words. I didn't take the difference into consideration. But we still have our supporters. Highly placed supporters. Duchesne is not the last word on Mars."

"Szalny and Forrest!" Klassen shouted. "They're the ones!"

Maranan rubbed the side of his nose. "What do you mean?"

"It must have been Hannik!" Klassen continued. "Somehow he escaped with the details of the Plan. Those cursed idiots didn't kill him after all." He clenched his fists. "They will learn what it

means to fail." He turned his back on Maranan and stalked out."
Szalny's in Lowell, but Forrest is here."

Maranan called Lin Grainger.

"There has been a change," he said when her face filled the
vidscreen. "The Plan must be advanced. I want you to ready a
pantrope for a surface test."

Lin goggled. "They're not ready! We haven't done enough sim-
ulations. I need to ease them in gradually, do gradated exposures."

"There is no time anymore, Lin. The world knows about
our plan. It is time for a demonstration, to show that humanity
is ready to live in harmony with Mars."

"But—"

"Do it, Lin." Maranan was firm. "No argument."

➤

"No!" Forrest cowered in the corner of his room like a pur-
sued rabbit, seeking cover where there was none.

"I swear to you! We killed him just like we told you!"

"So how did Duchesne find out?" Klassen rasped. "You and
Szalny were the only others who knew."

"Mmmmaybe it was Grainger," Forrest whimpered.

Klassen paused for a split second.

"She's too afraid. No, Forrest. It was you." Klassen stepped
forwards. "Now you'll find out what it means to disobey."

Forrest tried to bolt for the door. He was too slow. Klassen
grabbed his shirt and flung him back against the wall with teeth-
jarring impact. Forrest's head cracked against the rock. He reeled
and his eyes crossed. Forrest was bulky but no match for the
enraged Klassen. Klassen planted a fist in Forrest's solar plexus
and wrapped his hands around Forrest's neck.

His grip tightened.

Forrest's eyes bulged in their sockets. He fought for breath,
struggling in Klassen's iron grip. A harsh rattle came from the
dying man's throat.

Klassen shifted his grip and twisted.

Forrest's neck snapped with a crack.

Klassen threw the corpse on the floor and stared at it.

"You're next, Szalny," he swore. "If I get my hands on
you. . . ."

SIXTEEN

Arthur Thorston fulfilled his word. Within days he had the government up and running. To the Council Thorston appointed people he trusted who had occupied positions in the prior government, until such time as elections could be held. Security screened all applicants for Revitalist sympathies, remanding any suspects for further questioning and Rehab.

The renegade politicians who had joined Maranan in his quest for dominion had been taken into in custody, aside from a few who had escaped to the Enclave. Without exception, they refused to abandon the Revitalist cause.

The majority of the Marspolice, after being appraised of the situation, supported Thorston's provisional government. Only the highest echelon had been subverted or replaced. The return of the Marspolice to duty freed up Duchesne's troops.

After a few volunteers went first to act as test cases, the Christians were released to only rare incidents of harassment. It seemed as if the shocked population was unwilling to make the same mistake twice. A smoldering anger against the way the Revitalists had manipulated them created a subtle undercurrent of tension. Perhaps there was a feeling of guilt over how the Christians had been used.

The naval embargo became more of a nuisance than a serious hindrance to daily life. In the long term, however, lack of natural resources and rare elements could become a factor.

Duchesne would dearly have liked to talk to Forbes. But communications to Earth weren't going through. He suspected Commodore Washburn of jamming satellite relays.

It was a stalemate. Duchesne held Lowell, the major population center; the Revitalists held the Enclave, Phobos Navalport, and more importantly, the Colonial Board.

"Are you still busy reading?" he asked, entering the living room after changing out of his uniform. "Hasn't religion caused enough trouble?"

Carolyn set the Bible down on the floor by her side.

"Are you still upset?" she replied. "I thought we agreed that this wasn't to blame."

"I suppose not." He flopped beside her. "Anything the Revitalists hate, I suppose we should like." He held his head in his hands. "I need a vacation."

"Another trip to Iona?" Carolyn teased. "How about Lindisfarne this time?"

"Spare me."

Duchesne rested his head in Carolyn's lap and closed his eyes. She stroked his hair.

"How about we take a brief trip somewhere on-planet?" Carolyn suggested. "I know. Let's go to a resort. What's that one over toward Chryse?"

"The Golden Plain."

"Of course! You think I'd have remembered that. A weekend of swimming and tennis would do you wonders."

"I'd love to, but I can't. Maybe when this is over."

"You're still upset that I beat you last time. Come on, dear, there's nothing happening. Boris can cover for two days. We could be back within an hour if necessary."

"You're wrong there," Duchesne replied, opening an eye. "There is something happening. We just don't know what it is."

➤

The corridors of the Enclave were strangely deserted. The adherents had been confined to quarters for a period of meditation Maranan had ordered. Even Erik Klassen had to obey.

She was the only one exempted.

Lin Grainger propelled the covered tank along the corridor, alert for movement. Her footsteps echoed off the rock walls.

The lifter carried her toward the surface. She steered the tank into the motorpool. She chose an e-suit, made sure the oxygen tanks were full, and pulled it on.

She eased the tank into the airlock. The lock cycled, and Lin took her first walk on the surface of Mars in months. She relished the sense of freedom, even freedom of a limited nature, restricted to where her legs could carry her.

Why not steal a vehicle and escape?

She dismissed the thought even as it occurred.

Hannik hadn't made it.

She could try for the hoverjet, but she couldn't pilot it, and the autopilot probably had restricted access.

And even if by some miracle she made it to Lowell, what then? Szalny was there. Klassen would alert him to be waiting for her. She had no doubt what her fate would be at Szalny's hands.

Go to Security? She would find no mercy there. She had made her bed well. She had no choice but to lie in it.

She wished she had been happy working with plants and reconstructing extinct animal species.

She turned to the tank. Maranan had only given her so long for this first test. She couldn't waste the time in idle speculation or self-recrimination. She had managed to delay for almost a week, giving the pantrope a few more precious days in which to develop and mature. The genetic specifications had been reviewed repeatedly for the slightest flaw.

She didn't want this test. She had planned on introducing a pantrope stepwise, in environments gradually approaching surface conditions. That way she could monitor for problems and correct them as they occurred, before they became serious.

Maranan denied her such a cautious approach. It was all or nothing.

She slid the cover off and quenched the portable sleep field generator.

The pantrope stirred and then moved more vigorously at its first glimpse of natural sunlight, churning the viscous liquid in eagerness.

"You want to get out, don't you, Spock?" Lin asked. "I don't blame you. I want to get out too. I hope you like it."

The lid retracted at the touch of a button. The nutrient fluid began bubbling, boiling away in the low pressure. A parched, leathery hand gripped the edge of the tank, hoisting itself up. Lin gripped the thin wrist, helping the pantrope out.

With a convulsive jerk, Spock emerged onto the surface of Mars.

Lin held her breath.

The first life on Mars! And she had created it!

Her eyes were fixed on the being.

Spock coughed, expelling fluid from his lungs. His barrel chest inflated with the rarefied atmosphere. He took a few hesitant, unsteady steps, and then moved easier as his joints unlimbered. His heavy-boned head swiveled, deep-set eyes scanning the rocky plain.

Spock turned toward her, his narrow lips crinkled in a smile. His grin faded.

Lin's clapped a hand to her mouth; Spock's lips expanded in a wordless scream, a faint mewing in the thin air. He clutched his head with both hands, fingernails gouging into the flesh. From between his clenched eyelids blood trickled onto his cheeks. His nose erupted in a crimson stream.

"NO!" Lin's voice broke.

Spock rocked back and forth, head thrown back, hands over ruptured ears. Mouth working.

He stretched out a pleading hand toward her. Lin reached out to take it. The movement was never completed.

Spock pitched forward onto the dusty ground, fingers scrabbling irregular furrows in the dust. His hand clenched.

A convulsive gasp, and he lay still.

Lin buried her face in her hands and sobbed.

➢

"Are you sure?" whispered Maranan. The depths of the glade surrounded him. "I have never before questioned you."

"Do you deny that the mass of humanity is fit only to be exploited or ignored?"

"The idea is horrifying!"

"It is inevitable. It is a logical outcome of your teaching, Ghalji."

"That does not make it any less horrifying." Maranan stared at the bright, shimmering form of his Guide.

"Are you afraid to take the final step?"

The form pulsed with light.

"I am not afraid. But must it be so?"

"*Yes,*" replied his Guide. "*It must be done. Only those who are willing to be one with our Mother Mars will be allowed to live. Those who treat her with contempt will themselves be treated with contempt. Mars must be rid of all those who treat her improperly. You must respect your mother, Ghalji. All must respect her. You are her agent.*"

True, thought Maranan. And what do those people matter? They have rejected me, have spurned my message. Erik is right to hate Duchesne.

"Very well. It shall be as you say."

His Guide smiled.

Ghalji Maranan shivered with a sudden chill.

➤

Erik Klassen was glad to have something he could sink his teeth into. He had chafed unbearably, confined to the Enclave while Maranan was botching things in Lowell.

Removing Forrest had provided a certain satisfaction, but the pleasure had worn off.

He kept one hand in his pocket, caressing the cold stock of his laser pistol while responding to Maranan's summons. Almost he had used it. The temptation to incinerate his one-time mentor had been nearly irresistible.

He wondered if Maranan knew how near to death he had been.

But as the Revitalist spoke, Klassen grinned with fiendish glee. "It is perfect! It is what you should have done long ago instead of pussyfooting around with politics."

Maranan did not look so excited. "It is necessary, not something to rejoice over."

"I will make sure the arrangements are made. We still have a number of trustworthy members in the city."

"Szalny is still in Lowell."

"I have other plans for Szalny. But they can wait."

➤

Lin Grainger pushed the tray bearing the body of Spock into the doc unit in her laboratory.

"Autopsy program. Complete."

She waited for the routine to run its course.

A dull rage seethed, burning her belly, making her heart as heavy as lead.

Spock had survived a few brief, agony-filled minutes on the surface. Far longer than a normal human, but still only a few minutes.

And Maranan was to blame.

She had *told* Maranan the pantrope wasn't ready. But had he listened?

And she—the scientist—the one who should have known—had obeyed him.

Spock had died.

Maranan had killed him.

She could create another, but Spock had been her favorite, the most advanced of her creations.

She didn't turn around at the footsteps behind her.

"What happened, Lin?" Maranan asked softly.

"You killed him," Lin snapped.

"How did he die?" Maranan's voice remained soft.

Lin wanted to hurl herself upon him, make him feel a portion of the agony Spock had endured.

A part of the agony she felt.

Instead, she studied the readout.

"Massive cerebral hemorrhage. The dura wasn't tough enough and the middle cerebral artery ruptured."

Lin whirled around. "Why, Ghalji?" she cried, her emotions erupting in a flood of tears. "Why? I told you he wasn't ready. Why didn't you listen to me?"

"I am truly sorry, Lin," Maranan replied in a voice of infinite sadness.

He put his hands on her shoulders, turning her chin upwards, allowing her to see the pain in his own eyes.

"It had to be tried," he asserted. "But now—"

"Now?"

"I do not know."

➤

Earthdate: December 14, 2166

As the morning progressed, Duchesne became increasingly on edge. His stomach churned, a headache throbbed in his temples, his nerves quivered. He tried to place a finger on the reasons for his disquiet, but couldn't.

Lowell City was quiet. The Revitalists were confined to their Enclave. The Christians remained unmolested. Life returned to normal.

Why, then, the unease?

Carolyn pled fatigue and went home early. Duchesne suspected she still suffered aftereffects of the stunner. Sometimes they could linger for weeks, cropping up at odd intervals. She wouldn't admit to any ill health, but that was what he thought. Perhaps going away for a couple of days wasn't such a bad idea. Maybe he shouldn't have dismissed the suggestion so abruptly, thinking only of himself.

He still hadn't pinned down a cause for his unease when he, too, left the office early. He wondered if an evening of music and relaxation would help. Carolyn was undoubtedly right about the need for some time off, but he wasn't sure the situation was stable enough that he could spare it yet. She'd say he was being too compulsive, afraid to relinquish control for even a short time.

She'd be right.

He knew something was wrong as soon as he arrived home. As he regarded the slender spire of the apartment complex, the hairs on the back of his neck prickled like those of a dog in the night seeing something invisible to human eyes. He reached back a hand to brush the sensation away.

The sense of unease worsened into dread.

Half afraid of what he might find, he hurried through the halls, chafed as the lifter wafted him upward, and raced toward the apartment.

He drew his Enerweap. The smart gun recognized his handprint and readied.

Stupid! It's your own home.

He stood to the side of the door and murmured the code. The door retracted into its slot.

He tensed.

Nothing.

196 Andrew M. Seddon

His laser in a two-handed grip, hands sweaty on the stock, he swung around the edge of the door frame and dropped into a crouch.

His eyes flicked around the room.

Empty.

No sound beyond that of his own breathing and his heart hammering like drilling equipment.

"Carolyn!" he called. "You home?"

Silence.

He padded through the apartment, laser nosing into the rooms. Dining alcove, bedroom, rec room: empty. Carolyn was not home. There was no sign of anyone else. Satisfied that he was alone, he clipped his weapon back onto his belt.

Where could she be?

Back in the living room, a familiar object caught his eye. Intent on looking for people, he'd missed it on his initial survey. Carolyn's pistol dangled on the back of a chair. It wasn't like her to leave a weapon lying around; she hadn't ventured outside without it since the episode with the police. Even though that threat had passed, she had remained cautious.

Surely she would have told him if she had been going anywhere; that was a habit they both cultivated.

The sense of something being wrong grew stronger.

Metal glinted on the floor, buried in the carpet. He almost trod on it before the image registered. He bent over and picked it up. The cross he had given Carolyn as an anniversary present; the chain had snapped. And close by it—

He scrutinized the other object. A thin sliver of metal.

But not just any kind of sliver.

The kind of sliver used in a dart-gun.

Holding the cross tightly in his hand, over his heart, he cursed whoever had been there.

➤

The cargo flitter, its holds full of mining equipment, oxygen tanks, replacement e-suits, and portable rations, lumbered from the launch dock. Swinging around Lowell in a great circle, the flitter picked up speed and cleared the city, heading west.

"Remember," Szalny had said. "Head west until you're out

of range of the city beacons, just like you're going to Olympus. Then cut south and drop her at the Enclave."

"It's one ruddy-long detour, mate," the cargo pilot complained, rubbing a greasy hand on his coveralls.

"You're being paid well enough," Szalny reminded him. "When you get to Olympus, tell them sorry you're late, but you had engine trouble. You can rig that, can't you?"

"That I can." He fingered the credit chips in his pocket. The pilot grinned, "For this amount, I could rig almost anything. See ya."

The flitter disappeared. Szalny smirked. It had been almost too easy. Obtaining the apartment complex code had been a cinch. An adherent in CompCentral, one of those who hadn't fled, had provided it for the good of the cause. The apartment lock had been harder, but an instrument purloined from a dealer in such black market items helped immeasurably.

Once inside the apartment, he waited patiently. His only worry had been that husband and wife arrive together. But luck was on his side.

The woman came alone. She had her weapon off as she entered, moving to sling it over a chair. Obviously, she wasn't expecting trouble.

Szalny stepped out from the corner behind the door and shot her at point-blank range with the dart gun. The miniscule dose of hypneum worked instantly. She grabbed for her neck and then relaxed.

After that, he told her to lay down her gun, which she did willingly. They then strolled casually out of the building. No need to appear as if anything was out of the ordinary. She was just going out again, under her own free will, and Szalny happened to be heading the same direction. A waiting car, and that was that.

He smirked again. He had lost Hannik, but he had captured Carolyn McCourt.

A cinch.

Sometimes he was almost too good.

He had hoped it would make Klassen happy. At least allay Klassen's rage for a while, long enough for Szalny to consider his next step.

➢

In his office at Security HQ, Duchesne issued a stream of orders to Jacland.

"I want a forensic team to go through my apartment in minute detail. There's a needle-gun dart on the living room floor—tell them to pay particular attention to it, as there may be more than Carolyn's skin on it. What have I forgotten?"

Jacland consulted his workpad. "You've ordered a full-scale search for the captain, involving both Security and Marspolice. All nonassigned personnel to be involved. City locks and landing pads to be under constant surveillance. Her description to be broadcast over Marsnews." Jacland raised his eyes. "Any idea who could be responsible, sir?"

"No, I—" Duchesne broke off, a suspicion forming in his mind. "Yes, I do, Jacland. Add this to the list: an all-points bulletin for one Evgeny Szalny, former aide to Ghalji Maranan."

"He's distinctive enough," said Jacland. "He shouldn't be too hard to find."

"I hope you're right," said Duchesne. "I hope you're right."

"Don't worry, sir, everyone will do their best. We'll find the captain."

Duchesne appreciated the concern in the sergeant's eyes. "Thank you, Jacland. I know they'll try."

But a city, even of a million people, provided a wealth of hiding places. An elusive underworld character like Szalny would have no dearth of options.

He hoped Jacland's optimism was well-founded.

Carolyn seemed to have vanished into thin air.

As the night wore on without news, the strain took its toll. Duchesne stalked and muttered around his office, snapping at anyone who dared interrupt. Jacland remained at his post, handling all but the most urgent calls.

How could it have happened?

A kidnapping in broad daylight, in one of Lowell's best apartment complexes!

Szalny—if guilty—had nerve.

Duchesne swore to get the perpetrator, if it was the last thing he did.

Carolyn's necklace lay in his pocket, a mute reminder of her presence. It was no accident; she had left it for him, that he knew.

But as what?

A clue?

Or an encouragement to faith?

The long night passed without word of Carolyn.

SEVENTEEN

Duchesne still hadn't received news of Carolyn forty-eight hours later when the ultimatum arrived. He had a sneaking suspicion that his wife was no longer in Lowell; why, he wasn't sure, except that if anyone was going to use her as a hostage, they would be better off not keeping her right under Security's nose.

The major watched Maranan's latest broadcast in his office, along with Mikhaelovitch and Cohen. The three had spent the morning in a fruitless discussion of strategy.

"Greetings to the citizens of Lowell City." Maranan's recorded features beamed. His syrupy voice oozed charm. His face was placid, unworried, as if the preceding days had passed by without affecting him. "This is your Administrator, Ghalji Maranan, speaking to you from the Hellas Planitia Enclave."

A look of distress crossed the unlined face. The cultist's voice assumed a hurt tone which made Duchesne want to reach out and grab him by the neck.

"The current events have caused me intense pain and anguish. A few rabble rousers, posing under the guise of Security officers, have conspired to overthrow the freely elected government of Mars—the government that *you* chose. These men and women, unconcerned for our planet, seek to reverse the reforms we have instituted and send Mars down the path that Earth traveled, the path that leads to a ravaged and violated planet.

"I am disappointed that the populace has tolerated these malcontents, listening to their tissue of lies—lies that lack any foundation in fact. I am forced, therefore, to take drastic measures.

"The Red Planet is rising! Mars is once again shaking off unwelcome life, except for we who will become her caretakers. Those who would live in harmony with our Mother Mars are welcome to join the Revitalists and seek security in our Enclave. We do not have room for all, only the sincere.

"On the other hand, those who choose otherwise are not welcome on our planet."

Maranan's face hardened, his green eyes became cat-like.

"I am offering you this choice. Join us or face the consequences. Those who wish may leave the planet in peace. Go. Return to Earth, where humanity belongs. But one week from today our clemency ends. All who remain face destruction."

He smiled again, radiating charm.

"But it need not be so. Choose peace. Join us or leave while you may."

His smile lingering like that of the Cheshire cat, Maranan's image faded.

"He's mad!" exclaimed Cohen. "Stark staring mad! Face destruction indeed! Who does he think he is?"

"I wouldn't take him lightly, Nancy. He hasn't shown himself to be a purveyor of empty promises. From your investigation, Boris, can he carry out his threat?"

The big Russian rumbled, "Militarily, I would say not. Short of smuggling a thermonuclear bomb into the city, I do not see how the Revitalists could pose a significant threat—our defenses are more than adequate to keep that rabble at bay, despite the numerical differences. If you refer to something more exotic, such as a biological weapon, or terrorist tactics—?" Mikhaelovich shrugged. "Anything is possible."

"Would a man who professes a love for Mars unleash nuclear or biological weapons?" Duchesne asked. "What kind of a planet would he leave for himself to remain as caretaker over?"

"He's mad," Cohen repeated. "He could do anything."

"There's a call coming in from the Enclave," Jacland interrupted over the intercom. "Maranan wishes to speak to you, sir."

Duchesne arched his eyebrows. "The devil himself. Put him through, Sergeant."

Maranan reappeared. But this wasn't the same Maranan. This was not a politician trying to win over a population with charm and honeyed words. His expression caused a chill to creep over Duchesne. Maranan's eyes seemed inhuman, their unfathomable depths unworldly and alien.

"Major Duchesne," Maranan said, no trace of emotion warming his voice. "You have caused me great irritation. Let me tell you here and now that I will brook no further interference. I have given a week's grace period, which is more than you deserve. If you make any aggressive moves to provoke me, then I will act sooner. You cannot win, Duchesne. Leave Mars while you still can."

"Empty threats, Maranan? What action do you propose to take?"

"Do you think I would be such a fool as to tell you?" Maranan sneered. "But I say this: Every man, woman and child in Lowell will die, and their deaths will be on your head. There are ways to ensure your compliance."

Duchesne's eyes narrowed. "Do you have my wife?" he demanded. "Because if you harm her, I will personally see that you—"

"Tut, tut, Major. Would I be so crude?" Maranan shrugged. "But one of my more enthusiastic followers . . . Think well, Major. Noon. One week from today."

Maranan cut the link.

Duchesne couldn't think of an epithet vile enough.

"We can't just sit," said Cohen.

"Without knowing his plan, it is hard to take definitive action," Mikhaelovitch countered.

"What kind of twisted logic does he have, trying to blame me for the deaths of the populace?"

"I told you. He's mad."

"We need to take some precautionary measures," Duchesne said. "Nancy, I want you and Howard to take your squads with ground vehicles and air support and establish a perimeter around the Enclave. Don't get close enough to spook them but be close enough to take rapid action if needed. I wish we had satellite surveillance, but we don't. You'll need to establish a line of ground-based links.

"Boris, you and Reginald secure Lowell. Make sure the city defenses are prepared and on-line. If anyone has any suggestions as to what Maranan is up to and how to prevent it, let me know and check them out.

"We've got a week to discover his plan, but I would like to have some inkling well before that."

Mikhaelovitch and Cohen nodded and left.

Alone in his office, Duchesne slammed his hand on his desk.

What obscene plan was going to emerge from the twisted recesses of Maranan's mind?

What was he doing to Carolyn?

➤

Lin Grainger watched curiously as the two adepts conveyed a woman along the corridor toward a secure residential block and not toward the lab. The woman couldn't be for her.

Lin let out a breath and studied the woman's face as she passed by. She was striking—features best described as pert but framed by a shock of red hair the likes of which Lin had never seen. She felt a sudden stab of envy.

The woman's eyes fixed straight ahead, unseeing, pupils slightly dilated. Hypneum.

Klassen trailed the adepts, stalking along the corridor. He brushed by Lin and bumped her against the wall.

"Who is that?" Lin asked.

Klassen paused and laughed coarsely. He waited until the adepts rounded a corner, out of earshot.

"That," he smirked, "is Captain Carolyn McCourt, wife of our beloved Major Duchesne."

Lin gasped. "What are you going to do with her?"

"Wouldn't you like to know," Klassen scoffed, following the adherents.

"I have a very good idea what your intentions are," she muttered.

She hurried in search of Maranan.

She found the master reclining in his meditation room, eyes closed.

"What's going on?" she demanded, hands on her hips.

Maranan's heavy lids parted. "In what way, Lin?"

"I just saw Klassen going down the hall with a woman. Duchesne's wife."

Maranan's eyes narrowed. He remained silent.

"Are we kidnapping now, Master?" Lin accused. "Adding to our list of crimes?"

"Crimes, Lin? We are doing what our Mother desires."

"I have heard enough about Mother Mars! If Mars is a woman, she seems thoroughly confused about how to deal with humanity!" Lin pressed: "She is not to be cloned. There is not time for that. What are you going to do with her?"

"She need not concern you," Maranan soothed. "It is a . . . personal affair between Erik and the major."

"And so you let that animal do what he wishes? How can it be personal when it concerns all of us? I don't want to be a part of this, of what Klassen is going to do to her! I've had enough of manipulating and warping other people's lives—"

Maranan fixed his eyes on her, compelling attention. Lin felt herself falling into the icy green depths. Her will dissolved before an influence more potent, a personality so powerful that her resistance melted. A personality more potent than ever before.

"Trust me, Lin," Maranan said in a voice not his own, a voice that seemed to echo from the depths of space, a voice that froze Lin to her very being.

"Yes," she heard herself say, the words spoken of their own volition. "I trust you."

>

Earthdate: December 18, 2166

Erik Klassen gave the woman an extra shove as he burst into the lab unannounced. She took a couple of stutter-steps before regaining her balance. She made no protest at the rough handling. Lin looked up in surprise from a screen detailing a nucleotide analysis. She rose to her feet, her face flushed.

"What are *you* doing here?"

Klassen pushed the woman in Lin's direction. "What's wrong with her?" he demanded.

"Depends what you've done to her," Lin snapped.

Klassen stepped toward her, arm raised.

Lin retreated behind the miniscule safety of a nutrient tank.

Klassen turned the movement into a pointing finger.

"Watch your lip, Grainger! I haven't done anything to her. She's been like a zombie ever since the cargo hauler dropped her off."

"So? What do you want me to do?"

"Run her through the doc unit, idiot."

Lin studied Klassen's face, trying to judge his intentions. Warily, she circled the tank and took the woman's arm. The violet eyes had the same unfocused gaze as when Lin had passed her in the hall two days ago. Klassen made no move.

Lin waved a hand before the woman's face. She didn't blink. "It looks like hypneum," Lin said.

Klassen quivered like he was going to explode. "Of course! But hypneum should have worn off well before now, unless Szalny got the dosage all wrong."

"Come with me," Lin said to the woman.

The doc unit had two entrances, one into the lab, the other into the outside corridor. That way, any adherents needing medical attention could be examined without coming into the lab.

"Sit here."

The woman descended on the seat. Lin brought a helmet down over the patient's head and slid the woman's hands into twin receptacles.

"Don't move."

Lin closed the door and moved over to the console. She initiated the diagnostic routine.

In moments, the screen illuminated with lines of print and columns of figures.

"Well?" Klassen demanded, standing so close behind her Lin could feel his body heat. "What's the matter?"

Lin bit back another sharp retort and studied the readout. "Judging from this, it's an idiosyncratic reaction. The hypneum is lasting longer than usual for the dosage received. Based on the neural scan I'd say she was stunned recently, and that's affecting the effects of the hypneum."

Klassen cursed. "So how long before it wears off?"

"Impossible to say. An unusual reaction like this is very individual. She could be better tomorrow, or it could take several more days."

"Bah! Szalny, you're dead!"

Klassen spun Lin around, transfixing her with a deadly glare. "Not a word of this, Grainger, or you're dead too. Get her out. I'm taking her back to her quarters."

Lin rose to comply.

>

The interminable days ticked by one by one with nothing but silence from the Enclave.

Duchesne tried to contact Maranan, to keep some sort of dialogue underway, to gain a modicum of insight into the cultist's intentions, but Maranan refused all communications.

A trickle of people abandoned the city, fleeing to the Enclave and safety. Duchesne had everyone leaving Lowell searched but let them go. He didn't want anyone in Lowell who could cause trouble. He couldn't spare the manpower to incarcerate and guard the disaffected.

Anybody entering the city, even on legitimate business, underwent a rigorous search and interrogation. Most were prospectors returning to civilization, or cargo haulers from Olympus or mining outposts.

Cohen and Yellow Horse established their perimeter, keeping the Enclave under surveilance but making no aggressive moves. Lowell City became an armed camp.

Thorston went on the news immediately after Maranan's broadcast, trying to dispel fears. Most people accepted the situation, trusting in the power of Security to protect them.

Few believed Maranan had the power to carry out his threats; Duchesne was glad the populace didn't realize how limited were Security's resources.

Maranan had obviously contacted Washburn, since passenger shuttles were allowed to take off. Even if every citizen had wanted to leave, it would have proved impossible. There simply weren't enough passenger liners and transports available to move one million people to Earth. The limited number of available spaces filled in short order at exorbitant prices as the nervous, the timid, the vacationers who had no stake in Mars, fled the planet. Cargo freighters and ore transports loaded up with human cargo far more profitable than their normal freight.

Deimos Spaceport was crammed to capacity, but the exodus made little dent in the population.

Forensics identified minute fragments of skin found in his apartment as coming from Evgeny Szalny. Duchesne wondered what he had done to trigger such hatred in a man he didn't even know.

Fearful for Carolyn, his appetite vanished—as did a few pounds.

Paul Sommers tried to provide support.

"Why, Reverend?" Duchesne asked after Sommers had completed a reassurance of God's love. "Why would your God allow such a monster as Maranan to flourish?"

"God is sovereign, Major," Sommers replied. "Nothing happens that he does not allow. You may wonder why a man like Maranan can proceed unmolested, but I assure you that his plans will ultimately come to naught. It won't go on forever. 'Why do the wicked prosper?' is a question that has been asked for ages. The response is equally valid: 'The way of the wicked will perish.'"

"I wish I had your faith," Duchesne replied.

"You can, Major."

Duchesne let it go. It was a poor choice of words.

"Why doesn't He do something then? Will your god let the population of this city be killed for no reason by a madman?"

"I cannot tell you what He will do, Major, although I believe things will work out well. As to why He allows certain situations to happen, let me ask you this: What claim do you have on Him? You and the vast majority of people go on your way pretending that God either does not exist or is irrelevant. You don't seek to acknowledge Him or obey Him. Why, then, should He interfere every time humanity makes a mess of things? Do you think He should bail us out of our willfulness and let us go on our merry way without Him?"

Sommers regarded him steadily. "You should rather thank Him for His mercy, for providing the opportunity of salvation."

"If His salvation is so good, why are there so few of you?"

"Humanity believes what it wants to believe. Only a few hear and heed God's call. God's patience is wearing thin. Eventually the world will unite in final rebellion against God, led by one evil man."

"One man leading the world? Are you serious?"

"Never more so," Sommers replied. "Why do you find it incredible? We have a one-world government, a one-world religion—all that is necessary is that a charismatic leader step forward and seize the reins."

"Hmm. Maybe."

"Not maybe, Major—when. Is that time soon? I don't know. But I would urge you to accept God's offer now."

"Maybe later, Reverend."

"From what Carolyn has told me, 'later' has been going on for years," Sommers persisted. "How long do you think you can delay? Is time unlimited?"

"I appreciate your sentiments, but later, Reverend."

Sommers sighed. "You will have to choose sometime. A choice by default is still a choice."

➤

That evening, in the unbearably lonely apartment, Duchesne teetered on the brink.

He never thought he would reach this place. But without Carolyn, he felt lost, uncertain.

Why not? he thought. *What have I got to lose?*

Oh God, he prayed, standing before his window, eyes fixed on the cold, pinpoint stars. *I don't even know if You exist. But if You do, please help me. Help me to defeat this madman. And even more, bring Carolyn back to me. If You do, I will believe. I promise.*

Would Sommers say it was wrong to bargain with God? He thought so. But could he accept this God unconditionally, without guarantees? Even more, could he give himself to this demanding God who insisted upon repentance?

How long he stood there, he didn't know. But the pale pink of the sun began to encroach on the horizon, lightening the sky, driving the stars into obscurity.

The supports of the dome twinkled and glistened. The city came to life.

December 22.

Deadline day.

EIGHTEEN

The unit wasn't above 10 centimeters on a side, a rectangle, folded at the edges. The featureless gray plastic could have been almost anything, but a blinking red status indicator suggested otherwise. The bomb was armed and attached to one of the dome's supporting beams. Duchesne let his eye rove up the curving arch of the beam, tracing the delicate strand until it disappeared in the height to merge with the multitude of other supports high above the city center.

Lowell City's dome was the most impressive example of human engineering skill anywhere in the system. There had never been a problem with the dome in all the years of its existence. In a very real sense, the dome was Lowell City. No dome, no Lowell.

Duchesne pursed his lips. This was worse than he had imagined.

"Have you found any others?" he asked.

"One more," replied Sergeant Garth Bloundt, Security's top weapons expert. "About a kilometer round to the north."

Duchesne leaned closer to inspect the unit.

"Not too close, sir," Bloundt cautioned. He put an arm between Duchesne and the bomb. "These things are very unstable."

"How was it found?"

"A maintenance technician noticed it by accident. He had the sense to notify us. Probably made of plasekrexe." Bloundt pointed to the computer pad Duchesne wore around his arm. "You can mold it into any shape, like a flexpad. Stuff a casing with it . . ." He shrugged. "Who would know?"

"What kind of a detonator mechanism?" Duchesne asked.

"Carrier wave signal," said Bloundt. "Coded to prevent accidental or premature detonation." He gestured toward the unit. "You can see from the way the assembly is made that it was done hastily. Whoever it was knew what he was doing, he just didn't have much time. Given the right materials, you can make one of these in minutes. That's why I'd keep my distance. But it'll work. A few of these babies will be plenty to bring down the dome."

"No timer?"

"Not that I can see."

"Can you defuse it?"

"Sure. But it takes longer than it does to make and arm one. I can't rush it. And I can only do one at a time," he concluded pointedly. Bloundt gnawed on a fingernail. "There's no one else I'd trust with these."

"Meaning," said Duchesne gloomily, "that if there are enough of these things, we may find ourselves running out of time. Very well, Bloundt, good work. Get started on this one. Call for any help you need. Boris," he continued to Mikhaelovitch, who was standing close by, "concentrate your attentions on the dome. Locate as many of these as you can. But tell your people to keep clear of them, for pity's sake."

"Had you considered that they may not all be attached to the dome?" Mikhaelovitch asked. "All they need to do is be close."

"I know, but we must do what we can." He looked at his chrono. "Three hours."

"Sir," said Bloundt.

"Yes, Sergeant?"

"If you were Maranan, sir, where would you detonate these from?"

"Where? From the Enclave of course."

"Exactly so. You wouldn't wait in the city for the sky to fall in."

"So?"

"Well sir, if you don't want these to go off, then all you have to do is prevent the signal getting through."

"Jam it?" Duchesne suggested.

"Difficult, unless you know the precise frequency. And we can't cut off the signal at a satellite. No sir, to be certain, you'd have to stop it at the source."

Duchesne's mind raced. He clapped the sergeant on the

shoulder." Bloundt, you may have saved the city. Come on, Boris!"

He and Mikhaelovitch departed the scene, leaving Bloundt to his dangerous task.

"I can see your mind working," Mikhaelovitch said, climbing into the car. "How do you propose to stop the signal? Maranan isn't going to open up the Enclave and let us waltz in."

"Do you have any suggestions?"

"An attack on the Enclave is presumably out of the question. They'd spot us coming kilometers away. But Nancy and Howard are in position. How about pumping in anesthetic gas? A small team, two or three—"

"Same trouble. They'd never let us get close enough. And even if we were able to introduce gas, it would take too long to take effect. We need something instantaneous."

"Do you have a better thought?"

"Yes. But I have to convince an old friend to sacrifice his career."

➤

Duchesne had no idea if he could succeed. But he wasn't like Sommers. He couldn't sit, waiting for some kind of divine intervention to manifest itself, a *deus ex machina* to pull them out of the fire. He had to do something, even if it proved unsuccessful.

Bloundt would do his best, but one man against a forest of bombs was too little.

He urged his driver to greater speed than was safe, to get him back to HQ. Decorations hung from buildings and statues, reminder of Winter Festival time. Duchesne didn't feel very festive, and, from the scarcity of the decorations, most of the populace didn't either.

Normally the city would be running riot in an orgy of pleasure and festivities.

Winter Festival might never come.

"Communications," he ordered when back behind his desk.

"Yes, sir."

"I want you to try to raise Captain Samuel Benson, SSF *Collingwood*, off Phobos Navalport."

"We have no satellite access, sir."

"I know. Try for direct contact. Make it secure."

"Yes sir."

Duchesne had no inkling of Phobos's location at the moment. The little moon moved so rapidly that if it was in range it would not remain so for long. He would have to hope *Collingwood* was in a suitable position to receive a direct tight-beam comm laser.

If not, they were all dead.

They would not die immediately. Unless Maranan had planted explosive devices in lower levels, the city infrastructure would be intact. But the falling dome would cause terrible damage to surface structures. The power would fail; the oxygen plant would be rendered inoperable; hydroponics would freeze and die.

How long could a city of one million people survive without power or oxygen, subsisting on batteries, bottled air, rationed food? They would die, a slow lingering death without help from Earth.

Would Maranan be happy then, to see the planet cleansed of human life?

Please God, let *Collingwood* be in range. . . .

"I have *Collingwood*, sir. Captain Benson."

Benson's grizzled face appeared, beneath its mane of gray-white hair. His voice possessed the gruffness Duchesne had come to expect.

"What are you trying to do, Duchesne? Have me accused of complicity?" But Benson smiled abruptly—a good sign.

"Worse, I'm afraid," Duchesne replied. "How are the space rats?"

"You've met one of them. Wesley has tried hard to convince me that you're still sane."

"Do you believe her?"

"I'm tempted not to. What the devil are you up to?"

"Trying to save the city, Samuel."

"What do you want from me?" Benson glanced aside. "Wesley says we'll be out of range in a few minutes, so make it quick."

"I need your help. Specifically, I need your ship."

Benson's pupils dilated. "You *are* crazy! Washburn will have a fit! It's more than my job's worth!"

"It's not Washburn, Samuel. It's a *clone*! I don't know what happened to the real Commodore, but that isn't him!"

"Wesley showed me the chip. Clones. Brainwashing. It's pretty hard stuff to swallow."

"How about this then," Duchesne said desperately. "Maranan has explosives scattered all around the dome supports. We don't have time to defuse them. In just over two hours the dome comes crashing down, and we all die. I'm not bluffing, Samuel."

"I *am* listening, Wesley," Benson said off screen. "All right, Duchesne, what do you want me to do?"

Duchesne told him.

Benson snorted. "You sure know how to ask a lot."

"*Please*, Samuel."

"All right," Benson said slowly. "I'll trust you on this one. But you had better be right, or you'll have more than Washburn to worry about."

"Thank you. Believe me, Samuel, you won't regret it."

"Hah!" Benson swiveled his head. "You've got your way, Wesley. Let's get this ship underway. All hands to duty stations. Prepare to break orbit."

He returned his attention to Duchesne. "I'll call you when we're in position. Benson out."

"Out."

Duchesne breathed a sigh of relief.

Would it work?

At least they would go down fighting.

He wondered if God had heard him.

➤

Sergeant Garth Bloundt held his breath so his hand wouldn't tremble and applied an instrument to the casing of the bomb. If he cut the wrong lead, that would be the end of one munitions expert.

As he'd told Duchesne, the bombs weren't easy to defuse. A really good bomb-smith would make the workings so complex that an interior scan was confusing. These were thankfully, bare-boned models. But still, on occasion such devices could be detonated even by the scanning process. Though notoriously difficult to work with, Plasekrexe was malleable, cheap, and easily manufactured, and therefore popular with those who desired such characteristics.

He pressed the control.

The red light on the bomb winked out.

Bloundt breathed again. One done.

He detached the bomb from the strut, placed it in a sealed container, and closed the lid. Chemicals inside the container would degrade the plasekrexe in a few hours, reducing it to inert materials worth a few credits at most.

He handed the container to a waiting private.

"Put this in the van, Gregory. Carefully!"

Bloundt watched the man walk gingerly to the reinforced munitions vehicle, the container held at arm's length, as if that would make a difference.

One down.

He raised his eyes to the sky.

He hoped Major Duchesne had a good plan.

Because there was no way he could deactivate them all.

➤

Carolyn stirred as the door to her room slid open. She had hardly seen anyone since she had been locked in here. At first, she welcomed the quiet. Her head had throbbed unbearably as the effects of the hypneum wore off. She had found it difficult to think coherently.

Gradually, she pieced together what had happened—what she thought had happened. An attack in her apartment was the last thing she'd expected.

She wasn't sure how many days had passed since her abduction. Hypneum was normally a short-acting drug, but perhaps the lingering effects of the neural stun had contributed to her slow recovery. She had a vague memory of a medical exam— but had it been real or a dream? She couldn't tell.

Except for an adherent sliding a tray of unappetizing food through a slot in the door at regular intervals, she had been left alone. She must have eaten at some point, although she didn't remember doing so. Three meters on a side, the room contained a hard cot and a foldout hygiene cubicle.

A large man appeared in the door. He wore the pale yellow robe common to members of the sect, but unlike others, his had a frill of gold braid around the collar. He appeared to be in his late thirties or early forties. Curly black hair framed a face not easily forgotten, a face disfigured by a large scar running vertically down the left cheek.

Broad-shouldered and narrow-hipped, the man leaned against the doorframe. The door closed behind him.

"So," he leered. "Look who's here. Carolyn McCourt. Wife of our beloved Major J. I. Duchesne. I'm sorry we couldn't spend time together earlier, but I had other things to do, and I wanted to make sure you were in a fit condition to appreciate the honor."

Carolyn swung into a sitting position on the hard cot, her feet on the floor. She tensed.

"You're probably wondering who I am," the man continued.

"I know who you are," Carolyn replied. "Erik Klassen. Wanted for murder on two worlds."

"Only two? I'm disappointed."

"Low-life scum."

Klassen laughed.

He pushed himself off the frame and swaggered over to stand before her. Carolyn smelled the harsh odor of his breath. Klassen had been drinking. From his behavior, he'd obviously not used any Soberfast before coming to call.

"What do you want with me?"

"What do I want?" Klassen leered, planting his hands on his hips. "Two things. First, I want revenge on your husband."

"And second?"

"I want you. The two are not mutually exclusive." He reached down a brawny hand to stroke her cheek. "The major has good taste."

Carolyn pushed his hand away.

A backhand caught her blindside and flung her against the pillow. The salty taste of blood stung her tongue from where her lip had split.

"That wasn't very smart. I expected more."

Carolyn returned his gaze. "You won't get it."

Klassen hit her again. Carolyn's head swam from the force of the blow. She raised a hand to defend herself, but he swatted it out of the way and hit her a third time.

"I will," he said, fist clenched, his words more menacing for the quiet way in which they were spoken. "Erik Klassen gets what he wants." He grabbed the front of her shirt and jerked her toward him.

Carolyn spat in his face.

The next blow left her barely clinging to consciousness. Klassen's evil laughter came from a great distance.

➤

"We're in position, Major," Benson reported just before noon. He sat in the command chair of the System Security Frigate *Collingwood*. The frigate had dropped out of Phobos standby, into a lower orbit precisely above the Enclave. "Just give us the word."

"No sense waiting to the last minute," came the reply. "Cohen and Yellow Horse have withdrawn to safe positions. Just make sure you don't miss. We won't get a second chance."

"We won't miss," Benson replied.

"Coming over the Enclave now, sir," Ensign Lafferty said from nav. "Nearing weapons range."

"Target," ordered Benson. "Communications array first."

"Targeting now." Glenda Wesley had resumed her old position at tactical. She wasn't about to trust this operation to anyone else.

"Weapons armed and ready."

"Fire when ready."

Wesley's hands danced over her console, her eyes glued to the rapidly changing readouts.

"Firing now."

➤

Maranan paced back and forth in the upper-level control room as the deadline neared.

"There's no sign of major evacuation," said the adept manning the console.

"Duchesne is a fool." Maranan fingered the detonator resting in a pocket of his robe. The detonator was linked directly to the Enclave's communications array.

So Duchesne was a fool, and the people hadn't left. What did it matter? His Guide had told him they would all die anyway. Mars didn't want them. And Gaia? When Earth saw what her sister had done, maybe humanity on Earth was in for some unpleasant surprises if it didn't change its ways.

Maranan paused in his circumnavigation of the room. He drew the detonator from his pocket. His finger poised over the initiation button.

"Good-bye, Major Duchesne."

➤

Twin spears of vivid ruby light erupted from *Collingwood's* massive laser batteries and streaked planetward, unimpeded by the rarity of the thin atmosphere.

They found their mark.

The Enclave's communication array melted into fused slag. The power-collecting system disintegrated, erupting in a massive explosion that rocked the whole Enclave, unleashed power exploding backwards along overstressed conduits. Raining debris buried the ruin of the antennas. A cloud of dust poured into the sky, which sizzled with stray radiation.

Within seconds, the lasers had done their work.

"Status?" Benson inquired.

Wesley studied the scan data.

"Direct hit, sir. The Enclave's power and communications appear to be destroyed."

"Good," said Benson. "It's up to Duchesne now."

"Are we returning to Phobos orbit?"

"No. We're committed now. Let's remain here a while in case Duchesne needs any more help."

➤

The Enclave rocked and staggered as from the blow of a mighty fist. The floor heaved. The shock threw Maranan to the ground in a welter of tangled robes. The detonator flew away. The control console exploded, flinging back the unfortunate adherent with a blaze of flame. A high-pitched scream cut off short as the body crashed into a bank of equipment and slumped to the rocking floor.

Electronics shorted and arced. Flames showered hissing sparks across the room. The adherent's robe ignited; the wearer past caring. The ceiling buckled and sagged, dumping dust and rock, turning the air into a choking miasma.

A chunk of thermocrete clipped his skull. With a flash of light and pain, Maranan lapsed into unconsciousness.

When sensation returned, he saw a room utterly devastated, lit by the stuttering flashes of burning circuits. A cable hung precariously near his head, sizzling dangerously. As it swung, snakes-tongues of energy flickered.

Maranan raised himself to his hands and knees, gasping for breath, and swore in a torrent of blasphemy, cursing Duchesne.

The detonator lay on the floor close at hand. He put it back into his pocket.

He staggered to the door and gripped the wall for support. The door had wrinkled and buckled, but enough of an opening remained for him to squeeze through. Maranan had one destination in mind. Blackened and grimy, he pushed his way down the corridor that he knew like the back of his hand.

➤

Carolyn fought for breath as Klassen's big fists attempted to choke the life out of her. Suddenly, the room trembled. The lights flickered and died. As Klassen struggled for balance, his grip relaxed.

Carolyn took advantage of his distraction. She brought her knee up sharply. Klassen gasped and doubled over, retching. Carolyn chopped his neck as he pitched forward, and Klassen crumpled. His head cracked on the bed-frame. He hit the floor with a grunt and lay unmoving.

Carolyn massaged her neck. Her ribs hurt; conversely, her face was numb where Klassen's fist had struck her. She bent over the inert form and felt for a pulse, finding it strong.

She stumbled toward the door. Something soft touched her foot. She pulled Klassen's robe off him and draped herself in its bulky folds. The door was shut, but she felt for the hand-holds, and it slid open.

Only a few, dull glow-strips about shoulder height, running off emergency back-up power, lit the corridor. She wondered what could have happened to cause the Enclave power to fail. With Washburn in command in space, there was no way to shut down power transmissions from one of the orbiting stations. Lowell's fusion plant hadn't been affected by the embargo.

Confusion reigned in the corridor, a confusion of milling bodies, incoherent shouts and moans, mad scrambling in the dark. An adherent carrying a handlight bumped into her. Carolyn stuck out a foot, wrenching the light away as the figure fell.

She had only the haziest idea of which way to go. She had been too confused when brought here to form more than the dimmest notion of the layout.

Klassen would wake up shortly; he would not be out for long.

Up. She had to go up.

➤

Lin Grainger rubbed her forehead. Her hand came away wet and sticky. For a moment she panicked, unable to see. What was the matter with her sight? She realized belatedly that she *could* see; there just wasn't much to look at.

Her feet crunched broken glass and plastic. She maneuvered across the lab to a storage locker. She thumbed the access switch. The locker opened, and she pulled out a flashlight.

She swept the beam around the room.

The lab was a mess. The sensitive equipment had not tolerated the shock well. Mars was a geologically inactive planet— there had seemed no reason to build the Enclave with seismic stress in mind.

The nurturing tanks had cracked. Nutrient fluid sloshed in a sluggish stream across the floor. She looked in horror as a nearly grown organism, its lungs not adapted for a high oxygen environment, gasped its life away on the floor, flopping and writhing like a dying fish, choking in the rich air. Its mouth opened in a soundless scream.

Something else squished underfoot. She didn't look.

Monitor lights flickered in the low power and went from green to red. Alarms sounded a ghastly chorus. The backup systems must have suffered damage too; the lab was supposed to have adequate power no matter what.

EEGs and EKGs went flat-line.

Lin panicked. She reached for stimulants, pounded frantically on a still chest, administered fruitless injections, ran from one expiring form to another.

All around, her work was dying.

There's nothing you can do! said a voice in her head. *Get out! Save yourself!*

No! I can't leave them!

Don't be a fool! They're dead already!

Common sense prevailed. With a last despairing glance, Lin Grainger pried open the lab door and joined the melee streaming toward the surface.

>

What seemed like hours later, but was probably not more than fifteen minutes, Carolyn stumbled across the lifter bank. The door refused to open.

She leaned against the wall, trying to catch her breath.

The mad scramble in the dark corridors took its toll. Many adherents had panicked. Bodies littered the floor, trampled to death in the rush to escape. Carolyn herself had nearly been mown down by a mob rampaging along a barracks unit. There seemed to be no one in control.

She tried to remember the plans that Yellow Horse had brought back from his reconnaissance. She thought the sleeping areas weren't too far underground. Above them was the communications area and motorpool.

If she could make it to the motorpool and access a vehicle. . . .

There had to be another way up.

Of course.

She shone her light on either side of the lifter doors and discerned the outline of another opening. She braced her feet and pried as hard as she could on the edge. Grudgingly, the panel slid aside, revealing a yawning pit.

She aimed her light upward. A service ladder stretched as far as she could see, disappearing into darkness. There was no sign of the lifter.

Down . . . better not look.

She didn't look forward to the climb but saw no other way of escape.

She put the light in a pocket in the robe and hitched it up around her waist. Gritting her teeth, she gripped the stanchions of the ladder. She swung herself out over the void and began to climb.

She had not ascended more than a few rungs when a cry wafted up the shaft. Someone must have blundered into the open door and fallen down the shaft. She winced as a dull thud emanated from far below.

At first, the going was easy. But as the steps multiplied, it became harder and harder. Her arms began to cramp. She had no idea how far she had to go, no idea how far she had come. Each intake of breath burned her raw throat.

Up, always up.

She wrapped her arms around the supports and paused, waiting for her shaking to stop, the bitter taste of fear to leave.

Think of something! Don't give up.

> *Where can I go from your Spirit?*
> *Where can I flee from your presence?*
> *If I go up to the heavens, you are there;*
> *if I make my bed in the depths, you are there.*

Heaven above, hell below.

She forced her legs to move against the agony that assailed them and urged her body upward.

➤

Erik Klassen vomited twice and groaned as he rolled over. Even in the dimness of the room, he could see that he was alone.

She was gone.

He rose to his feet, calling Carolyn McCourt every expletive he could think of.

The door stood open.

He almost tripped over a body lying in the corridor. He noticed his own robe was missing and stripped the body at his feet of its robe and covered himself.

"Get out of my way!"

He shoved an adherent aside and forced his way through the milling forms, heedless of whom he bludgeoned.

He didn't care about escaping.

He didn't care about Maranan.

But he would find the woman.

>

She raised a hand tentatively above her head and touched the coolness of a hard surface. Rock or plastisteel, it didn't much matter. Carolyn had reached the top of the shaft. The access panel should be close by. A few moments probing located the hatch. Thankfully, it wasn't as tightly closed as the one below.

She squeezed through the opening and emerged onto a level floor.

Her wobbly legs threatened to give way. Her arms ached.

The air stank with smoke. She coughed, her nose and eyes on fire. She risked using the torch, which failed to penetrate far, lighting up a storm of dust particles.

Which way now?

She chose a direction at random.

"May I help you, my dear?"

Carolyn jumped at the voice, whirling around too fast. Her head swam.

But there was no mistaking the laser pistol pointed squarely at her midriff.

"I should kill you now," said the ragged, dirt-besmirched figure of Maranan.

"Why don't you?" Carolyn asked, suddenly weary. Maybe J.I. had been right. They wouldn't get out of this alive.

"Because I still have need of you. Turn around and walk." Maranan gestured with the pistol.

Carolyn hesitated and then complied.

There were few people in the passage they traversed. Eventually they arrived at an airlock. The doors stood open. From a viewing window, Carolyn could make out the stream-lined fuselage of a hoverjet, affixed to the lock by a connecting tunnel. The sun was a wan orb overhead, visible through the retracted hanger doors. The sight of daylight was welcome after the travails of the dark corridors.

Maranan gestured again. "On board."

"Drop the gun!" commanded a hoarse voice.

Maranan turned slowly.

"Drop it!"

Maranan let the gun slip from his fingers. "Erik? What is the meaning of this?"

Klassen moved closer. Carolyn noted with grim amusement that he walked stiffly, one hand over the stomach she had kicked. Green tinged his pale cheeks. But the expression on his face instantly quelled any humor. Never had she seen such a look of pure hatred on a human face. Gone was any veneer of humanity. The raw fury of naked evil blazed forth.

Klassen meant to kill them.

"The meaning is that you are both going to die. You first," he said glaring at Maranan, "and then you," to Carolyn. "Slowly, piece by piece."

His finger tensed on the trigger. "Good-bye, Master," he snarled.

Carolyn looked around desperately. Maranan's pistol lay out of reach. There was no cover to try for. Klassen stood too far away. She'd be shot before she could reach him.

So this is how it ends? she wondered. *Shot down like a dog?* From the gloom and shadows of the connecting tunnel, a laser bolt flared. Klassen's pistol flew across the hall. He sank to his knees, clutching his side. A stream of blood darkened his robe, growing even as Carolyn watched, horrified.

"You!" he hissed. He mouthed one of the foulest curses Carolyn had ever heard.

From the hoverjet lock stepped a petite woman. A trickle of blood from her forehead matted her long flaxen hair. She held a laser rock-steady in her left hand.

"Yes," said Lin Grainger. "Surprised? You shouldn't be." Being careful not to draw too close to Klassen, she leveled the gun at his forehead. "Do you want to beg, Klassen? Beg for your life!"

"Lin—" began Maranan. "Don't—"

"Don't interrupt!" retorted Grainger. "This is my moment. My revenge. This *animal* has abused me too often."

"You deserved it! You enjoyed it," Klassen taunted.

"Liar!" Grainger howled. It was more like a sob. Her finger convulsed on the trigger.

224 of his head.

Klassen fell back, a smoking hole drilled through the ruin of his head.

Grainger slumped for a moment, then she swung around to cover Carolyn. "Don't try anything."

"Come on," said Maranan, stepping over Klassen's charred corpse. "Let's go."

He led the way down the tunnel into the hoverjet. Carolyn followed, watched closely by Grainger. Maranan sat in the pilot's seat. Grainger took the co-pilot's, swiveling around to keep Carolyn, seated behind, under cover.

Maranan pulled an instrument from his pocket and rested it on the console. Carolyn recognized a detonator.

But a detonator for what?

Maranan activated the communications-console.

"This is Maranan," he coughed. "Are you reading me?"

There was a brief pause, and then the screen winked to life.

"This is Lt. Nancy Cohen. Give yourself up, Maranan. The Enclave is surrounded."

"Cut the military jargon," replied Maranan, his voice jagged, "and get me Duchesne. Or your precious Captain McCourt dies here and now."

"Wait."

Carolyn intercepted a glance that Grainger sent toward Maranan. Puzzlement? Surprise? Uncertainty?

Her husband's face appeared. He looked tired, haggard.

"This is Duchesne. What do you want, Maranan?"

"I'm coming out in a hoverjet, Duchesne. If you're smart, you'll let me."

"We found the bombs you planted on the dome supports."

Maranan laughed horribly. "There are too many. I've got your wife, Duchesne. Tell your troops not to try any surprises."

Carolyn's eyes flicked toward the detonator. The dome!

"J. I.!" she shouted. "He's got a detonator!"

Maranan cut the link with one hand.

"Shut up!" He seemed to have snapped; his face wore the same contorted expression that Klassen's had.

He turned to Grainger. "Kill her."

"Master?" Grainger queried, alarm evident on her face.

"Kill her!" Maranan almost screamed. His mouth foamed. "You want Mars to be free again of the human scum infesting her, don't you? We can still succeed! We can rebuild the lab, rebuild our human constructs!"

Grainger looked from Maranan to Carolyn. Maranan brought his fist down on the comm panel, which erupted in a shower of sparks.

"KILL HER!"

He turned away from the women, beginning the pre-flight check.

Carolyn thought desperately. What was the woman's name?

"Do you have family, Lin, back in Lowell?"

Grainger hesitated before answering. Her pistol pointed directly at Carolyn. "Yes. But they don't believe," she added bitterly.

"You heard that, didn't you? Bombs on the dome supports. And a detonator on the console. He's going to blow the dome, Lin!"

Again the look of uncertainty. "They don't believe," Grainger repeated. "None of them."

"Is that a reason to *kill* them, Lin? Because they don't agree with you?"

Carolyn gazed into the other woman's eyes, reading the confusion, the anguish, trying to compel her to listen. "You aren't a killer, Lin. Klassen abused you, as he tried to abuse me. We're talking about your *family*, Lin. And one million other people. Can you kill a million people, Lin?" Carolyn pointed to Maranan, finishing the check. The jet's engines powered up. "Because he will."

"Pre-flight check completed," came the computer's metallic voice. "Automated liftoff and flight sequence verified and locked in."

The lifters began to whine. The connecting tunnel prepared to disengage.

They had only a few moments left.

The muzzle of the gun shifted away from Carolyn, rotating in a semicircle.

It pointed at Maranan.

➤

In a blinding swirl of dust, the hoverjet lifted into the sky. The main engines ignited and it streaked northward, away from the smoldering ruins of the Enclave, heading toward Lowell.

From the Security positions another jet roared off, burning in pursuit. The air reverberated with the scream of the planes. The faster, high-performance Security hoverjet gained, closing the distance.

"This is MacKinnon," the pilot opened comm-channels. "Do you read me, Lieutenant Cohen?"

"This is Cohen. Loud and clear, MacKinnon. What's your status?"

"I'm in pursuit of the hoverjet. Range twenty kilometers and closing."

Duchesne had been anxiously monitoring the field squad's transmissions. He broke in.

"This is Duchesne, MacKinnon. How long to Lowell ETA?"

"Expect Lowell ETA in twenty-five minutes, sir."

"Maranan will be within detonation range well before then," said Mikhaelovitch. "I'd estimate fifteen minutes max."

His eyes met Duchesne's. Both men shared the same thought.

Carolyn is on that plane.

"Sir?" came MacKinnon's voice. "Do you have an order for me?"

Cohen came on-line again. "You have no choice, sir. Bring the plane down."

Duchesne looked at his chrono. Another minute ticked off.

Carolyn.

"What are you waiting for?"

Mikhaelovitch laid his hand on Duchesne's shoulder.

"I'm sorry," he whispered, his voice husky. "But there's no choice. There are no other options."

Duchesne's chrono ticked remorselessly. In just a few minutes one million people would perish.

Unless he did the unthinkable.

Carolyn, would you understand?

He pounded his fist on his desk.

It couldn't end like this!

"J. I." said Mikhaelovitch, looking nervously at the chrono. "We're running out of time."

"I know," said Duchesne, his mouth dry, voice almost inaudible. His eyes turned toward the screen, showing MacKinnon in her cockpit.

Carolyn . . .

"Down it, MacKinnon. Down it."

The view changed to a wingtip camera.

The Security hoverjet accelerated, crossing the desert with blistering speed. Maranan's plane swelled, its course steady, unswerving. The course that would bring it in range of Lowell.

"Closing," said MacKinnon. "Entering firing range."

The jet bore down.

The laser batteries fired. The shots impacted the rear engines. The eye-searing glare of an explosion was followed by a cloud of dense black smoke. Maranan's plane staggered under the impact and then rolled out of control. A wing sheared off from stress. The nose dipped, and the plane dove earthward, shedding pieces of skin and fuselage.

It plowed vertically into the ground and disintegrated in a final burst of fire and smoke.

"Downer," came MacKinnon's unemotional voice. "That's funny. He made no move to escape."

But Duchesne wasn't listening.

He buried his face in his hands and sobbed.

"Carolyn. . . ."

NINETEEN

D own it."
Would he ever be able to erase the fateful words from his mind?

Two simple syllables that took but a fraction of a second to utter.

"Down it."

And in that fraction of a second his wife had died.

Duchesne's driver pulled to stop a block away from Pat Maloney's, one of the rougher bars on Lowell's seedy, lower south side. The invaluable Jacland had relayed a message from an off-duty trooper, acting on his own, named Doggan. It seemed he had spotted Evgeny Szalny entering a bar known as a hangout for unemployed and off-duty freighter crewmen. There had been no sign of the bald man until now.

Duchesne guessed instantly what Szalny was up to—Lowell was undoubtedly the last place Szalny wanted to be now that Maranan's latest plot had failed. When the bombs failed to detonate, he would have known Security had caught onto Maranan's plan. Szalny could only hide for so long; eventually either the police or Security would catch up to him. Lowell was not like Earth, where you could find someone with a smattering of medical training or a fringe medical clinic to alter your appearance for the right price. Lowell was too small, med centers too few.

Ergo, Szalny was trying to run. Finding passage off-world wouldn't be too hard. There was always a captain down and out on his luck willing to pick up a well-paying passenger without asking awkward questions.

Duchesne wondered why Szalny had left it so late. Perhaps he had intended to leave earlier but had been unable to.

"Keep him in sight but don't move in until I arrive," Duchesne ordered. He wanted to do this one himself. He had a score to settle with Szalny.

The Security man, wearing a nondescript jumpsuit of indeterminate color, lounged by the door, leaning against a battered dispenser selling single-dose vials of Soberfast. He jumped up as Duchesne arrived.

"He's been in there a good half hour, sir."

"Then he should be out soon." Duchesne looked around. He spotted an alcove a few meters away where he could hide. One glimpse of his uniform and Szalny would be gone. He wished he'd had time to change but didn't want to miss the opportunity of apprehending Szalny.

"I'll wait over there. You stay here."

Doggan slouched back against the wall.

Another half hour passed before Szalny emerged. His bald headed swiveled as he scanned the street. His gaze slipped over Doggan, who appeared to have lapsed into an alcoholic coma.

"Come on, Brutus."

Followed by the dog, Szalny set off along the street. When he was sufficiently far ahead, Duchesne trailed in pursuit. The comatose Doggan made a miraculous recovery and followed suit.

Szalny slipped around a corner and disappeared. Muttering an imprecation beneath his breath, Duchesne quickened his pace. He rounded the corner. The street split into a Y.

"Take the left, Doggan. I'll go right. I think these join back together again."

He broke into a trot. The street took another bend. Szalny was dead ahead, strolling nonchalantly. He evidently had no idea he was being followed.

Duchesne closed the distance. His fingers tingled with nervous excitement, and his heart rate sped up.

He drew his laser.

When he was but a step behind the smaller man, he rammed the muzzle into Szalny's spine.

"Freeze, Szalny!"

The bald man stopped in mid-stride. Duchesne ran a hand over Szalny's pockets, removing a small, palm-sized weapon. He put it in his own pocket.

"Turn around slowly. Hands on your head."

Szalny pivoted.

"Thought you could get away?" Duchesne asked.

Szalny spat on the ground. "I almost made it, didn't I?" Szalny's eyes were curious; Duchesne had never seen such a lack of expression. No fear, no anger, nothing. He felt as if he was looking into a vacuum.

Szalny's lack of emotion made his own rise higher.

"Give me a reason to blow you away, scum."

Szalny said nothing.

"You sent my wife to her death."

Down it.

The first warning Duchesne had was a woman's scream. He heard a growl and spun on his heel as a black streak leapt for his throat.

He'd forgotten the dog!

Instinct saved his life.

He dropped flat on his back, bringing his feet up. His boots met the dog's chest, and he pushed up as hard as he could, sending the surpised animal into a wild tumble. Cartwheeling, Brutus crunched awkwardly a few meters away.

Seizing the opportunity, Szalny wheeled away from Duchesne. He bolted down the street, legs pumping.

Duchesne rolled as he hit the ground and brought up his pistol. He snapped a shot after the fleeing Szalny. The shot took the man behind the knee. His leg buckled, and he fell heavily into the ground.

Duchesne jumped up and sprinted over to Szalny. The dog rose slowly, favoring a paw. Brutus had apparently been winded in the fall. The animal's lips peeled back in a snarl. Szalny tried to rise but fell back with a moan, spitting dust from his mouth.

Duchesne leveled his gun at Szalny. "Tell the dog to stay back or you both die."

Szalny licked his lips. Hackles raised, the dog tensed, preparing to charge.

"Stay, Brutus," Szalny said finally. "Lie down."

Duchesne watched out of the corner of his eye as the dog lay down and licked its leg. He turned his attention back to Szalny.

He grabbed the front of the man's shirt and hauled him to his feet, flinging him back against the side of a building, where he leaned, a gaping hole where his knee had been. Brutus growled but stayed put.

Duchesne jammed his pistol under Szalny's jaw, forcing his head up and back.

"Give me one reason why I shouldn't kill you now," he snarled.

Szalny's face went white, from pain or fear or both. His lips twitched nervously. Duchesne had the satisfaction of seeing a flicker in the man's eyes.

So he *could* fear.

"Well?" he pushed harder, the laser grinding into the soft tissues of the neck. All the bitterness and rage welled up into a red mist through which he could barely see.

Szalny gulped. His mouth worked, but no sound came forth.

Duchesne's finger tightened. "Good-bye, scum."

He heard feet behind him.

"Don't do it, J. I."

Duchesne blinked. That was Carolyn's voice! Unearthly, incorporeal. But she was—where?

Heaven? Hell?

Dead on the ochre sands of Hellas Planitia.

He shook his head.

"He's not worth it," her spectral voice continued. "Don't let his blood be on your hands."

He wavered.

"For me, J. I."

"Bah!" He lowered the laser. Szalny's eyes rolled back, and he crumpled into an insensible heap on the floor. "She's right. You're not worth the trouble."

He turned to Doggan, ignoring the crowd of spectators that had assembled.

"Call for backup and get this scum out of here."

➤

That evening, Duchesne stalked the shattered corridors of the Enclave nursing his wounds.

A mask of anger concealed the bitterness of his defeat, a mask that threatened to crack at any moment, revealing the pain and hurt beneath, pain that he'd vented at Sommers earlier.

"I was ready to believe!" he had shouted at Sommers in a sudden outburst, tears trailing down his cheeks. "I was *this* close! I even prayed!"

"What stopped you?" Sommers had asked. "Self-sufficiency? Pride?"

Duchesne's voice had failed. "She's gone."

What good was anything anymore? What good was anything compared to the awful coldness inside, the coldness of knowing what he had done?

I killed my own wife!

The lives of all those in Lowell didn't matter.

How could you, God? How could you be so cruel?

From deep inside, a quiet prompting told him how senseless it was to be mad at God. But he hurt so much he didn't care. He had to be mad at somebody. God wasn't there. He couldn't hear. You couldn't hurt God.

"You can hurt God," Sommers had contradicted, bearing Duchesne's anger patiently. "You *have* hurt Him."

"That's absurd. How have I hurt God?"

"You haven't cared that His Son died. Died for *you*, Major. Died because of your sins and mine."

He tried to comprehend that, but found it impossible. One didn't think of God in those terms.

It's *your* fault, said another accusing voice. You waited too long. You put off and put off making a decision.

Now it was irreparable.

What if he had acted differently? What if he had decided? Would things be any different now?

"Who gives the orders here, Major?" Sommers had asked.

"I do, of course."

"Do you expect your subordinates to dictate the terms of their obedience?"

"Of course not."

"It's the same with God. You cannot approach Him on your terms, as if He's some friend you met in a bar; you must go to Him on His. What claim do you have on God? He's not a puppet on a string that you can invoke with a few magic words or bargain with by making promises."

Sommers had spoken softly. "Christ suffered the ultimate loneliness, Major. The loneliness of a horrible death, suffered in the knowledge that the majority of people would reject that sacrifice."

Duchesne had no answer.

Duchesne had ordered the troops to hold positions after the downing of Maranan's plane. The Revitalists had stockpiled weapons; he didn't want to risk any more lives than necessary. A frightened and confused rabble could be dangerous by their sheer unpredictability.

They didn't give up without a fight. Several hundred made a break for it, foraying in a motley assortment of speeders, crawlers, and flitters. Refusing repeated calls to surrender, they had assailed the Security positions. The Revitalists had been defeated in a fierce firefight that cost the lives of several of Duchesne's troops.

Air superiority proved decisive over mere numbers. MacKinnon and the other pilot, Solveg, strafed the suicidal cultists with a murderous barrage.

Darkness, cold, and a diminishing supply of oxygen in the Enclave had done the rest. A multitude of half-dead adherents emerged and surrendered. A few diehards preferred death and deliberately exposed themselves to the harsh embrace of Mother Mars.

After capturing Szalny, Duchesne had arrived to oversee the final mop-up.

The Enclave was bigger than he had envisioned, even having seen the plans and Yellow Horse's scans.

Temporary lights dangled in the major passageways. Power had been supplied to the life-support units, and the air was breathable again. But not for long. Once they had finished here, the Enclave would be totally destroyed. Duchesne swore that never again would such a situation arise.

It had been a costly victory.

He would trade it all to have Carolyn back.

The Enclave was a shambles. What the initial attack hadn't demolished, the resulting panic and mop-up had. Bodies lay where they had fallen. Duchesne noticed one corpse sprawled near the hoverjet bay. A big man with a scarred face.

He pointed the body out to Yellow Horse. "Erik Klassen. Looks like somebody did us a favor."

Howard Yellow Horse walked silently beside him. The news of Carolyn's death had spread rapidly. Yellow Horse, like most, acted as if he was afraid to speak in Duchesne's presence.

"Show me where the concealed rooms were located," Duchesne requested. "We've come this far; I suppose we ought to see what Maranan was doing."

"They're along here, sir."

Yellow Horse led him through the devastated communal rooms and beyond, down to a small featureless chamber with dark holoscreens on the walls. A faint odor—incense perhaps?—lingered on the air.

"This was Maranan's private meditation chamber," Yellow Horse explained. He pointed to the opposing door. "You'd expect that to lead into the corridor on the other side, but it doesn't." He yanked the door open. "After you, sir."

Duchesne entered the room and looked around.

It had once been a highly sophisticated lab. Computer banks lined the walls, the consoles dark and silent. Several padded couches surrounded a central console. Each was wired into the terminal and supported a helmet-like construction.

A body occupied one couch, strapped down, the helmet in position over a bare scalp. The face had frozen in a death-mask of agony.

"This was where they 'educated' the clones," Duchesne murmured. "Strapped into couches, being fed the memories and lives of the persons they were to replace. Can you conceive of it, Howard? What must it have been like for them, being forcefully turned into an artificial person?"

He shuddered with the enormity of the idea.

"What do you suppose will happen to them?" Yellow Horse asked.

"It's a tough problem. Maranan had the originals eliminated. I suppose it all depends on whether they can be successfully deprogrammed." He shook his head. "Maybe they can become the people they are—or think they are."

"The legals are going to have some real headaches."

"You can say that again."

"I feel sorry for them. How do you tell Sue Li-Shin that she's not really Sue Li-Shin?"

"Physically, she is."

"You know what I mean, sir. How do you tell her she's a clone?"

"Beats me. And this has been going on for years. There's no telling how many of them there are."

"CompSci will be down to access whatever files are salvageable," Yellow Horse commented.

A secondary lab housed the facilities for creating clones.

"Imagine creating a fully grown adult in just two or three years!" Yellow Horse exclaimed.

"What's in there?" Duchesne asked, pointing to where a trickle of dark liquid seeped from the wall.

"Don't know, sir. I hadn't seen that one."

Duchesne strode over and examined the wall. "It looks like another concealed door." He pulled on it, but it remained closed.

He drew his laser. "Let's cut our way in."

The two handguns focused on the locking mechanism, eating into the metal. The circuits sparked; with a creak the door opened a foot, releasing a whiff of stale, chemical-laden air.

Duchesne choked. "It stinks. What's that?"

Fragments of a slippery material stretched and broke in the opening.

"Looks like some kind of sealer," Yellow Horse replied.

"Give me a hand."

With both men heaving, the door opened far enough for them to enter. Duchesne took a torch from Yellow Horse and shone it inside.

"Looks like another lab. Come on in."

Duchesne considered himself to be a tough man. Battle-hardened, he had seen death in many forms, facing it himself on many occasions. But what he saw in the lab left him speechless, too shocked even to swear. He heard Yellow Horse gag and had to restrain the impulse himself.

The figures sprawled in death on the floor of the lab were vaguely human in outline. Beyond that. . . .

The one nearest him, arm outstretched as if in supplication, had a barrel-shaped chest cavity at least twice the size of Duchesne's own. The skin looked like leather, although he wasn't about to touch it to make sure. Outsized ears framed a face in which the mouth was the merest slit.

But it was the color that was most astonishing.

The creature—male or female?—was green. Duchesne thought immediately of the ancient science fiction concept of "little green men from Mars."

What could make a skin that color?

Surely it hadn't been long enough for mold or fungus to grow.

Chlorophyll?

Perish the thought. . . .

The other creatures were roughly similar. Some were nearly fully grown, by the look of them; others appeared barely out of some fetal or intermediate stage.

Carolyn's dream of the Clone Wars returned in full revolting force. What horribly distorted mind could have concocted such a gruesome scenario? Maranan's dream of creating a 'new humanity' able to live unprotected on the inhospitable surface of Mars had ended here in death.

Trying to improve on the Creator's design . . .

A crash of breaking glass.

The two men whirled, weapons at the ready.

A figure lurched from the darkness.

"Hold your fire." Duchesne raised his torch and shone the light toward the head of the figure. The torch slipped from his fingers to clatter on the floor.

With a hoarse cry he rushed forward, catching the form before it crumpled to the ground.

"Carolyn! I thought I'd lost you."

He had to strain to catch the words.

"You. . . . Did you think I'd make it easy?" Her voice faded. "Lin . . . help Lin. . . ."

EPILOGUE

Carolyn flashed a perky smile as Duchesne bounced into the room. "Hi, lover!" Her voice was hoarse, but there was no mistaking the emotion.

"Hi yourself."

Duchesne cast a questioning look over the bewildering array of medical gadgetry enveloping her bed, half hiding her. "Are you in there somewhere?"

"I think so. The doc unit seems to think I'm who I think I am."

Duchesne leaned over. Their lips met, lingering long over the kiss. Carolyn's color had returned. She had lost the pasty, chalky-white color symbolizing her close brush with death.

"I almost forgot." He brought his hand from behind his back, presenting her with a bouquet. "To brighten the accommodations."

"They're beautiful!" Carolyn breathed, inhaling the soft fragrance of the variegated flowers. "Where did you get them?"

"That would be telling."

"Tease."

She patted the bed beside her.

"Are you sure it's safe?" Duchesne asked. "I don't want to be mistaken for a patient."

Carolyn wrinkled her nose. "Let me assure you that any self-respecting doc unit would turn up its nose at you."

"Thanks. How are you feeling?"

"Like a million-credit deficit. Other than that, fine."

Duchesne stroked her hair. "You don't know how glad I am to have you back. I was sure you'd gone down in Maranan's plane."

"I very nearly did. We barely got off in time. Boy, is it cold out there!"

"I have a sure-fire method for warming you up," Duchesne suggested, leaning over.

Carolyn snickered, pushing him back with a hand on his chest. "Later, lover-boy." Her pert nose wrinkled. "How's Lin Grainger?"

"Not as good as you," Duchesne replied. "Early exposure, dehydration. Lung irritation from nutrient fumes. The medics think she'll pull through, but it may be touch and go."

"She saved my life," said Carolyn. "It was her idea to hole up in the lab. We had no way to notify you, so we didn't want to risk being shot down. Without e-suits, we couldn't make a break on the ground and didn't want to be mistaken for hostiles."

Carolyn coughed. "There was a trickle of power, so we weren't completely cold, and there was a supply of oxygen. We sealed the door to preserve as much as we could."

She shivered. "It was creepy in there."

"Creepy is hardly the word for it. It was the most hideously nauseating thing I've ever seen."

"What will happen to her?" asked Carolyn.

Duchesne was pensive. "She's guilty of some pretty serious crimes."

"Klassen deserved it."

"Oh I don't care about Klassen. She warrants thanks for that. But she broke all kinds of genetic engineering prohibitions—"

"We had a long talk there in the dark. Lin is brilliant in her own way. She really thought she was doing good, J.I. Maranan had her completely duped. She thought he was going to be the savior of Mars."

"That doesn't excuse—"

"She's good at heart—she cared for those pantropes. She thought of them as her children. She's not some kind of mad scientist trying to create Frankenstein—just misguided."

"That's hard to stomach."

"It's true, dear. Could you—?"

"I don't know—"

"Please? For me?"

"If she has truly repented. . . . She'll need an extensive period of rehabilitation, of course. Okay. I'll put in a favorable recommendation."

"Thank you." Carolyn kissed him. "Hey, look at this." She touched a bedside control. The room ceiling dissolved into space. The night stars blazed in undiminished splendor. "Nifty, huh?"

Carolyn craned her neck to peer upward.

"Do you have a poem for this?" Duchesne asked.

Carolyn reflected for a moment.

In all your life have you ever called up the dawn
or assigned the morning its place?
Have you taught it to grasp the fringes of the Earth
and shake the Dog-star from the sky;
to bring up the horizon in relief as clay under a seal,
until all things stand out like the folds of a cloak,
when the light of the Dog-star is dimmed
and the stars of the Navigator's Line go out one by one?

"I wish I could do that," said Duchesne wistfully. "Remember poetry."

Carolyn pulled him closer. "You just have to have the memory for it. It's beautiful, isn't it?" she remarked, still gazing upward.

"Definitely," he returned, his eyes on her.

She caught the location of his look and laughed. "I wonder what's happening there," Carolyn sobered, regarding the bright point of light that was Earth. "It can't really be him, can it?"

"I sent a forensics team to examine the wreckage. They found a few charred human remains in the crash. ID positive for Maranan."

"So then, unless he really found a way to rise from the dead, like he claims—"

Carolyn stopped in mid-sentence, her mouth hanging open.

"What is it?"

Carolyn's violet eyes were wide. "Oh, J. I., what if he cloned himself? Sent a copy to Earth to carry on his work there?"

Duchesne pursed his lips. "With the right influence, a ruthless enough man could deceive enough people. With the UWC behind him, he could even take over the world."

"Who could resist a man who seemed to have cheated death? You can bet he wouldn't advertise himself as a clone. A reprieve. That's all we've gained."

"Do you know what day it is today?" Duchesne asked, changing the subject.

Carolyn regarded him quizzically. "December 25," she replied. "Do I pass?"

"And?"

"Winter Festival."

"Okay. What else?"

"I don't know. What else?"

"It's Christmas. It's early yet. What do you bet Reverend Sommers is home?"

Carolyn's eyes danced. "Do you mean it?"

He held her hand, squeezing gently.

"When you were gone—when I thought you were dead— I realized how right you were. I had nothing, Carolyn, *nothing*. No faith, no hope, no love, nothing. I've never been so scared in my life. I even thought I heard you speaking to me." His voice dropped. "I looked into the face of an empty eternity. I didn't like what I saw."

He gazed at Carolyn. She smiled radiantly back at him.

"I don't want to lose you again. Ever."

"Nor I you." She enveloped him in a tight hug. Breaking the embrace after a long moment, she nodded toward the screen. "Go call."

Paul Sommers looked like a new man, bursting with new-found vitality. "Major," he grinned, "Merry Christmas! It's good to see you. How's Carolyn?"

"She's fine, Reverend. Nothing a few days rest won't cure. Say, I was wondering if you could do something for us."

"Anything, Major. Name it."

"Would you mind coming over?"

"Be glad to. Is there a problem?"

"No, not at all." Duchesne turned and smiled at Carolyn. "There's a decision we'd like to make. Together."